The
Protector

Critical acclaim for **Madeline Hunter** and

By Possession

"With the release of this new volume, [Madeline Hunter] cements her position as one of the brightest new writers in the genre. Brimming with intelligent writing, historical detail and passionate, complex protagonists . . . Hunter makes 14th-century England come alive—from the details of its sights, sounds and smells to the political context of this rebellious and dangerous time, when alliances and treason went hand in hand. For all the historical richness of the story, the romantic aspect is never lost, and the poignancy of the characters' seemingly untenable love is truly touching."
—*Publishers Weekly*

"A poignant tale that readers will treasure . . . with scenes that show the writer's brilliance."—*The Oakland Press*

"Ms. Hunter skillfully weaves historical details into a captivating love story that resounds with the sights, sounds, and mores of the Middle Ages. This is another breathtaking romance from a talented storyteller."—*Romantic Times*

"*By Possession* is a compelling read with a difficult but well-handled subject matter. Fans of medievals will particularly enjoy it—especially those who crave 'meaty' reads."
—*All About Romance*

"Dynamite-packed from beginning to end, *By Possession* is a tremendous tale. The strong characters and tumultuous plot make this an outstanding story. Ms. Hunter's talent shines as she climbs the road to success."—*Rendezvous*

"Madeline Hunter's exciting new trilogy that started with the stunning first novel *By Arrangement*, continues in September with *By Possession*. A remarkably talented writer with a deft hand, Ms. Hunter shines brightly with the second installment of this tantalizing series. This is truly an irresistible story that should NOT be missed."—*New-Age Bookshelf*

"With elegance and intelligence, Ms. Hunter consolidates her position as one of the best new voices in romance fiction. I'm waiting on tenterhooks to see what is in store for readers in her next book, *By Design*."—*The Romance Journal*

By Arrangement

"Debut author Hunter begins this new series with a thoroughly satisfying launch that leaves the reader eager for the next episode in the lives of her engaging characters."
—*Publishers Weekly*

"The first in a marvelous trilogy by a fresh voice in the genre, *By Arrangement* combines historical depth and riveting romance in a manner reminiscent of Roberta Gellis. Ms. Hunter has a true gift for bringing both history and her characters to life, making readers feel a part of the danger and pageantry of the era."—*Romantic Times*

"*By Arrangement* is richly textured, historically fascinating, and filled with surprises."—*All About Romance*

"Splendid in every way."—*Rendezvous*

"*By Arrangement* has action, adventure, political intrigue, humor, passion and secondary characters that compliment and fill out the tale. If the titles that follow are written like this debut, Madeline Hunter is an author to watch for. I am one fan that is waiting anxiously for her next title."—*Under the Covers*

"*By Arrangement* is a fast-paced treasure that marks the beginning of a terrific career. Ms. Hunter is bound to be added to many an auto-buy list—including mine!"
—*The Romance Journal*

"I recommend this book to any romance reader. Ms. Hunter has a skillful pen and is particularly good at characterization in her debut novel. There are plenty of events to keep the reader involved, but you'll read it for the love story . . . and I can't wait to read the others."—*Old Book Barn Gazette*

The Protector

MADELINE HUNTER

Bantam Books

New York Toronto London Sydney Auckland

THE PROTECTOR

ISBN 0-7394-1775-4

Published simultaneously in the United States and Canada

Bantam Books are published by Bantam Books, a division of Random
House, Inc. Its trademark, consisting of the words "Bantam Books" and
the portrayal of a rooster, is Registered in U.S. Patent and Trademark
Office and in other countries. Marca Registrada. Bantam Books, 1540
Broadway, New York, New York 10036.

PRINTED IN THE UNITED STATES OF AMERICA

For my mother, Anna,

who really believes that all of her children are beautiful

Author's Note

Brittany was France's Scotland, choleric, Celtic, stony, bred to opposition and resistance, and ready to use the English in its struggles against its overlord as the Scots used the French in theirs.
—Barbara Tuchman, *A Distant Mirror*

TODAY BRITTANY IS the northwestern province of France that pokes out into the sea. In the Middle Ages, however, it was a duchy struggling to maintain its independence. Although bordering French territories, it had more in common with the nearby British Isles. England and Brittany shared a strong Celtic culture, the legends of King Arthur, and even the names of cities and places.

In the middle of the fourteenth century, Brittany was torn apart by civil war. In 1341 the duke died, leaving no children to succeed him. Two of his relatives claimed the ducal crown. One was Jean Comte de Montfort, the dead duke's half-brother. The other was a woman, Jeanne de Penthièvre, who was married to Charles de Blois, a nephew of the French king.

England supported the Montfort succession while France supported the Penthièvre. The two great nations became involved in a ferocious war that ravaged Brittany. The death of Jean Comte de Montfort did not end things. His wife continued the fight in her son's name. Charles de Blois's wife did the same after he was captured by the English.

In the midst of this chaos, a new threat appeared. In 1348 the plague known as the Black Death began its first devastating sweep through Europe.

CHAPTER 1

1348

IT WAS ONE HELL OF A WAY FOR the son of Hugh Fitzwaryn to die. Killed by a mob of Breton peasants in a house that stunk of cows and dung.

Morvan kicked a bench over to the wall that faced the longhouse door. He sank down on it and rested his sword across his lap.

To his right, in the stable area of the house, his destrier snorted and stamped, aroused by the danger. To his left, on a bed near the hearth, the youth William moaned in pain and madness.

This end would probably be a mercy for William. Better to face a quick death than to endure the agony that burned your brain and deformed your body with black sores.

Where had they come from, this clutch of peasants who shouted curses and threats? He couldn't hear them distinctly, for the walls of the longhouse were stone and the door and one small window were closed. The only light in the chamber came from the fire he had built in the hearth when he had dragged William in.

The whole village had appeared deserted when he had led his men here seeking shelter for William. The disease had manifested itself yesterday, just in time for the gate guard at Brest to deny them entry to the port city. And so they had continued north along the coastal road.

It was only after he sent his men back toward Brest that the villagers had emerged. He had nailed a black cloth on the door in warning, and so they knew that the disease lurked within. These peasants had a right to be angry. The death had already run its course in Brittany and they knew all too well the danger lying in the long-house.

He eyed the thatched roof above him. They could not risk entering. It would be fire. They only lacked the leader to emerge who would rouse them to it. And the night. It was always easier to do these things at night.

He could have left the squire and gone on, of course. It had crossed his mind, unworthy thought that it was. But he had held William on his horse and the disease would claim him too. The men would wait for him at the last crossroad as planned, would wait, he knew, the full day or even more. But if he went to them he would carry the death with him. Better to stay and die here. John would get the men back to Brest and across the sea to England. They didn't like John much, but they would follow him that far.

The noise outside changed. The cries fell into pauses and shouts. One voice yelled and then the crowd responded. They had found their leader.

William thrashed on the bed, his breath rasping. He

called out several times to Sir Richard, the Gascon lord whom they had served until the plague had claimed Richard and his household and Morvan had taken the responsibility of getting William home.

The crowd grew more raucous. Their leader called something over and over and they picked up the chant. Morvan only understood a little of the Breton language, but it sounded like "No more!"

Maybe they wouldn't wait until night.

The chant soared, reaching new levels, the emotion of the mob thundering off the door. He gripped the hilt of his sword as the pounding of his blood matched the rhythms of the screaming peasants. Louder and higher and faster the yelling roared until it doubled in on itself and became an unending violent noise.

Then suddenly it stopped, swallowed in an instant by a hollow silence.

He waited, tensed for an attack. They hadn't left. He could still hear some movement. Compared with the previous din, however, the quiet possessed a physical presence.

The door of the longhouse opened a handspan. A slice of brilliant light fell on the floor. He rose and held his sword ready, to protect the villagers as much as himself.

The door swung wide. Two knights stood at the threshold, in the blinding glare of the afternoon sun. They appeared as silhouettes surrounded by halos, but their bearings and weapons proclaimed their status. Both had swords in hand.

One looked to be in his late twenties. Golden hair swept back from his forehead to his shoulders. He wore full armor except a helmet and was of medium height and build. His dark, deep-set eyes contrasted strangely with the fair hair.

The other was harder to see since he stood farther in the doorway. The sun picked up a glow of blond curls tumbling about his head and shoulders. He was taller than the other, but more slight of build. This one wore no armor, but instead a gray cotte and a black cloak. From his clothes and youthful frame he might have been just a squire, but the authority of his stance said otherwise.

The younger one spoke. "Put up your weapon. No harm will come to you here."

Morvan peered past them through the open door. The villagers were gone. He sheathed his sword. The young knight strode through the shadows toward William's bed. "Go no farther," Morvan warned. "Your people were right. It is the death."

"I do not fear it." The other man joined him and together they examined William. Then the older knight went back outside.

"Were you alone?" The voice was young, yet full of authority and command.

"Nay."

"Where are the others?"

"Waiting. About an hour hence."

"The death spreads quickly and they may be carrying it. We must bring them back. I promise you and yours care, but they must return."

Morvan told him about the crossroad.

"Will they obey you?"

"Aye."

"Then give me your cloak, so they know we come from you."

Morvan unfastened the brooch and handed over his cloak, then followed the young knight to the doorway.

Outside, in addition to the older knight, were six mounted men-at-arms and a youth no older than a squire. Two riderless horses waited nearby, one a handsome bay mare that appeared almost motionless.

The older knight came forward carrying a small box.

"Ascanio, here is his cloak," the young knight said. "The others are at the first crossroad toward Brest. We will wait here for the boy to pass, and then meet you at the keep. Tell the servants to have all prepared."

Ascanio took the cloak and handed it up to the youth. Then he returned to the doorway. "I must shrive him."

"Aye. But say the sacrament quickly."

So the older knight was a priest. It was not unheard of, but rare.

Morvan stepped outside into the sunlight. The men-at-arms eased their horses away. The young knight followed and spoke. "The squire is far along. I am sorry, but I have seen this many times. He will die soon."

Morvan turned to respond. What stood there stopped the words in his mouth. In the clear afternoon light he saw that the young knight was not a knight at all, but a woman.

She presented a startling sight. For one thing, she was very tall. He was a big man, bigger than most, and he judged that she would reach his nose. Her blond hair fell in a tumble of unruly curls around her face and just past her shoulders. The face itself was oval-shaped, with high cheekbones and a straight nose. She was dressed all in men's clothes, the cotte too large and bagging over the belt that held her sword. Soft high boots reached almost to the hem at her hose-covered knees. The loose clothing and black cloak hid the bulge of her breasts, but here in the sun her woman's slender form was unmistakable.

Large sapphire eyes gazed back at him, compelling his attention. "What is your name, sir knight?" The voice should have told him. It was deep and throaty, but possessed a velvet softness. She and Ascanio spoke French to him, the language used by the Breton nobility.

"Morvan Fitzwaryn, my lady."

"You are English, but Morvan is an honored name here in Brittany."

"It is a family name. My ancestor rode with the Conqueror, but hailed from the Breton marches near Normandy."

She smiled, and he realized that she was probably younger than her manner and authority implied. "Well, Morvan Fitzwaryn, you need not stare. Surely you know that our civil war has made some Breton women very strange."

She was referring to Jeanne de Montfort, the last duke's wife. While her husband was imprisoned by the King of France, she had taken his place at the head of his army. Morvan had met her once in England before her husband had died and she had passed from strange to mad, leaving her son, the young duke, in King Edward's care.

The young woman before him held herself as proud and tall as any man. "I am Anna de Leon. You are on my family's lands. Since you are English, you may be glad to know that we are Montfortists and not supporters of Charles de Blois and the Penthièvre claims to the ducal crown."

He hadn't even thought about it, and did not care overmuch. Considering the likelihood of his imminent death, the war of succession in Brittany seemed insignificant.

The priest-knight Ascanio emerged from the long-house. "It will not be long." He looked skeptically at Morvan, and then at Lady Anna. "You will be well here?"

"Sir Morvan has nothing to gain from harming me, and his immortal soul to lose. Go now, and find the others." She turned to the youth. "Josce, they are our guests, not our prisoners. Follow Ascanio on this."

They rode off, leaving the bay mare, who had not moved a hair the whole time. "Your horse has no saddle," Morvan observed.

"She will take one, but prefers not to. I did not expect a battle today." She walked back into the longhouse.

She hadn't meant it as a jest. Clearly some days she did expect to be in battle.

When he followed he found her at the boy's bed, laying a wet cloth on his brow. William accepted her ministrations. His delirious moaning ceased and his fitful movements calmed.

Morvan gazed at the young, anguished body. Was this what awaited him? He would choose ten deaths in battle compared with this pitiful, ignoble exit. He suddenly wished that this woman had not spared him from the villagers' fire.

He watched slender, feminine hands do their work. "You said that you do not fear the death. If so, you are the only one who does not."

"I do not fear it because I have already suffered it. It does not claim the same body twice."

"You were ill but survived?" Over the course of the summer, as this plague ravaged all of Christendom, he had heard tales of whole villages killed, of cities losing half their people. He had never heard of survivors. "Are there others?"

"A few in our villages and the town. Very few."

"The priest? Ascanio?"

"Nay. He tempted fate repeatedly, but it never claimed him. There are a few others like that too."

"Why . . . How did you live?"

She looked at him with that level gaze. No feminine artifice. No coy glances or veiled expression. She looked at one as a man did. Straight, frank, and honest.

"I do not know how. As to why . . . sometimes I felt that I was spared so that there would be someone to bury my people."

She had been gently stroking William's hair and face. A peaceful sleep had claimed the youth.

"He can go at any moment, or it could take hours. We could hold a death vigil all night. I would get some rest, Sir Morvan. If the madness comes again, I may need your help."

Morvan glanced at William's face, angelic in its newly found repose. He looked at the half-hidden face of the strange woman whose touch had brought this peace. Then he retreated to the bench across from the door.

Anna sank down on the floor and leaned her back against the bed. She had learned during those horrible months of fighting the plague to take her sleep when she could get it. She closed her eyes and calculated the calendar of her guests' confinement. If no one besides Sir Morvan got sick, it would be simple. But if it spread through his company they could be in very cold weather before it ran its course. She hoped that none of the villeins or tenants had come in contact with these men.

The boy's uneven breathing broke her thoughts. She was impressed that this knight had stayed with him.

While nursing the plague-stricken she had seen mothers abandon their children, husbands their wives. This curse from God had shown the human soul for the frightened, pitiful thing that it was. She had thought that they were finally done with it, and could go back to rebuilding their illusions. She frankly wished that this knight had performed his noble Christian duty on someone else's lands.

She turned on her hip and looked down the room. Sir Morvan sat across from the door, his eyes closed and his body slouched against the wall. The door stood ajar and the light barely reached him, but it was enough for her to study his face.

It was a handsome face, and had probably been beautiful when he was a boy, before battle and time had hardened it. Now weather-bronzed skin stretched from strong cheekbones to square jaw, creating shadowed hollows between. He had a fine nose and a well-formed mouth, and no scars marked him. His black hair, unkempt from life in the field, hung beside his face in slight waves. His beard showed only a stubble, meaning that normally he was clean-shaven.

She regretted that his eyes were closed. They were remarkable eyes, dark and bright and expressive beneath their straight brows. When he smiled they sparkled like black diamonds and when he frowned a different, deeper fire burned in them. They were almost mesmerizing. Since she and Ascanio had entered the longhouse they were almost the only thing she had seen when she looked at this knight.

She had no interest in men as lovers or husbands, but she was not immune to male beauty. She could enjoy it, briefly and analytically, the way she enjoyed the colorful paintings in some of the Mother Abbess's books. This was a stunningly handsome man. She looked at him a long time before she rested her head against the side of the straw mattress.

Anna woke him with a touch to his shoulder. "He is gone. It was peaceful."

Morvan went over and looked down on the wasted body. "It happened very fast. He appeared well yesterday."

"Sometimes it goes like this. We sent some villagers to prepare a grave. It is consecrated ground. Put him on your horse, and we will walk there."

After they buried William they trailed through the forest until they reached the coastal road. There they mounted and rode in silence. Lady Anna controlled her animal with a calm authority. She sat very straight and held the reins expertly. The cotte hitched up her legs and pulled tightly around her hips, creating a long curving line from her waist to her boot. Anyone paying attention would know at once that this was a woman, with legs like that.

She gave a command and the horse moved quickly to a gallop. Morvan pushed Devil until he rode beside her again. As they flew past the flanking forest, she raised her face to the wind, which blew back her hair and billowed her cloak. The expression in her eyes as her horse charged forward was one of dazzling, uninhibited pleasure. His blood stirred in response to her private abandon.

Finally she reined in her horse and pointed to a road heading west. "That will take you to the town of Ville de la Roche. We could get home that way, but this is shorter." She led him to a forest path farther down the road.

The trees eventually thinned, then fell away. Across an open field, an old triangular castle stood on a rocky rise of land. A large tower formed the gatehouse at its front point, and a large round keep filled the northern angle. A wall stretched from the gatehouse for a goodly distance to the north.

As they neared he realized that the coast formed a cliff here. The castle had been built on a promontory of land jutting out into the ocean, and most of its walls rose above sheer chasms. A deep, wide ditch had been carved into the rock at the base of the walls facing the field.

"It is impressive," he said. "Has it ever been taken?"

"Nay. My family has held La Roche de Roald for over three hundred years. With the sea at our backs we can always be provisioned, so a siege is useless."

They rode through the gate into the bailey. It was empty of people, and eerily silent. The world of the living had retreated from the death that he carried. He peered at the upper reaches of the keep in time to see a young blond girl pull back from an open window.

A small portal stood open in the northern wall, too low for a man on horseback.

Anna dismounted. "Please leave your horse here and take what you need."

The gate gave on the section of field enclosed by the long northward-thrusting wall. It extended about two hundred yards before curving to meet the cliff, which made a natural boundary on the west. The enclosure served as an outer bailey, and small houses and service buildings hugged the wall.

In its middle, busily posting canvas lean-tos, worked the twenty men who had come north with him from Gascony. Each man's camp was separated from the next by a fire and they and the fires had been placed in neat rows, chessboard fashion.

"We have given them plenty of blankets, and canvas to protect them from rain. Food will be brought to the perimeter of the camp at meals," Anna explained. "They are far enough apart to avoid the disease's spreading if one succumbs, I hope."

"Why so many fires?"

"My brother told me that in Avignon the Pope was kept between two fires and he did not get the death. I have no idea if it really does any good, but we will try anything."

At the edge of the field, twenty paces from the cliff edge, was a wooden-roofed structure fitted with canvas walls. Anna brought him there. She pulled aside a canvas flap and secured it open.

Morvan stuck his head in and looked around. Three cots formed a U in front of a rude hearth. There was also a table, chair, and stool, and some buckets and rags in a corner.

A void opened in the pit of his gut.

"So, this is the death house," he said.

Anna built up the fire in the hearth and tried to act as if she hadn't heard him. She knew too well what he was experiencing, and it wasn't a moment for strangers to see.

This shelter represented the reality of his future, and he was facing it in his soul. It was one thing to know that you were going to die, and it was another thing to *know*. It had been too much to hope that he would be one of the many who were too unimaginative to ever fully know.

Memories of her own knowing, of waiting for the

death while huddled like a baby in Ascanio's arms, forced themselves on her. She fought back the desperation.

He still stood at the entrance. Those wonderful eyes stared dully, with all of his vision turned inward.

"I survived, Sir Morvan."

A bit of spark returned. He stepped into the shelter and gestured to the cots. "You expect others. When will you know?"

"When ten days pass and no one has shown the illness, your men can leave."

"And if one does?"

"He comes here and we begin the count again. Set down your possessions and I will help you remove your armor."

He permitted her to unbuckle the breast plate and help him lift it from his body. He sat on a cot and went to work on his arms and legs.

"Tell me, my lady, what is the name of your lord?"

"My lord?"

"Aye. I would know his name if I am to be his guest. What is your husband's name?"

She smiled at that. "Sir Morvan, look at me."

He glanced up as he set aside the plate.

"Nay. I mean *really* look at me."

"Aye, my lady." And he did. A speculative, amused expression passed on his face, and then a different one that left his jaw set and his eyes burning. The look unsettled her. She wondered if she had angered him somehow.

"Well, Sir Morvan, in all of your experience, have you ever met a man who would have a wife such as me?"

"My lady?"

"Think about it. If I had a husband telling me what to do, do you think that he would be telling me to do this?"

He smiled slowly. "Perhaps your husband is an unusual man."

"In this, there are no unusual men." She had removed her cloak on entering, and now swung it back over her shoulders. "I must go. Ascanio will come to you soon."

He accompanied her outside. Someone had placed little pennants around the structure, and others flew at the corners of the men's camp. They were blue and gold, not black, but their message was still a warning to stay away. Combined with the noisy camaraderie shouted over the fires, they gave the field almost a festive mood.

He faced her with eyes full of black fire. "Will you be back?"

"Someone will be with you," she said, promising comfort since she could offer little hope. "Either Ascanio or myself. You will be cared for. You will not be alone." She forced a cheerful smile of farewell, then walked away toward the castle. She sensed his gaze follow her until she passed through the bailey portal.

CHAPTER 2

LOOK AT ME, she had said. Really look at me. And he had. He had looked and the specter of death had slipped away as he suddenly saw the woman beneath the man's clothes and behind the wild mane of curls.

She was very beautiful, but not in a fashionable or predictable way. No tweezed brow and forehead, no elaborately coifed hair, no flowing gown. Her beauty was as honest and natural as her manner.

And as he looked desire had entered his head and shown him images of her dressed in thin silk, and then in nothing at all. He had been unprepared for that, and for the reaction of his body. He had no doubt that his unbidden thoughts were written on his face, but she had seemed oblivious to them. Or indifferent. He found that interesting. He almost never looked at a woman that way and have her fail to look back.

He judged her to be about eighteen, but it was hard to tell with the hair half hiding her face. When she gave orders to men or cast that level gaze she appeared older. The occasional smile lightened her eyes and features, however, and then he saw a girlish, almost childlike quality.

He watched her until, a proud gray and gold form, she disappeared into the inner bailey. She didn't walk like most women, but it wasn't a man's stride either. Rather, she had a purposeful, fluid movement, with all of her limbs working together in graceful coordination.

A strange woman. Interesting. He had never met one quite like her before, and he had known many women very well. The one constant in his life besides his skill at arms had been his ability to attract women. They came to him because of his face and body and stayed because of the pleasure he could give them. As a youth he had reveled in those conquests, but the predictability of success had made the sieges less interesting of late. It was, in the end, a cheap form of power.

A voice calling his name roused him from his thoughts. At the edge of the camp a familiar figure waved to him. Morvan walked to the boundary marked by his own pennants and found himself thirty feet from Gregory, one of the archers in his troop. A good man, Gregory, strong and honorable and a plain speaker who had aided Morvan in keeping the men in order during the past months. When life got hard as they crisscrossed their way up the coast from Gascony, trying to avoid the plague outbreaks, it had been Gregory whose voice always supported him as he convinced the men not to resort to brigandage. And yet, that week when no town would receive them and there was no food, it had also been Gregory who disappeared for a day and returned with a cloakful of bread and fowl. No one had asked him how he came by it, least of all Morvan.

"Well, you've finally led us to paradise, Sir Morvan," Gregory called with a grin.

Morvan smiled back at the graying beard and thickening form of his friend. "Was there any trouble?"

"Not to speak of. We outnumbered them and they were just boys, but they caught us napping, so we had to listen. Even Sir John, who argued long and loud that they might have taken your cloak from your dead body and that we couldn't trust them. But the knight, the one called Ascanio—he's a priest, did you know that?—he promised us hot food and soft blankets and, well, soldiers like us live to be bought."

"Try to keep things orderly. If they stay apart and all goes well, you can be on your way soon."

"Oh, they'll be orderly. There's archers on that wall and those bolts can come this way as well as outside."

"Have you learned anything of our hosts?"

"We spoke with some servants who brought us supplies. A few speak French and some of the men know a bit of Breton." Even from thirty paces Morvan could see his eyes twinkle. "It is a strange place you've brought us to. There is no lord here. A Lady Anna is mistress. A saint, to hear them speak of her. She defends the castle, manages the farms, cures the sick, and probably walks on water and makes the sun move. Some have seen divine light glow from her at night, ever since they say an angel saved her from the death. Seems her father died in battle and her brother of the plague and she's all that's left, her and a younger sister. Dedicated to God, too. Convent-raised and convent-bound, once she gets the young duke to settle things here."

"I have met her. Hardly saintly. Just a woman in man's clothes."

"Was she that lad who brought you in? She must be taller than me."

"A tall woman, and formidable, but still a woman."

"That's what Sir John said. He speaks Breton well, and he also learned that there is a legend of a treasure hidden here, brought back from the Holy Land by an ancestor."

John was bound to be trouble. He was too full of youthful conceit and arrogance not to be.

"He also," Gregory continued, "has studied the castle closely and, I figure, has realized as I have that there be no more than twelve men, along with the priest and the lady, holding the place. And most of them are green."

Morvan didn't like the implications. The castle was unbreachable, but that wasn't a problem if it was lightly defended and you were already inside. "Did they let you keep your weapons?"

Gregory shook his head. "Sir John was indignant when they took his too, but this Ascanio isn't stupid."

"You must watch John. Do not let him influence the others. Make sure that your voice is heard, for I'll not be with you."

"If he plans something, he'll wait until you are sick or dead," Gregory said bluntly.

"Go to your meal now. I see it being brought. If God is generous, I'll speak with you in the morning."

Morvan waved him off and walked to the cliff edge. This section of the coastline shot farther out to sea than the promontory on which the castle stood. From here he could see the back of the keep.

It was built right into the cliff, with heavy buttresses supporting the foundations. Above that curved the living quarters, marked by small windows. Then a newer level rose, with larger windows and the unusual feature of a gallery hanging off one room, its openings neatly arched and roofed.

Something else caught his attention. The rock of the cliff below the castle had been worked, and a narrow staircase carved into the living stone. It zigzagged up from the small beach until it disappeared behind one of the foundation buttresses. There would be a postern door there. A secret way out and in, and inaccessible to an enemy even if he knew of it.

He walked back toward the shelter, staying near the cliff. The sun was setting, and he sat on a large rock that still held its warmth. He looked out to the sea, feeling empty and exposed in a way that he had never experienced when facing death in battle. But he'd had some control over his fate then.

A sense of utter isolation descended on him. The sounds from the camp dimmed and disappeared. He had become accustomed to being alone in the world, but this was growing more intense and essential than that. It was as if an invisible hand was drawing a circle around him that prevented even tenuous connections to the other men, leaving him with only his soul for company.

Nay, not only his soul. The sea and the sky were still alive for him, surrounding him with their sounds and vastness. The western horizon became streaked with brilliant pinks and purples that reflected like colored ice on the throbbing eddy of the water. Even the crests of the breaking waves were touched by the colors, and the dimming light itself seemed tinted. He was momentarily awed by the beauty, and entranced by the slowly sinking disk of fire on the edge of the world.

His tired spirit rose and stretched in response to the view. Like something out of his control, it grew until it contained his body and not the other way around. In an unnatural silence profound for its stillness, his invisible self reached out and touched the beauty, feeling it as something physical. In that instant of breathless transcendence, another presence met his in the glory. It was human, not godly, of that he was sure, for he at once knew its essence even if he did not know its name.

It was a stunning moment of connection that ended almost as quickly as it came, but which contained a sense of infinity while it lasted. Its passing left him suddenly more alone than before, and more aware of his separateness, and drenched with painful resignation.

So, it would end here. The Fitzwaryn name, ennobled by the Conqueror himself, would die in obscurity on this rocky Breton coast. The lost lands would never be regained, his sister's sons would never be knights, the entire family wealth would never be more than the gold and emerald necklace buried in his bag. He would have to tell the priest about that, and ask to have it sent to his sister in London.

Would that merchant husband of hers let her keep it, or take it to finance yet another expansion of his trade? Did it matter? In a generation the family's nobility would be no more. His failure to his family's honor was the only real regret that he had about his life. He had always carried that like a glowing ember in his heart, but now it flared to engulf him.

"Sir Morvan."

The blaze subsided. He turned to see Ascanio approaching. The armor was gone but he still looked more knightly than priestly. He wore a friendly expression and not the suspicious one from the village. Sitting on the grass near the rock, Ascanio said, "I have come to ask if you want to confess."

"Under the circumstances, I think that I had better."

"Probably so."

It did not take long. There had been little opportunity for his normal sins during the months of running from the plague. He included a litany of earlier ones of the flesh, in case he had forgotten them at previous times. The priest kept silent when he was done.

Morvan finally spoke, to break the confessional mood. "You are from Italy? How came you here?"

Ascanio's pose relaxed, and he became a knight again. "Two years ago I decided to take the coastal pilgrimage route to Santiago. I stopped at an abbey called Saint Meen. There was trouble in the area, with free companies raiding villages. I convinced the abbot to form a defense and hire some men."

"It was good advice."

"They had a sister abbey for women a few miles away. Fifteen nuns and some girls. Brigands attacked it. One of the girls, no more than sixteen, knew something of weapons. She held the men off with a crossbow, wounding four including the leader, and the others fled."

"Lady Anna? Did they turn her out after she saved them?"

"Nay. The abbess had been frightened witless. She asked my abbot for a man to train the girl further. He sent me."

"The world has truly turned upside down. So you, a priest, were sent to teach a novice nun weaponry?"

"She was not a novice. She had taken no vows yet. What was the abbess to do? This civil war has made Brittany a lawless land. Unprotected women are safe nowhere, not even in an abbey. Word that the place was armed could perhaps deter the overbold."

Morvan shook his head in amazement. "It is a strange story, but then these are strange times. So you went?"

"Aye. She had hunted as a child and her bow eye was superb. She did not need my help there. We just worked with the sword."

"Is she any good with it?"

"She is skilled and quick. But armor weighs her down and extended swordplay in it requires more strength than she has."

Morvan pictured that. The image was not nearly as fantastic as it should have been. "Why did you both come back here?"

"After her father died in battle, her brother requested her return while he attended to some business in Avignon. When he came back, however, he was sick with the plague. The town priest would not attend, so she sent for me. When I arrived, she wanted me to shrive him through the closed door." He shrugged. "I confess that I considered it. But I made her let me in and together we helped him to die. Then we waited."

"You did not get sick. Are you blessed?"

"Just fortunate."

"She was not."

"Nay. But no one else died. This was in March. Then in June it reappeared, and it hit like a wave. One quarter of the town perished. One in five on the estate lands."

"I have heard worse."

"As have we. Even so, it is difficult to be grateful after such a curse." He rose to his feet. "Now I must go see to your men and other duties. Someone will come to you later."

Come to see if he was dying yet.

He walked with Ascanio toward the camps. "Do you stay to protect her? Until she returns to the abbey?"

"She protects herself. But there are no knights here—the few remaining died—so, I have stayed for a while.

Until the young duke appoints a warden, or until the boy Josce earns his spurs."

"Then she will return to the abbey?"

Ascanio shot him a penetrating glance. His eyes showed the memory of what he had just heard in the confession. "She will return. She is resolved."

In any other circumstance it might have been a warning instead of a flat statement of fact.

But there was no need to warn a dead man.

CHAPTER 3

ANNA BENT HER KNEES and scooted forward so the water would cover her shoulders. Only God knew when she would have time to bathe again. The next week promised to be one of sleepless nights and duty-packed days.

She ducked her head and rinsed the soap from her wet curls, then stood and wrapped the towel around her. She moved the stool to the fire and began the horrible process of combing through the snarls made by wind and water.

When she was young an old servant had done this, loudly bemoaning the condition of her hair every day. Then she would cluck over the bruises Anna's adventures had raised and, when she thought Anna wasn't looking, shake her head over the body itself. A lot of people did that, for she was always much larger for her age than other girls, and even most boys. For as long as she could remember, she had expected startled looks when people met her.

Only her father hadn't seemed to find her grotesque. The last Roald de Leon in a line of Roalds, he had been bigger than life and full of the Viking blood of the first Roald, who had planted a fortress on this cliff rock. He had found joy in her size and strength, and had shown delight in her horsemanship and good bow eye. The only attention she received from him came because of her unwomanly skills.

She went to a trunk and found some clean clothes. After dressing she returned to the fire to let her hair dry, combing through the curls so that they wouldn't be too wild. As always she did this herself, without the aid of a mirror.

There had been no mirrors at the abbey either, but she had ceased looking in them long before she entered that world of women. She knew what she looked like, and as a young girl had seen her lack of beauty in her mother's regretful eyes as surely as she had seen it in her own reflection.

When people glanced with astonishment at her height and face now, it mattered not to her. Beauty would avail her nothing in the life she would have, a life delayed only briefly by her current duties at the estate. She looked forward to returning to the abbey. A world that suited her waited there.

The light told her that the sun was setting, and she went to the gallery. A glorious sky greeted her as she stepped out onto the covered balcony. Blues and pinks and purples streaked the sky, and the sun itself appeared as a huge orange circle skimming the edge of the horizon. The air filled with color and the light transformed the sea. It was the sort of beauty that showed God in all of his magnificence in the world, and her spirit stretched and melted into it as the sun finished its slow descent.

She glanced down. A solitary figure sat on a rock by the cliff's edge, his arms resting on his knees, his body poised in reflection. From her perch, Sir Morvan appeared desperately isolated and vulnerable.

Her heart wrenched with astounding empathy. She might have touched his soul for an instant, so profound was her understanding. The spike of connection assaulted her as if her separateness had disappeared, absorbed by the glory filling the sky.

It frightened her, and she was grateful when it quickly passed. But its power echoed in her emotions as she watched Sir Morvan. Had they told him that she was supposed to be touched by the angels? She doubted that this knight would believe such nonsense, but if he chose to because it gave him hope she wouldn't argue the point.

Two hours later, Anna sat at the high table nibbling her supper. The meal was symbolic of their lives. In reverse of normal practice, the meat was plentiful and the bread sparse. Animals of the hunt had survived the summer's neglect, but the fields had not. The household's grain had to be rationed carefully.

As the noise in the hall flowed around her, she tried to calculate how she would arrange to nurse Sir Morvan and still manage the estate. There were horses at the stud farm that needed her hand, that needed to be trained and sold in order to buy grain for the villages.

The horses promised to be their salvation. Their farm bred and trained the best in Brittany. Secluded and accessible only by secret paths, it had been safe from brigands and thieves. Just as well, for she could spare only two men to protect it.

Her sister Catherine tapped her arm for attention. "Tell Josce that I'm right. I said that Sir Morvan is the most handsome man on the estate, with eyes like a dark angel, and he doesn't agree."

Anna looked past her younger sister's delicate, pretty face and cloud of fair hair. On Catherine's other side Josce fumed silently. "Don't tease him. I know girls think it is a game to make boys jealous, but it isn't worthy of you."

Catherine rolled her eyes. "You are always so serious, Anna. You have to be the most dull sister in the world."

"Perhaps I'm just a sister with a lot to do. Are you getting the women on with the Nativity sewing?"

"Aye. There will be new clothes for everyone." Catherine turned away to flirt with Josce. He lowered his sandy head and whispered something in her ear. He also nibbled that ear.

They were sixteen and old enough to marry. It was what her father had wanted and what the estate's future required. Then La Roche de Roald would pass through Catherine to Josce. Perhaps she should just let them marry and forget about obtaining the duke's permission. He was only ten years old, after all, and over in England. Neither he nor his guardian, King Edward, had responded to her letters, assuming that they had even received them.

The question of the estate's future was a weight that never left her shoulders, and this evening it pressed heavier than ever. She needed to settle things. La Roche de Roald needed to be secured to a Breton lord, so that it did not get swallowed by either France or England in these squabbles and alliances over titles and land. The plague had given them a perverse security, but chaos stirred on the edges of their world, threatening to engulf them.

Ascanio entered the hall and approached her table. "One of us must bring Sir Morvan food. The servants were too frightened to leave it near the shelter."

She ordered a servant to place food and wine in a basket. "You have not eaten. I will go. I had planned to visit him this evening anyway."

That was not entirely true. She recognized her duty to visit him, but had been trying to justify not going. Being close to the man unsettled her. Riding back to the castle, she had sensed that large presence, and it had put her on her guard the whole time. It was foolish, of course. He represented no danger and appeared to be an honorable knight. Still, he unaccountably made her wary.

She sent for her cloak and a box from her chamber, then took the basket and headed out.

CHAPTER 4

MORVAN SAW ANNA AS SOON as she passed through the portal. He stood at the entrance to the shelter watching the night sky, identifying the constellations that had been taught to him by his tutor when he was a boy.

He had known that she would come. He had been waiting for her.

Her hair had been combed into something smoother and less wild, and a band of silver circled her forehead and tamed it further. She had changed into a blue long-sleeved tunic that fell just past her knees, leaving a glimpse of hose-clad legs above felt shoes.

"I have brought you supper," she said.

Morvan held open the canvas and she swept inside. He moved the table and chair near one of the cots by the fire as she set aside the box she'd been carrying.

"Will you join me?"

She shook her head but accepted some wine. She settled into the chair, back stiff and knees together. He
could barely keep his eyes off her as he set out the food.
She sat like a queen. Like an ancient warrior queen.

She leveled that gaze at him. He realized that it wasn't
so frank and confident as he had thought, but contained
a guarded caution.

"Sir Morvan, I do not know you well. If you would
prefer to be alone, I will leave. But if you desire company,
I will stay a while."

"I would have you stay."

He sat on the cot and picked at his food. The silence
stretched, and he was grateful that she made no attempt
to fill it with witless chatter. This woman was not afraid
of quiet. She would not speak until she had something
to say. In the meantime the mood was companionable
and relaxing.

He looked at her on occasion while he ate. The blue
tunic fit better than the afternoon's clothes and she had
removed her cloak, but her form still looked ambiguous,
as if her woman's body took refuge beneath the loosely
shaped wool. Her lovely face wore a mask of serene calm.
In a curious way her arrival had made this death house a
friendly and natural space. He felt more ease than he had
experienced in many months.

"Where is your home?" she finally asked.

He would have her stay, but not to talk about him. On
the other hand, she had a right to be curious. After all,
he'd made it a point to find out about her.

"My family lived in the north near Scotland. An estate
called Harclow."

"Lived?"

"Fourteen years ago, during the Scottish wars, our

lands were besieged by a lord from across the border. My father died defending the castle. I was a boy at the time. It was left to me to surrender in order to save my mother and sister. We went to King Edward, who was campaigning in the north, and he gave us refuge. He had been my father's friend."

She waited for him to continue. He paused a long while, then relented. "My mother died soon after. Edward took my sister and myself into his household."

"You lived at court?"

"When of age I went into service with Sir John Chandros. Later I became one of the King's household knights. But most of those years were spent at court."

"What was it like?"

"It is a false place with false people. Your future hinges on a word, a gesture."

She looked straight at him and he looked straight back. Her eyes were almond-shaped, and her brows angled like the wings of a falcon in flight.

"Did a word or a look unhinge your future?"

Damn, but the woman was sharp. "Three years ago I fell out of favor with the prince. Around the same time I realized that the King would not help me regain our lands. When the army went to Normandy to fight the French king, I rode with Edward, but I knew that I would not return to the court with him. I earn my living by my sword now. It is honorable."

She sipped her wine thoughtfully, holding the cup with both hands. Her rod-straight back had not moved an inch.

"Did you have many tournaments and jousts at the court? I have heard that many kings no longer permit them because they waste knights. Fewer men to die in their battles then."

"Spoken like a woman, my lady."

"You think so? This woman would like to fight in such a festival. One where all weapons are used. Jousts rely on the lance too much. Do you favor the lance?"

"I prefer the sword, but the lance is still considered the most chivalrous weapon." He couldn't believe that he was discussing weaponry with this woman, and thoroughly enjoying himself doing so. "Which weapon do you favor?"

"The bow. The coward's weapon. I am a woman, Sir Morvan."

"I would say that is obvious."

"Hardly. Many people don't notice. Even you at first."

She had missed both the compliment and the appreciative look he had given her. Utterly oblivious to both. Amazing. "The longhouse was dark. I saw what I expected to see."

"Most do. It is very useful. When I ride alone, strangers see what they expect to see too."

"Do you do that often? Ride alone? It is dangerous. The roads are full of displaced soldiers and peasants. With the war and the plague—"

"I have duties to perform, and too few men to always bring an escort."

She had finally relaxed, and her long, lithe body had fallen into sinuous lines. He noticed again that the legs visible below the tunic were slender and shapely. Firm straight shoulders balanced the gentle flare of her hips. He wondered what her breasts looked like. The rest of her seemed beautifully proportioned to her height.

"You find me amusing, don't you?" she asked, misunderstanding his scrutiny. "The clothes and sword. My questions about tournaments. You think that I am a girl playing at being a man."

"I find you unusual."

"Unusual. A kinder word than most would use."

"Does that offend you?"

"Not at all. I do not care what people think. A woman who looks like me must learn that. Unusual. Not a bad word. Still, you do not approve."

"You are very brave. Who can disapprove of that? Still, I am accustomed to women being protected."

"Aye, protected. And commanded. They go together, don't they?" She turned her head to the fire for a moment, and then looked back and deliberately changed the subject. "You intend to try and regain your lands still."

"It has been my hope."

"But each year that passes, it becomes more unlikely." She said it like she was finishing his own thought, and she was, but it was a thought that he rarely admitted to. Still, he found that he couldn't summon any anger.

Since she had come he hadn't felt like he was with a stranger, but rather in the company of an old friend. That first long silence had been filled with an oddly familiar connection that had gotten deeper as they spoke. Every passing moment had served to ply an invisible cord, like a tether between their souls.

Was it her frankness? His need for distraction? All he knew was that his sense of this woman's spirit was heightened. The air in the shelter was heavy with a peculiar intensity. An intimacy. He felt raw and oddly free.

"Why do you wear men's clothes?" he asked, much preferring to talk about her than himself.

She raised her eyebrows in amusement. "Why do *you* wear men's clothes?"

"I am a man."

"Nay. You wear them because they suit men's work. That is why they are men's clothes. I find myself doing men's work now." She smiled. It was a nice smile. It animated her face. She didn't smile often these days. He just knew that. "They were my brother's garments. I began wearing them to work with our horses. Then, with the death, gowns became impractical. I didn't come home with many gowns anyway."

"From the abbey? Did you live there from girlhood?"

"Nay, only four years. When my father went to fight in the duke's cause, he put me there for safety. One of his vassals gave a home to Catherine, my sister, but I was not welcome. I did not like the abbey at first, but I found contentment there."

"Ascanio says that you will go back. That you will take vows."

"Aye."

"Why?"

She looked away and did not answer at once. He sensed vulnerability in her, and was pleased to find it. "I belong there. There is no place for me in the world outside of there," she finally said.

"There is here. With your people."

"There is no place for me here. I won't marry and I do not like women's things. You kindly call me unusual. My people think that I am unnatural."

"They think that you are *super*natural."

"It is the same thing. Today I am a saint. Next year the crops fail and I am a witch. It is a thin line that I walk through no choice of my own."

She abruptly rose and fetched the box she had brought. "Your meal is done? Then let us play draughts."

He poured more wine while she set out the pieces. He had expected a desperate night, but the shadow of death had been banished by this woman's presence and the strange bond he felt with her. He made his first move and watched as she considered her own.

He had to know if she was with him in the way that he thought.

"It is strange, but since you came I have had this feeling that I have known you . . . years." He spoke words that he had used before in flattery and seduction. This was the first time he had ever meant them.

"Aye. It happens sometimes." Her gaze rose to meet his, and it was as if she could see into his heart and knew him like a mother knows a son, or a woman her husband. "It comes from you. You expect to die. You have nothing to lose. You are open. I am just the one who is here. If Ascanio had come instead of me, it would have been the same. But I know what you mean."

She had felt this before. It was an astounding thought.

He continued the game in silence. He could tell she did not want to speak of it.

She may have been here before, but she was wrong about one thing. If Ascanio had come it would not have been the same. Because Anna was a woman, and Morvan had been aware for some time that he wanted her more than he had ever wanted a woman before in his life.

"Tell me about Josce," he said, in a futile attempt to distract his thoughts from that. But his blood told him how this night should end. He needed to touch her. He wanted to take the silver band from her head and stroke out her curls with his fingers until her hair swept wild and free again.

"He is a kinsman. Distant. He came as a page, to be fostered. He was my father's squire, and at his side when he died."

He wanted to kiss her. Taste her mouth and her neck.

Smell her. He wanted to bend that rigid back over his arm and have her look up at him as he caressed her, as his hand found the lacing to her tunic. . . .

"He is like a brother to me. But his relationship with Catherine has been something more for several years."

He would undress her and discover the body beneath those loose garments. He imagined her hidden breasts as he held them in his hands and took them in his mouth. Her moans of desire filled his head. In his mind's eye, a veil of yielding passion softened her penetrating gaze. He would lay her down, and cover her with his hands and mouth and finally his body. . . .

"My father's will assumed my brother would inherit and that I would take vows. Now, with my brother Drago gone, when Catherine and Josce marry, Josce will be the next lord of La Roche de Roald."

He had seen her ecstasy when she galloped her horse. He wanted to watch her as he took her and that sensual oblivion claimed her for him alone. He would control her and bring her with him, their union finishing what he felt here tonight. Completing it . . .

"Sir Morvan," her voice intruded and brought him back.

Was he mad? He had confessed and was clean. Yet here he sat, contemplating the seduction of a virgin touched by angels and dedicated to God. But it felt as though heaven itself was part of this temptation.

"Sir Morvan," she repeated, tapping the board. "It is your move."

He shifted a piece and then watched her again with that unsettling gaze. Anna had been trained in restraint and serenity at the abbey, but her studied reserve hid dismay.

She had lied to him. She had suggested that she had felt this before, but she had not. The connection was always a possibility when she cared for the dying, but this had been more immediate than ever before. Even with Ascanio, when they had both reached out in their fear of the abyss awaiting them, even then it had built more slowly.

Later, during the plague, she had feared this unnatural intimacy and the love and pain that it brought. It made the death harder on her. She had been grateful that with most of the sick she could just be mistress and nurse and nothing more.

And now this. Different. Stronger. Somehow even dangerous.

He wanted something more. She could feel his spirit stretching toward her.

She kept the conversation going, because the pauses became filled with an acute expectation that unnerved her. She told of her attempts to settle the estate's future so it would be secured for Brittany. She told him about her many letters to the duke in England, asking for a warden's appointment, and for permission for Catherine to marry.

She described her problems keeping the estate protected. How, when her brother took sick, some men-at-arms fled and how, with the death, more died. In the end Ascanio had recruited and trained some sons of free-holders on the estate. The plague had given them a respite of sorts, but already problems were starting again and a band of thieves had been harassing the area.

And then, in the middle of her description of the castle's history, Morvan asked, "Why won't you marry?"

"If you marry," he went on, "the estate would be yours."

"If I marry, the estate would be my husband's."

"Still, you would have a place."

She did not want to talk about this. She could never expect anyone, let alone this *man,* to understand. "Only the place my husband let me have. A woman's place, serving him. I would rather serve God."

"If you want freedom, there is little of that in the abbey."

"More than you think. For a married noblewoman there is none. The villeins in the fields and the merchant's daughter in town have more. My nature is not suited for such a life and I will not turn myself into something I am not to please a husband."

He appeared to study the draughts very closely. "Will you not miss things?"

He glanced up at her, his eyes as fiery as they had been when she'd left him in the evening. For a moment she felt mesmerized by that gaze. A peculiar excitement coursed through her. The sensation wasn't unpleasant.

"I will have to give up the horse and the hunt again. Someday I may regret not having children. Besides that, what is there to miss?"

His wonderful eyes sparkled. He smiled slowly. "I think," he said, "that you do not know what you are talking about."

She felt trapped by his attention. That exhilarating sensation shot through her again. A power emanated from him. It was strong and willful and very male. Her own will and strength retreated from it, leaving her vulnerable and exposed.

Instinctively, she knew that she had to leave. Now.

She rose abruptly. "It is very late and I have much to do on the morrow. More important is that you rest."

Her cloak lay on his cot. He stood with it in his hands

and came over to her. She barely resisted the urge to back away.

He draped the cloak around her shoulders and fastened the brooch under her neck. She became uncomfortably aware of his closeness as she submitted to his slow actions.

That strange sensation shook her again.

He placed his hands on her shoulders and looked at her, his eyes sparkling like dark jewels.

He lowered his mouth to her lips in a soft kiss.

A tremor shot through her like a physical scream.

His gaze captured her again. She realized that she was staring back like a stunned animal, and shook off the effect. The eyes of a dark angel, Catherine had said. Or maybe just the beginning of a fever. The nurse in her placed her palm on his jaw to check.

He grabbed her wrist and held her hand on his face.

"I would have you stay," he said, kissing her palm, sending chills up her arm. She gasped at the intensity of her reaction.

Suddenly, she understood. It was so unexpected, so *preposterous,* that she froze in amazement. It had not been unusual during the plague for men to decide that they would await their fate on top of a woman, but she had certainly never been the woman whom they had in mind. It wasn't just her status protecting her. She simply wasn't the kind of woman whom men desired. But this knight probably thought that she was the only one available.

She gently extricated her hand. "I cannot." She walked away, feeling strange and shaky. She was not insulted, just surprised. She knew that men had this need and that there were times when it would not be denied. His had to be very great if he was approaching one such as her.

At the threshold to the shelter, she paused. He joined her, and his presence warmed her shoulder and side. The air around them weighed heavily with their raw awareness of each other. Looking out into the night, she spoke. "In the town there is a woman who is forever free of the disease and does not fear it. I could send for her. She would come."

She could tell that he was watching her. Perhaps he was shocked that she would offer such a thing.

"I have no interest in the whore."

That confused her. Had she misunderstood? She touched his arm lightly to acknowledge what had passed between them, and stepped away.

A strong hand grabbed her arm, stopping her. With breathless astonishment she felt herself pulled back and turned. The face that she met looked severe in the faint light from the distant hearth. He held her upper arms as if he would lift her from the ground.

"You do not have to go. Stay with me."

"You ask too much. There are limits to Christian charity."

"I ask only that you stay until I sleep. Your presence eases my mind. I would have you here only to keep the demons away. I will not offend you."

She thought about his death watch, and again remembered her own. How much harder to be a man, who could not show fear or even admit it to himself. What would it have been like without Ascanio there to comfort her?

That invasive intimacy flowed, heightening her empathy. What could it hurt to sit with him a while longer? He'd promised not to offend her. If he tried . . . well, she had dealt with that before and always could again.

"If you will take your rest, I will stay a little longer."

Feeling extremely awkward, she followed him back inside. When they reached the cots he turned to her. She hesitated, not knowing where to go or what to do.

She remembered Ascanio's physical closeness during those desperate hours, and how it gave her such comfort. She could not embrace this man or lie beside him as she had with Ascanio, however. The way he watched and waited looked anything but priestly. She walked over to one of the cots and perched stiffly on its end.

"Sleep now, Sir Morvan. I will sit by your head."

He sat and removed his boots. Unfurling a blanket, he stretched out. He was a tall man, and his head settled not beside her on the cot, but on her lap. She stiffened even more in surprise.

He reached up and guided her head down. He gave her a long, sweet kiss before releasing her lips. He held her thus, inches from his face, and his dark eyes gazed into hers. She worried that he could hear the clamoring pulse of her heartbeat.

He smiled ruefully. "It appears that I will die with two regrets instead of one, my lady. When the angels visit you next time, you must demand that I get full credit for my restraint."

He dropped his arm and turned on his side, his head cradled on her thighs and his hand resting on her knee.

She sat motionless, awed by the sensation of his weight on her, stunned by the physicality of it. Still confused by that kiss, she barely breathed until she sensed his body loosening as sleep began to claim him.

The low fire sent dim lights and shadows down his resting form to his face. He looked younger now with those planes softening in his repose. She reflected on this poignant friendship which the plague had brought her and would soon take away. A dagger, edged with regret and resentment, pierced her heart.

She raised her hands without thinking, and they hovered in the space above him. Hesitant and awkward, she let her hands fall and come to rest on his shoulder and in the black waves of his hair.

CHAPTER 5

SENSATIONS ASSAULTED HIM as he drifted on the edges of the black fog. Restraining weight . . . Slick, moist heat . . . A few flashes of light . . .

He struggled toward wakefulness, but only touched it, barely. A smell was all that he reached—the stench of corrupted flesh and death. His spirit recoiled, retreating from the odor, but it followed him into the fog, bringing new images that flew at him, filling the blackness, merging into memories worse than any vision wrought by the demons. . . .

The chamber stunk of corrupted flesh and death.

Two eyes gazed up from their sunken hollows. A hand summoned weakly, no more than a vague gesture.

He swallowed sickening bile and leaned over his dying father. How unfair that one chance arrow could lay waste to such a man as Hugh Fitzwaryn.

"Has Edward come?" The chest wound made the question little more than a gasp for breath. "They know I am dying, so I think that they lie to me. I ask you for the truth."

He should lie too, he felt, but he could not. He shook his head. "He has not come. Nor has word that he will."

Lids lowered over eyes glazed with pain. His father grew so still that it appeared death had grabbed him.

The eyes opened again, and bored into him. "It is left to you, then, because my time is over, boy."

"I promise you that we will hold. No matter how long it takes, until help comes we will hold, or else we will fight to the last man—"

"Nay, you must petition for terms. With me gone, the men will break. Hunger would have defeated them already, but for their loyalty to me."

"It is too late. What terms can men get who surrender on the brink of defeat?"

"Not for you and the men. For the women. Get that laird's word that they can leave. Send them to Edward. A knight must protect the weak, boy, and now you must do what must be done to save the ladies."

He barely got the last words out. He closed his eyes again. His whole body seemed to shrink, like speech had robbed it of substance.

Another weak gesture, telling him to leave. He did not. He called for his mother and sister, and held the death vigil with them while the sounds of battle poured in through the windows. He stood there, holding that still hand, hoping that the bravery and strength of the great Hugh Fitzwaryn would pass into his son when he breathed his last.

In the hour before dawn he left the chamber and went to the lord's solar, no longer a boy. He ordered the steward to send a herald to negotiate, and then prepared himself. He dressed in his

*finest garments, and strapped his father's sword to his waist. He
was tall for his age, but the tip still scraped the floor.*

*He sought out the priest and confessed, then prayed in the
chapel. He did not visit his mother, for she would try to dissuade
him.*

*The castle yard fell silent when he emerged from the keep. The
men watched solemnly, embarrassed that a ten-year-old boy
must offer his own life in a desperate bid to save theirs.*

*He marched on bravely, the way his father had taught him a
knight walks. He passed through the yard where five months ago
he had played with a ball and where he had practiced with a
sword made of wood.*

*He paused at the open gate, and glanced back to the keep. His
mother stood at its threshold, gauntly pale from hunger, dark
eyes glowing like jewels. The child in him wanted to run back to
the comfort of her arms.*

He faced the gate. Death waited on the other side. . . .

The chamber stunk of corrupted flesh and death.

He awoke to dampness, heat, and unbearable weakness. It took him awhile to recognize the canvas walls
and wooden roof.

With effort he turned his head. A man twisted
painfully on the cot beside him, half exposing his naked
body. Dark boils marked the hairy arm and flank. The
man mumbled, and he tried in vain to recognize the
vague voice. He hoped that it wasn't Gregory.

His own cot was soaked and clammy and his body was
drenched in sweat. Several furs weighed on his weakness
and smothered him with their heat. He considered
throwing them off, but every muscle shrank from the
thought of moving.

Was he almost dead? He felt more tired than he had ever been in his life. Even a day of fighting did not leave his body this useless.

The cool air on his face was delicious, like a drink of ale after battle. Focusing his strength, he pulled his right arm from under the furs and let it fall limply. His fingers, free now, stroked the fur's rich nap.

He touched something silky and fine mixed with the fur. Wrapping his hand in the new texture, he rubbed the soft threads between his thumb and palm.

Hair. Woman's hair. He slowly shifted his body and bent his neck until he could see.

Anna sat on the floor beside him, her body turned so that her sleeping head could rest on the cot's edge, nestled in the crook of her right arm. She wore only hose and a man's undertunic. Her upraised arm pulled the fabric around the curve of a breast. A round, full, feminine breast. He could see part of its swell through the gaping neck of the tunic. She bound herself when she wore men's garments, he realized.

The hose displayed shapely hips and legs. It would be very pleasant to caress those sinuous curves. He decided that he must not be almost dead if he was imagining such a thing.

Her sleeping face, luminous in the fire glow, looked peaceful, young, and mysterious. He could have looked at her forever if the back of his neck had not pained him so. He collapsed on the pillow.

She had been with him before during this illness, but his memories were mere phantoms. His last lucid sight of her came from the day after he arrived, when he woke briefly to see her sitting on the nearby cot. There had been trouble on the estate in the morning and she had ridden out with the guard to try and catch the thieves who once more harassed them. While they were gone the fever had slammed into him, and by the time Ascanio had come to check at midday he was a shivering mess. After that all was darkness and fearful dreams, except for one clear moment when he'd fought to consciousness and seen her there. "I am with you" was all she'd said before the black cloud claimed him again.

Now he stroked her hair, enjoying its texture. She had not been here the whole time. Others had come, Ascanio and another woman. Perhaps the whore whom she had mentioned.

Images from that night flew past his inner eye. He had frightened her. She was totally unawakened, no more than a child in these things. Only as she'd sought to run like a rabbit facing a fox had she been able to name what was happening. Even then she had misunderstood it as base and desperate lust. Never before in his life had he put aside his desire as he had forced himself to do with her.

Her curls felt soft as they wrapped themselves around his hand. She was a unique woman, strong and self-possessed, but he had seen the child in her.

She was practically alone, like him. She indeed walked a fine line, as she had said that night. She had been lucky thus far, but luck never holds forever.

The fog began clouding in again. He unwrapped his fingers from her hair but placed his hand flat against the silky strands. Silently, as he sank into oblivion, he swore an oath to protect this strange woman who stood so bravely on her own in a dangerous and graceless world.

The canvas walls blocked the sun, and the shelter was lit mainly by the fire. It took Anna's eyes a moment to adjust to the dimness as she slipped inside.

What she finally saw made her halt in her tracks.

Morvan had risen from the cot. He stood naked in front of the hearth, facing it, legs parted and arms spread low and wide. His head was angled back, and she imagined that his eyes were closed. He appeared as if the sensation of the heat had created an ecstasy.

He had not heard her enter. She should leave, or make herself known. She should at least look away.

She didn't.

The plague had cost him some weight, but it had not diminished his strength much. He was still a beautiful animal, more like the courser she had just ridden at the farm than a warhorse. His torso and legs were muscular but without exaggerated bulk. His shoulders stretched straight and hard and a series of flat angled planes defined him. His body was chiseled in stone rather than molded of clay, and now it stood in its glory in the fire glow, like a statue given life.

She had come to know that body well while she cared for him during the fever and deliriums. More than once she had needed to bathe it. After the first day she had ceased being embarrassed. During his illness he was both with her and separate at the same time, and his ignorance had made her fascination with his beauty dispassionate.

It had been different since the fever had broken, though. Very different. Suddenly Morvan became a man conscious and alert, regaining his vitality with every passing hour. The slightest touch had turned awkward and embarrassing. For her, not him. Those diamond eyes had reflected vague amusement at her predicament. Ascanio had guessed, and taken over the more personal duties. That had helped, but the last two weeks had still been difficult.

She suspected that the next few would be impossible.

His arms fell. He looked over his shoulder. His fiery gaze met hers, and she felt her color instantly rise.

He stepped to the cot, unembarrassed by his nakedness, but then they both knew she had seen him thus often enough. He sat and pulled the blanket around his hips. "You said that I will move to the keep today. Now, I hope. I am done with this death house."

She brought over the garments that she carried, and tried to look like someone who had just arrived. "These were my father's. There are more in a trunk in the chamber you will use." She moved a pail of warm water from the hearth to the cot. "After you wash and dress, I will take you there."

She fetched a clean rag. His fingers closed on hers as he took it, gently imprisoning her hand. "Aren't you going to do it? I'm not sure I can spare the strength." His expression appeared innocent, but his eyes sparkled.

"You appeared strong enough to me just now."

"I was enjoying the sensation of the warmth. Such commonplace things are like new to me."

She understood what he meant, but her instant comprehension annoyed her. She did not want reminders that they had shared this experience. She did not want the empathy born of his illness to continue. "If you need help washing, I will send for Ascanio. It is his duty."

The lights in his eyes turned mischievous. "It has been recently, but was not always."

He could not know that for certain. He had been unconscious when she tended him thus. Or so it had seemed. It horrified her that he might have been aware of all of it.

She pulled her hand away. He was teasing her, and toying with the silly way he could fluster her. He kept acting as if they shared a special familiarity. They did, but he had survived, not died, and it was time to put that behind them.

Fortunately, once he moved to the keep he would be distracted by more appealing women and could test his resurrected powers on them.

"Either do for yourself, or wait for Ascanio."

He grinned, pulled the pail closer, and cast aside the blanket. She turned on her heel to leave him to it.

At the entry she glanced back. Morvan sat, wiping one outstretched arm. Water glistened off its taut muscles. His eyes burned with contentment and triumph as he felt and watched the rag's progress.

She understood, too completely. He was reveling in being alive.

Surviving the plague humbled most people. Morvan Fitzwaryn looked as if he thought it meant he could conquer the world.

He let the warm rivulets drip, relishing the meandering sensations. He took his time, and tasted it fully while he could. This sharp awareness of the little things would not last, he knew. Already it had begun to pass.

Old things had been made new. Smells and touches. The beauty of a flame's dance. The confusion of a woman unsettled by a man's gaze.

That would pass too, if Anna had her way. For the last few days she had been almost officious in her dealings with him. But her curt instructions could not hide her discomfort, and her impassive expression could not mask the reactions that he sensed more than saw. Inside the dutiful lady of the manor was one very uneasy girl.

When he stepped out of this shelter today, she would be waiting. She would escort him back to the world of the living. And she would expect him to pretend that nothing had passed between them.

It would not happen that way. He could not undo things, any more than she could be a stranger with Ascanio after her own fight to live.

He finished washing and pulled over the garments. They were lordly enough, but old-fashioned. He dragged an undertunic on, and a long cotte, and reached for the hose.

Light split through the shadows, then disappeared. He turned to the entry, expecting to find Ascanio. Instead a different blond-haired man walked over, grinning. It was John, the other knight in his troop.

"I see that God has blessed you, Morvan. It is being said that the lady's prayers brought the angels here."

"Since two others perished on that other cot, John, I do not think the angels came."

"Still, you appear hale and fit for one who almost died."

Morvan continued dressing, while waiting for John to explain why he had come. They were not friends, and John would have not mourned his passing.

John moved the chair closer and sprawled in it. "Her lordship says we can leave in three days."

"The men will be glad for it. I will not be fit for travel yet, however, and will follow later."

"I have been thinking it might be better to stay here too. For all of us."

Morvan did not reply. He finished with the hose and pulled on his boots.

John glanced to the entry and pitched his voice as low

as possible. "I have been speaking with the servants. There are two poorly defended outlying fiefs. The land goes east for miles."

Morvan gazed at the young knight and waited for the rest.

John smiled slyly. "There is no lord and a weak defense. We are inside already, and getting weapons should not be hard with guards as green as this. Fortunes have been made thus, and there is enough for us all."

"How many are with you?"

"Enough."

"With me dead, perhaps, but not now, unless I approve it. Most will not stand against me, which is why you are here."

John shrugged a grudging acknowledgment of that.

"You describe thievery, and a violation of the lady's hospitality and help."

"She will not be harmed, I swear."

"Put this idea out of your head. Anna de Leon is under my protection. If you try this, my sword will be waiting. If you do anything to put her in danger, I will kill you."

John's face twisted in annoyance. He rose. "You are ever the fool. If you want that giantess, I would gladly let you have her. You could be the lord here, and truly protect her. Think about what I have said. Fortune led us here, and offered this gift. It is all ours for the taking." He strode out, muttering a curse.

Morvan rose and threw a short cloak around his shoulders. John had spoken so boldly because the two of them had one essential thing in common. They were both landless. Marrying property was unlikely. They could either buy it with war booty or take it through force.

He crossed the shelter and stepped outside. The light blinded him and the crisp air shocked his skin. He adjusted to the raw reality, and surveyed the yard and keep, and thought of the forests and farms beyond.

Despite his attempts to keep it away, John's temptation worked on his mind. Vague considerations crystallized into an inner debate. Right here, within reach, was the answer to fifteen years of prayers. With an estate like this as his base, he could plan to regain his family's honor. He could get Harclow back, and restore the nobility of the Fitzwaryn name. He could undo what fate had wrought so brutally all those years ago.

He had not needed John to point out the possibilities. He had been aware of them since he'd first ridden in the gate and learned the situation here.

Servants were bringing fresh water to the camps' edges. Anna was lending her strength to the chore, taking the pails and delivering them to the individual men.

You could be the lord here, and truly protect her.

There was that appeal too. She was very vulnerable, and La Roche de Roald was a tempting prize. How long could she hold the world back? He doubted this lawless country would let her return to the abbey as she intended.

But even if she changed her mind about the abbey, she was not for him. If she did not take the veil her duke would give her to one of his barons in a political match.

Except that the young duke was in England, and those barons were at war. He was here.

He could make it happen before the outside world could stop it. He could claim her.

It would not take the conquest of a castle, as John planned. He need only breach one woman who blushed whenever he wanted her to.

That woman noticed him, and joined him at the shelter.

"Can you walk on your own, or should I call for some men?"

"I will do it."

She fell into step beside him. Close enough for him to smell the soap that she used to wash. He looked at her profile, and the eyebrow shaped like a falcon's wing. He glanced down to the woman's form hidden beneath the cotte and cloak.

Memories from the shelter loomed in his mind. His awareness, even in his delirium, when it was her hands that bathed his body. Her eyes widening in surprise at the pleasure of a touch. Her lips trembling beneath his kiss. The glow of firelight on the half-hidden swell of a woman's breast . . .

CHAPTER 6

ANNA GAVE MORVAN A CHAMBER off the ancient hall. She called for a bath to be prepared, showed him the chest of garments, and left. She expected him to sleep out the day.

He didn't. He emerged for the midday meal, jaw freshly shaved and hair newly trimmed. He managed to make her father's old garments appear courtly. She put him beside Josce at the high table and turned her attention to making plans with Carlos, her head groom, regarding the training of several stallions.

"You are scowling," Carlos said. "It is very unattractive. It makes you look like your father, and no girl wants that."

She had to smile at him. He liked to tease her with advice on her appearance and behavior. It was a private joke because Carlos of all people knew that she had never cared about either.

Their familiarity came from spending years together as children when his father had served as head groom. Her father had brought them back from a trip to Castile along with the Saracen horses that fed the bloodline of their palfrey stock. Short and wiry, with a close-cropped beard and dark expressive eyes, Carlos left the estate as a young man only to return three years later to take his dying father's place. He was an excellent horseman skilled in training destriers. Since the plague he had helped run the estate farms and was much more than just the head groom.

"I am scowling because there are not enough hours in the day, Carlos. The stallions need more time than either you or I have. This morning's work proved that."

She was lying. She was really scowling at herself, and her constant awareness of Morvan. His presence distracted her. As he ate, he was observing the workings of the household and studying the faded paintings barely visible on the ceiling beams, but he was very much *there*.

"Well, now that your English knight has recovered, your hours are your own again," Carlos said. "He no longer needs your attention. It is said that he has already asked for his weapons, and sought out a swordsman for practice."

"He has regained his strength more quickly than most."

"As you did, Anna. Now, let us decide how to handle that white courser."

Halfway through the meal, Ascanio entered the hall, accompanied by a young guard. The priest wore an expression that immediately had Anna rising from her seat with concern.

"We may have trouble," he said.

"The thieves again?"

His eyes silently communicated that it was much worse than that.

"We will discuss this in my father's solar." She gestured for Carlos and Josce and led the way to the stairs.

The solar was a large room on the second level with a row of windows overlooking the walled field. Here her father had managed the estate and planned his campaigns. On its bed her brother Drago had breathed his last and she herself had fought the death. Although she slept elsewhere, she used the chamber as a place of consultation and decision.

She sat in the only chair, a richly carved half barrel that could easily fit two. Even her father had barely filled it.

Ascanio and the others entered the room. A fifth man followed: Morvan had decided to insinuate himself into this council. His gaze passed over the large, high bed surrounded by drapes, the table and stools, and the two handsome tapestries. It finally came to rest on her.

She thought that she detected amusement in him at seeing her sitting in the lord's chair. She straightened, preparing to put him in his place by asking him to leave.

Ascanio saw it coming. He caught her eye and shook his head. "We may need him," he muttered.

Her attention snapped back to the matter at hand. "What is it?"

Ascanio turned to the guard. "Tell her."

The guard was younger than she, not much more than a boy. She recognized him as Louis, one of the farmers' sons whom Ascanio had recruited and she herself had trained in archery.

"Well, my lady, you know that my family lives close to

the manor's north end. I went to visit them, because I got word that my father was ill. While I was there, a man passing through their village said that he had seen a small army moving in our direction. So I rode out and looked for myself."

"It sounds like another free company," Carlos said.

That was indeed bad news. Such companies, made up of knights and soldiers under no lord's command, had been plaguing Brittany with their brigandage for years.

"If so, it was a big one. There were over a hundred men, well provisioned."

"They may not be coming here," Josce said. "They may only be aiming for the coastal road, to go south."

"If so, they will still pass through these lands, even if you are not their goal," Morvan said. "Did you see any colors, boy? Any banners?"

Anna's annoyance with Morvan spiked again. He demanded answers as if he had the right to do so.

"Aye. Red and black, quartered, with castle and dragon."

The words penetrated her head like darts. All thoughts of Morvan's presumptions disappeared in an onslaught of shock.

"You are sure?" She did not hear her own question, and wondered if she had even uttered it.

"I watched from a hill as they passed. They are moving slowly, because they have the wagons and foot soldiers, but—"

"How far away?" Morvan again. At least she thought so. The chamber had become distant and dreamlike, as if the pulse pounding in her head left it no room to absorb forms and sounds completely.

"With the wagons, six days, more if it rains."

A visceral chill clutched her chest with hundreds of

icy fingers. She could not conquer the horrible sensation of having the breath squeezed out of her.

Fear. This was what fear felt like.

Someone else spoke. The men moved. A hand touched her shoulder, and she jolted alert. She looked up into Ascanio's concerned face, then glanced around. Louis, Carlos, and Josce had left, but Morvan remained, and his dark eyes studied her.

Ascanio squeezed her shoulder in reassurance. "There may be no real danger here. There is no indication they will even cross your lands. Still, we should take precautions."

Morvan moved closer. He took her chin in his hand and raised her head so he could look into her eyes.

"This army is indeed coming here, isn't it? You know it is."

"Aye." She brushed his hand away. "We have lived through hell these last months, but I never expected the devil to arrive at the gate."

"Then you had better explain who the devil is, lady, so we know what we face."

"She will do so when she has calmed herself," Ascanio said sharply. "This has unsettled her badly."

"I know that, priest, as well as you—"

"His name is Gurwant de Beaumanoir," she interrupted. "It is his banner that Louis described."

"I know the Beaumanoir family," Morvan said. "They are among Brittany's leading allies of the French king, are they not? The Franco-Breton lords' taking of a strong coastal fortress would have important strategic implications. Still, trying to conquer an estate so far from their holdings is overbold."

"Gurwant could have once had a claim on this estate. That is why he journeys so far, and dares to be so bold."

"What claim?"

"The claim was through me. We were once betrothed. It was annulled."

Both men reacted with surprise. Ascanio in particular appeared astonished. He was her closest friend, but there were some things she had never shared with him.

The fear tried to spread again. She managed to force clarity on her thoughts. Later she would contemplate what she really faced, but right now there were more immediate concerns.

"Ascanio, we will double the guard. And we do not ride out over petty thefts. It will draw off what few men we have and leave even this castle vulnerable. Tell Josce to personally oversee the gate tower. No one is to enter who is not known to us. I will send messengers at once to my father's closest vassals, summoning them to our aid. They should arrive before Gurwant."

She dismissed them, strode from the solar, and went to her bedchamber, where she fetched up her bow.

"What are you doing?"

She pivoted in surprise. Morvan stood at the threshold. His sharp gaze took in the weapon that she held.

"I am going back to the horse farm, to warn the men there." She was not going just for that. She practiced with her arms at the farm, and had been lax these last weeks.

"Carlos can warn them. You must stay in the keep now."

It sounded a lot like a command. She inspected the string on her bow. "They are still days away."

"An advance guard could have been sent ahead, to assess your strength and the terrain. The thieves who have been harassing you might not be mere brigands. You must stay here."

"I will be careful." She slung the bow over her shoulder and grabbed up her sword and quiver, then walked quickly to the doorway.

He did not move. Which blocked her way out.

She glared at him impatiently. He returned a severe gaze.

"Since you will not see to your own safety, Anna, have a groom prepare my horse."

Another command. A stupid one. "You are too ill to ride yet, and I do not need your escort."

"My strength returns with every hour, and it is not for your escort. I will go and meet this Beaumanoir, and deal with him knight to knight."

"He has an army behind him, and that he comes at all speaks of his lack of honor. He will have them cut you to pieces if it suits him. Now, stand aside. I have things to do."

He didn't budge. That infuriated her enough that she almost gave him a good shove.

He moved closer until she had to look up to see his face. A handsome man, she found herself thinking despite her vexation, handsome even when stern like now.

"While I recovered I swore an oath to protect you," he said.

An oath to protect her. *Saints.* Small wonder he was being so overbearing.

"You are released from this oath."

"It is not for you to release me."

"I am its object. I can and do release you. You were ill when you made it. You cannot be held—"

"It is not a matter of your choice. It is done."

An assault of rage hit her. *It is done.* That was a phrase her father had used to end discussion. The lord's will is done. How often she had heard that imperious statement. And now, from this man, a stranger almost . . .

"Sir Morvan, your oaths are between you and God. But know this. Do not expect me to conform to your ideas about protection. I discovered long ago that the price of a man's protection is too high and its value very dubious." She turned away from his burning eyes.

He did not leave. He just stood behind her, filling the room with that damned male presence of his, glaring at her no doubt. But she refused to look and see.

Finally, she heard him walk toward the door.

"Morvan, know something else. Within these walls, no man commands me, no matter what his oaths. Not even Ascanio, and certainly not you."

CHAPTER 7

ANNA SPENT THE AFTERNOON at the horse farm, training the stallions and using her bow. Carlos arrived near evening, and she used the last hours of light to practice her sword with him. Ascanio was the better teacher, but with Gurwant on the way he could not spare the time for this.

The activity kept the fear at bay, but the icy fingers again wrapped her heart once she was alone in her chamber that night. She hated the way it made her feel.

The confining walls seemed to make it worse, so she slipped from her chamber, took a torch from its ring, and mounted the winding stairway up to the roof of the keep. A wind blew off the sea, raising her hair around her head.

She climbed up to the battlements and positioned herself to look out over the sea. It was a dark night, but the clear sky shimmered with starlight that etched silvery highlights on the incoming waves. Setting the torch in an iron ring, she huddled in her cloak.

This was where her brother had found her that morning, all those years ago. She had hidden here to avoid the silence in the hall. Even her father had acted cold to her. She realized later that no one had known what to do about what had happened, and so, by silent agreement, they had decided to do nothing. But at the time she saw the reaction as blame aimed at her.

Only Drago had understood. When he had found her here, still in shock from the night's events, he had taken her in his arms and soothed her. He was only three years older than she, but she had let herself be a child with him.

He had held her and promised to speak with their father, and swore always to protect her. Then his voice had become hard and old. "Next time, Anna, if you have to stop a man, go for his neck."

She shook off the memory, for it threatened to drown her in that childhood terror. Her mind surged up out of it like a body gasping for air.

If Gurwant was coming here, there would be no negotiation. Nor would they be able to repel his army forever. He was counting on that, on the plague and the absence of a lord finally making the impregnable fortress of La Roche de Roald vulnerable.

A sound pulled her out of her reverie. She turned and saw a shadow emerge from the stair opening in the roof. Tall and erect, the form paused there in the darkness.

She knew who it was. She sensed the confidence and strength that he exuded even in the dark. This afternoon she had found that dominating aura infuriating, but she did not feel strong right now and her spirit lifted with something like relief.

She said his name.

"My lady."

"Join me. The sea is beautiful tonight."

He climbed to the battlements and circled toward her. A body's breadth away he stopped and turned to the sea, raising his gaze to the sparkling sky.

"Do you believe that one can read the future in the stars?" she asked.

"I had a tutor who did, and he taught me some of it, but the stars always neglected to warn me of the important things, so I lost interest in such matters."

"I wish you had been a better student. It would be nice to know what the future holds."

"Would you be less fearful then? You are still badly troubled. You hide it well, but all who know you closely can tell."

"What woman wouldn't be troubled to learn that an army marches on her home?"

The torch gave enough light for her to see the planes of his handsome face above the red cloak. She stayed silently by his side, relishing a soothing sense of sanctuary.

"Anna, there is more to this than you revealed, I think. Tell me the rest."

She realized that she was going to obey. Even Ascanio had been spared this story. She didn't doubt Ascanio's love and friendship. When the time came he would fight to save her and die by her side. But this other knight had a power about him that suggested that no one who stood by his shoulder needed to die at all.

"My mother passed away when I was ten. A year later,

my father decided to marry me off. Gurwant's father approached him. It was a profitable match for both families. Gurwant's branch of the family is rich in nobility but poor in property. My father would forge an important alliance, and Gurwant would receive some lands we own inland near Rennes."

She collected her scattered memories. "I was twelve when they came for the betrothal. Gurwant was sixteen. I was to return with them to their home to be educated by his mother. We would marry in three years."

"Gurwant was not pleased when he met me." She smiled thinly at the memory of his astonishment. "I was as homely then as now, and already unnaturally tall. I had learned nothing of grace and charm. At the betrothal it humiliated him to have to stretch up to kiss me."

"Girls often reach their height before boys. And you are not homely."

It was a chivalrous denial of the obvious truth, but it was kind of him to try. "I remember only one thing distinctly about his face. His eyes. They were pale blue, vacant and cold. The feast went on well into the night. Finally, the castle slept."

"What happened?" His voice came tight and low, as if he guessed the rest.

"I remember being asleep, and then they were there. Gurwant and his father. His father held me down, his hand over my mouth. He told Gurwant that he wanted the sheets well bloodied so the betrothal could never be annulled."

Morvan placed a hand on her arm. His eyes burned and his mouth formed a hard line.

"I fought them. Finally, Gurwant told his father that he couldn't. I thought he had taken pity on me. I realize now that he didn't mean that at all. And so his father decided to do it for him. I was in my own chamber in my father's castle, but no one could protect me but myself."

"And did you protect yourself?" It sounded like he hoped that she had.

"Aye. I managed to move my hand to a table beside my bed where my dining dagger lay. I stabbed his father with all of my strength. In the back, below the shoulder. He never used his sword arm again. I caught Gurwant too, and sliced his face. And then, my mouth free at last, I screamed and screamed."

She could hear her quick breath and pounding heart. She could feel the terror anew, but she would never let it own her like it had that night. Not ever again.

"My brother heard. He burst through the door with his sword. I kept screaming until my father found us, my brother's sword at Gurwant's neck, the sheets well bloodied indeed, but not with my blood. When his father could travel, Gurwant's family left, but without me."

"And the betrothal was annulled after all?"

"Not right away, and not because of that night. My father had it annulled by the bishop two years later. By then the succession war was raging, and he wanted no ties to the French-allied barons. I think that Gurwant's father wanted my maidenhead because he guessed that when the old duke died the lords would split in their alliances, with the result that my father would not go through with the marriage and the Beaumanoir family would lose my rich dowry."

"Could they have bribed the bishop and had the annulment set aside?"

"My brother thought of that. It is why Drago went to Avignon. He brought back a papal annulment. It cost him his life."

Morvan battled an explosive anger. His hand still lay on her arm and he felt her tremoring. Facing these memories, he knew, had cost her dearly.

He pulled her to him and wrapped his arms and cloak around her. When he eased her head to his shoulder, his thumb felt the wetness of silent tears. She didn't resist, but lay against him, her hands on his chest.

"You have the papal letter?"

"Aye. I sent copies to Gurwant and to the bishop. I was sure that would end it for good."

With an honorable man, it would. But her brother's death had raised the stakes. She was the heir now.

"Once he defeats us, he means to kill me. For what I did to his father and him."

He rubbed his cheek against her hair. "He does not plan to kill you, Anna. You are the key to his plan. He seeks to enforce his old claim, so the estate becomes his and his hold on it cannot be undone. If he takes the keep, he will declare the papal letter a forgery. While it is sorted out in Avignon, he will have you here. If he gets you with child, the annulment will not stand."

He could imagine what would happen if Gurwant got his hands on her. There was more than a lust for property driving the man. She had shown him as weak and impotent in front of his father. She had marked his face with her blade. He might well want her dead, but would exact his revenge in other ways.

Her fear of this other fate must have been bigger than that of death, for it demolished her defenses. She huddled closer. He held her tightly, swaddled in his cloak. The mood from the shelter, so open and close, surrounded them as surely as the wind and wool.

He was aware of the slight curve of her hip under his

arm, and the warmth of her slender back, and her breath near his neck. His senses filled with her.

He reined in his impulse to caress her. He was not well practiced in self-denial, but he would not betray her trust this night. Still, he wanted to kiss the face nestled close to his, and stroke the strong body curving naively against him. He wanted to take possession of her, and with her the right to defend her.

Nay, he wanted more than that. Not all of his reactions to her were gentle like the one restraining him now. But tonight her weakness spoke only to his protective instincts, and not to the darker, more primitive ones evoked by her strength.

"You must leave tomorrow," he said. "Ascanio can take you back to the abbey."

"If I leave, the estate will be surrendered."

"I will stay and defend it for you."

She pulled away. "You are one man. The others will not fight for a lost cause. If the lord has run away, why should they risk their lives? I am not the lord, but I am the closest thing. You know that I cannot go. It would mean abandoning La Roche de Roald and its people to the Beaumanoirs and the French. Brittany might never regain it."

She regained her composure, and her strength. She set off for the stairs. He walked her back to her chamber. At the door she turned to him. "I did not think that we could have a friendship like I share with Ascanio, but I was wrong."

He looked down at her troubled face. And then, as he had done that first night, he placed his hands on her shoulders and lowered his lips to hers. He did it because he wanted to taste her. He did it to seal the friendship she spoke of. But he also kissed her to remind her that he, unlike the good Ascanio, was not a priest.

In her distraction over the more immediate threat, she was oblivious to the message. "Maybe I worry for naught. Perhaps he does not come here."

CHAPTER 8

HE CAME.

Anna watched the army move toward La Roche de Roald, banners flying.

Her knights flanked her on the southern wall walk. Fouke and Haarold, the vassals of the adjoining fiefs, had both answered her summons, bringing a handful of men each. Haarold was a tall, bony man in his middle years with a permanent scowl carved on his face and a censorious set to his mouth. Fouke in comparison seemed placid and smiling, his squarish body going a little fat, his pale scalp gleaming through thinning pale hair.

Haarold had also brought his son Paul, who had just earned his spurs. The black-haired, heavy-browed young man had spent the better part of the morning staring at her. She had spent most of that time in council with the

knights, making it clear that their sparring for leader-
ship was pointless because she would make the decisions.

The front lines of Gurwant's army drew closer. She
could see flashes of armor and weapons, and the black
and crimson of his coat of arms on the banners.

Over a hundred marched with him. She had but fifty,
and that many only because Morvan's men, finally free
of quarantine, had agreed to fight in exchange for silver.
She had sent Carlos to Brest to beg aid from the English
garrison there, but he had not yet returned.

Three hours later, encased in armor from head to toe,
she positioned her stallion in front of the gate between
Fouke and Haarold on her left and Ascanio and Morvan
on her right.

The portcullis slowly rose. Two servants carrying her
banners led the way across the drawbridge. On the field
five mounted men approached. The middle one would
be Gurwant.

She squinted at him in the afternoon sun.

The man bore little resemblance to the youth who
had stretched up to give her a betrothal kiss. He was as
tall as Morvan, a full head higher than his knights, and
possessed a breadth of shoulder to match. Pale blond
hair swept back from a sharp peak on his forehead and
reached to his chin. He was handsome in a forbidding
way, his face made harsher by the thin long scar slashing
across his left cheek.

He stopped fifteen paces away. And then she knew
that this tree of a man was truly her adversary, for the
eyes that surveyed her knights looked pale, blue, and
cold as ice.

Morvan and Haarold stepped their horses forward,

and Gurwant's flanking knights did the same. The parlay formed a rough circle.

"I am Gurwant de Beaumanoir. I have come to speak with the Lady Anna de Leon."

Fouke leaned forward in his saddle. "You have brought an army for a conversation? What do you want with the lady?"

"She is my wife."

"She is not. Your betrothal was annulled. Twice. Last by the Pope himself. A copy of the document was sent to you."

"I know of no annulment. Is there a witness here to it? Nay? I would speak with the lady. Let me enter or call her out. Tell her that her husband has come for her."

Anna lifted her arms and pulled the helmet from her head. Her blond curls tumbled out, the breeze drying their dampness.

For the briefest moment Gurwant's face showed surprise, then he examined her with narrowed eyes.

"I did not expect to find you armored. You should be glad that I have come if your brother's death has forced such unnatural behavior on you. When La Roche de Roald has a lord again, you will be free of this."

"The steel on my body matches the steel of my resolve that you will never have La Roche de Roald, Gurwant."

He moved his horse up beside her. "I will have the castle, Anna. And I will have you." He reached out and caught one of her flying curls in his gauntlet.

She sensed her knights moving to protest. She raised her hand to stop them, and extricated her hair from Gurwant's hand.

Those icy eyes examined her face. "You have changed. Calmer. Beautiful."

"As have you." It annoyed her that he would try to woo her with lies in such a public way. "I see that you've grown."

"Aye." His gaze drifted down her long length. "Enough man even for you."

She held her tongue, but the memory of his impotence must have shown in her eyes, for his own narrowed dangerously on her.

"Yield now. I know that your defenses are pitiful. You can save your people."

"Regarding my defenses, things have changed. Look you to the wall, and the number of bows sighted on you now. This castle has never fallen, Gurwant, and it will not fall to you."

He smiled. "You will yield. Before the week is out you will be in my bed."

His gaze raked the length of her body. He raised his hand and brought it down hard on her armored thigh. The sound of metal impacting metal rang loudly over the cold, silent field. "Look at us, lady. We were born for each other. Think of the sons we will make."

He backed up his horse, then turned and rode away with his knights.

After the evening meal, Anna escaped to her chamber for some solitude. The castle seemed very full to her, what with the additional men in the barracks and Fouke and Haarold crowding the high table. She had grown accustomed to privacy and silence at the abbey, and now found that she could not think clearly without it.

She sat on her bed and brushed a clump of hair smooth, then rolled it toward her head. Grabbing some pins from a box by her lap, she tried to secure the hair to her scalp.

She heard a scratch on her chamber door and called back permission to enter. That would be the servant returning to say that she could not find Catherine. Catherine was getting harder and harder to locate these days.

She continued sticking the pins into her hair, trying to hold the fat rolls in place at the same time. Errant curls kept escaping her grasp. This really was a job for two people, which was why she wanted Catherine.

Her back was to the door, but she heard the servant's footfall. "Come here. Hold this in place for me."

Hands took the roll of hair and held it firmly against her nape. She stabbed in several pins, then felt the halo of hair that she had created around her head. Very proper. Very sedate. She lifted a thin veil and pinned it on, letting the silk drift down her face.

"What do you think?" she asked, turning.

No servant stood there. It was Morvan.

She felt herself blush. "What are you doing here?"

"Ascanio sent me. He himself was called away by Josce. There is some news. The other knight in my troop, John, has gone over the wall."

"No doubt he thought his chances better with Gurwant. But, if he is not loyal, it is better to have him gone."

"Aye. The other news is more heartening. Your groom Carlos just returned. He sailed up from Brest. He brought ten longbowmen, and they are quartered in the town. They will look for movement from Gurwant's camp and come out if they see an attack. The town will not commit their own guard, but Carlos said that a merchant offered to pay any man who would fight for you. Maybe five or six will do so, no more. They are not soldiers."

"Still, that is indeed heartening."

He eyed the veils and ribbons strewn on the bed, then the serviceable light brown gown that she wore. It was fitted at the shoulders, from where it flowed down in full soft folds. Snug lacing closed its high neckline. "What are you doing?"

He had never seen her in a gown before. That must account for his scrutiny. "Getting used to woman's things." She reached for one of the veils and folded it. "It really is a chore."

He joined her in stacking the thin cloths. "Most ladies have servants to help them."

"I could arrange that. But there was only one old one left trained as a woman's maid after the death, and I gave her to Catherine. I don't like having servants underfoot anyway. They never leave a woman alone. They are always there." She got up and returned the veils to their chest.

"And why are you getting used to woman's things?"

She crouched and rummaged through the chest, searching for her mother's silver chain. "Well, as for the gown, I expect that I will be wearing them again soon. Walking with all of this fabric takes a certain knack, and I've lost it."

He came and stood over her. His leg almost touched her shoulder. She grew very alert to that.

"And the rest? The hair and jewelry?"

She rose and faced him. "I am confident that God is with us and that we will win this ordeal with Gurwant. But I should be prepared to negotiate terms with him, if it should come to that." She made a gesture at herself. "It occurs to me that if it does come to that, I might get further if I dress thus."

He stepped back a pace and examined her. "I assume

that you have already decided your terms. If it comes to that."

She licked her lips and knew that she was blushing again. She really felt very inadequate dressed like this. She wasn't very good at being a woman, and all of the gowns and veils in the world wouldn't hide that. But Gurwant wanted the estate, not her. The clothes would just be a bid not to antagonize him.

"What terms will you ask for?"

"I will ask that all of the knights, your men, and Catherine and Josce be allowed to leave the castle and estate. I will ask for the protection of my people and the town from pillage."

"What of yourself? What terms will you negotiate for yourself?"

"Nothing. He would not honor them even if he agreed." She walked to the hearth. It was one thing to go over this in her mind and another to talk about it. It seemed more real, and more possible, when she talked about it.

"So, you have decided that you will submit to him. If it comes to that, of course."

"I said nothing of submission." She glared at him over her shoulder. "It is a long way from my gallery to the rocks below."

He was behind her in a flash, his hands on her shoulders, turning her to face him. "You cannot be serious. You cannot be planning to throw yourself from the gallery."

It had been a mistake to say that. She would never get any of them to leave if they thought she was planning such a thing. "Throw myself? Nay, I was thinking more in terms of pushing Gurwant."

He obviously thought that murder in a just cause was preferable to suicide, for he let his hands drop. "I think that by the morrow we will not be so outnumbered. I spoke with a German knight at the parlay and let him know about the recent plague outbreak here. I will be surprised if at least ten of them do not drift away during the night. I have no doubt that they are brave, but you cannot fight the plague with a sword."

He was clever. Probably the cleverest person she had ever met. And so handsome. She was always aware of that, but tonight she found herself especially noticing the beautiful planes of his face and the lean strong lines of the body that she knew better than a maid ought. Maybe it was the clothes. Perhaps wearing a woman's stupid gown caused her to think like a stupid woman.

"That is welcome news." She flounced her skirt. "Then I don't need to practice with the gown yet."

"Nay, your precautions are sensible. You are just going about it wrong. If it comes to it, if you have to negotiate with Gurwant, you do not go dressed like that."

"Should I go in armor? In a tunic and hose? What is wrong with how I am dressed?"

"You do not negotiate with a man dressed like a nun. Is that gown from the convent? It is too much like a robe, and at least twenty years out of fashion. Now gowns have less fabric."

He stepped toward her. "Here, I will show you." He gathered the material of the dress on either side of her until the folds fell along the swells of her body. "Surely the servants could cut some of this away."

She looked down. The lines of her breasts and hips were vaguely visible. "More like Catherine's gowns, you mean."

"Even hers are fuller than the style I speak of."

"How do you know so much about women's clothes?"

He angled back to see the effect he had created. "I did live at court, where such things are major topics. Also, my sister married a mercer."

He stood very close to her, and the hands that grasped the fabric rested lightly on her hips. An unsettling excitement scurried through her. She tensed to keep from shivering. Her subtle flex was a reaction, however, and she knew, she just knew, that he noticed it.

She hid her embarrassment in a display of examining the gown. "I see what you mean. I should have the gown altered. Just in case." She pulled the material from his hands and made to move away.

He would not let her go. His left hand slid firmly up her back to hold her in place. His manner quickly changed, and there was no deference in the way he stood with her now. He looked into her eyes, and she saw a deep fire in his own. His jaw and mouth were set in firm lines. His expression made her breath catch.

He glanced up. With a quick pull he whisked the veil from her head. She watched it float to the floor as his fingers removed the pins that held her hair. Her curls began tumbling down, grateful to be free.

"Also, when a woman goes to negotiate with a man, she does not hide her glory." His fingers stretched along her scalp, searching for the last of the pins, sending wonderful sensations down the flesh of her face and neck. "We are weak in this one thing, and inclined to be most generous when we are most pleased."

He took a handful of curls and held them to his face, smelling their scent. The gesture pulled her closer to him. "When did you cut it? At the abbey, or because of your illness?"

Her voice almost wouldn't come to her. "The abbey."

"It is beautiful. Never cut it again."

But we always cut it at the abbey, she wanted to explain. Only this time the words truly would not come, because he was looking at her again, his eyes searching hers for something as they sparkled. Suddenly the abbey was a thousand miles away and her return there a lifetime in the future.

He had been playful when he redesigned her dress, but the laughter had disappeared and his expression had turned fiery-eyed and severe. She should push him away, but she could not. She felt his hand burning on her back, and her own body waiting, achingly alive, for something to happen. It seemed a long time that they stood thus, slightly stiff and apart.

He looked to her neck. "And that lacing was never meant to be so tight, strangling you."

She watched wide-eyed as his fingers slowly pulled at the tie and then, level by level, dragged the laces open. Their snaking movements matched the exciting spirals winding down her body. He did it very slowly, very deliberately, as if he knew how it was affecting her.

The heel of his palm rested above her breasts as the fingers did their work. When he finished he did not move his hand, but left it there, his fingertips lightly stroking the line of skin he had revealed.

His touch felt so wonderful. Exciting and comforting, dangerous and reassuring, all at the same time. They still stood slightly apart and only his hands touched her, but a power flowed from him and engulfed her and her awareness dimmed of everything but him and his touch and her own painful anticipation.

She looked up at him. His jaw clenched.

"When you negotiate with a man, never look at him

thus," he warned quietly. "He will see it as a challenge, and feel the need to put you in a woman's place."

"And what place is that?"

"This." With a quick movement he pulled her forward and molded her against his strength and heat.

She fought the overwhelming reaction of her body, but the hands that she raised to push him away suddenly grasped his shoulders as tightly as he held her. She gave up her will then, and her self to his control.

His fingers separated the cloth where they had un-laced her, and he lowered his mouth to her exposed skin. His gentle kisses shot hot bolts through her and she gasped and gripped his shoulders tighter. He stroked his fingers into her hair and held her head as he brought his lips to hers.

It was her first real kiss, and it completely undid her. It took her to the stars somewhere, far from La Roche de Roald and its troubles. No one existed but this man who filled her with such stunning sensations.

The kiss was soft as he brushed her lips with his own and nibbled gently at the corners of her mouth. But then the pressure became more insistent and his embrace more demanding as he pressed her body against his until her breasts felt the tense muscles in his chest. He ran his tongue over her lips and she instinctively opened to him and he was in her then, rubbing against her palate, send-ing marvelous tremors through her.

His mouth moved slowly to her neck and ears before returning to her lips in a demanding, hungry way. His hands began caressing her, moving over her back, wan-dering down to her hips. Waves of pleasure eddied out from his touch.

She thought that they were as close as humanly

possible, but then he ran his hands over her bottom and pulled her to his hips. She felt his arousal pressing against her, and the reality of what it meant made her tense.

He sensed it and paused, looking down at her, absorbing her with his blazing eyes, claiming a part of her that no one else ever had. "Do not be afraid. I will never hurt you." One hand moved up her body in a long, sinuous caress. His fingers splayed across her midriff and finally closed on her breast.

She wasn't prepared for the intensity of the pleasure. She cried out a gasp that brought his mouth over hers again. His fingers found her nipple through the soft material and gently rubbed. An oblivious madness fogged her mind and she clung to him fiercely, aware only of the heat of his mouth, the pleasure at her breast, and the ache growing low in her belly.

His fingers played at her in wonderful ways, increasing the pleasure to something sharp and tight and needful. She opened her eyes to see him watching as she reacted to each new caress. She reached up and felt the warmth of his face.

"Aye," he said, as if her touch had asked a question or led him to a decision. He gave her a possessive kiss. As it lengthened and deepened, his hand slid down the length of her body. He began stroking her thigh, skimming up the skirt of her gown.

She pressed into that exciting, exploring touch. A thrilling expectation spread through her hips and thighs. His hand exposed her skin and its rough warmth smoothed her thigh and she groaned softly in relief. His own deep sigh responded and he pulled her closer while he caressed up to the swell of her bottom.

A physical, throbbing desire burst low inside her,

making her frantic. She grabbed at his head and show-
ered kisses on his face and neck. She rocked her body
into his. In her delirium she silently urged that tantalizing, wandering touch toward the center of the torture
hidden between her legs.

And then, suddenly, a sound from another world
broke into her awareness and she tumbled from the
stars. She landed disoriented and confused in front of
the hearth of her chamber in La Roche de Roald.

He wrapped his arms around her breathless body.

"Finally, I have your attention," Ascanio said from behind her. He sounded exasperated. "Have you two gone
mad?"

Anna buried her head in Morvan's neck. Dear saints,
how long had Ascanio been there?

"Leave us, priest," Morvan said.

"I don't think so. And it is not the priest who stops
you, Morvan, but the knight who sees all too well the
lady's precarious position."

Need still racked her body. All the same, her senses returned. She looked up at Morvan and saw his furious
glare. She glanced over her shoulder and saw Ascanio
standing legs apart and arms stiff by his sides, ready to
fight if he had to.

She pushed against Morvan's embrace. "You must go."

The glare turned on her, but faded quickly. He looked
down at her, then kissed her softly. His arms fell away,
and he strode from the chamber.

She fell to a heap on the floor, crossed her legs beneath her, and stared at the fire in the hearth. The room
throbbed with silence.

"The door was left open," Ascanio finally said. "The
servant returned and saw you, then came for me."

"She will gossip."

"I will see that she does not. I will threaten her with eternal damnation. That usually works."

A sensual stupor full of Morvan's presence still filled her. She wanted to preserve it for a while. "If you are waiting for me to confess, come back tomorrow."

"Actually, I am waiting to make sure he does not return. A man like Morvan is not accustomed to denial. Besides, you have nothing to confess. It was not your will at work here."

Nay, it hadn't been her will. She had possessed no will. None at all. He had absorbed it, overpowered it, stripped it from her as neatly as he had removed her veil. She didn't care about that now, but she suspected that quite soon she would decide that she hadn't liked that part of it.

"I'm sorry that you came," she admitted.

He knelt beside her, taking her hands in his. She continued gazing into the mesmerizing flickering flames, so like the lights in those black eyes.

"Anna, I do not seek to prevent you from knowing a woman's feelings. If you choose the abbey, it should not be out of ignorance. But your position here is a delicate one. If your people know that you bed a knight whom you cannot marry, it will change how they see everything about you. You can only flaunt so many customs before they turn on you."

She faced him, and at once lost the phantom arms that had continued to hold her.

"Anna, do you think that you want this man? Would you marry him if you could?"

She thought about that. She liked being in Morvan's arms, but she wasn't at all sure that she would like being under his thumb. And that is where marriage would put her, she had no doubt of that. She had learned tonight that he had only to touch her and she would lock the

shackles on herself. The senses were indeed very dangerous things.

And yet, dear God, it had been a form of ecstasy. It
saddened her to realize that she would never feel it again.

"I do not want to marry anyone, Ascanio. Even tonight
has not changed my mind about that. Besides, if I were
willing to marry, I would not be allowed to choose the
man. The duke would decide, or perhaps Fouke and
Haarold would even reach a settlement with Gurwant.
They would find a way to rationalize it if it preserved their
rights and lands. I have not forgotten that my decision to
take the veil protects me from that. And Morvan is English. This estate must remain with a Breton family."

Ascanio's face was full of concern.

"Do not worry yourself so. I have no illusions about
Morvan, and what a woman like myself could mean to
him. I will not live out some foolish jongleur's song, pining for a man I cannot have and who does not want me."

"I would say it is very clear that he wants you, Anna."

Did he? No man ever had before. Nay, he only wanted
La Roche de Roald. She recoiled from that thought, but
there it was, explaining too much, tainting the sweetness
of what had just occurred with a bitter reality. Gurwant
had brought an army to gain this estate, but Morvan had
decided that his eyes and touch could accomplish the
same goal.

She stood and smoothed her skirt, the magic sadly
gone now. "I must see him and settle things."

Ascanio put a restraining hand on her arm. "I will
speak with him. It is late. Go to sleep."

Morvan lay in his chamber off the hall. In front of his
half-closed eyes floated the image of a long naked leg

and the raised fabric of a gown barely covering paradise. The memory of her skin, the color of old ivory, and both soft and taut under his fingers, threatened to inflame him again. His dreams had been frustrating enough, but with reality to feed on the torture would be unrelenting.

He had told himself that she was a woman he wanted but could never have. He thought he had accepted her godly future, had rejected the lure cast by John's words, but today had shattered his resolve.

He knew he should have controlled himself, but he could not. Saints help him, he had enjoyed controlling her, had reveled in the way she trembled in his arms and in the sight of her breasts arching forward. He had expected pieties or outrage when he touched her. Instead he had discovered a fire to match his own, and an untapped sensuality aching to drown them both.

The memories of her surprised gasps and aroused tremors floated back into his mind.

Suddenly the door to the chamber crashed open, scattering the drifting images.

"You self-centered, arrogant bastard!" Ascanio yelled, slamming the door behind him. Then his French left him and he added a string of insults in Italian.

"You are brave to come here, priest. Don't start with me."

"Aye, it is well that you call me priest, for remember that I am the one who has heard your confession. Isn't it enough that you have bedded most of the women at the English court and half the females in Gascony? Aren't you content to have fornicated your way through Normandy and France? Your men pass their time regaling each other with stories of your women. The maids here throw themselves at you, but you must turn your lust on an innocent with no knowledge of men!"

"You exaggerate my experience," Morvan said, throwing his legs off the bed and rising to meet the onslaught.

"Barely. What were you thinking of?"

"I wasn't thinking at all, or have you been a priest so long that you forget how it is."

"Are you so jaded that only destroying a woman can give you pleasure?"

"It isn't like that. I have wanted her since the first day I came."

"Do you always take what you want?"

"If I did I could have taken her that first night," he snapped. "She is a maid still only because I have permitted it."

"You think so? Well, I have bad tidings for you. She learns quickly. She is your match in everything else and will be in this also. Your game with her is over and a draw at best."

"You will force a baseness on this, won't you? I have feelings for this woman."

Ascanio's shock took the wind out of his fury. "God help us," he said. "You know it is impossible, don't you? That you must stay away from her?"

"So that she can return to the abbey? Or die in battle? She is your creation, isn't she? A man does not fit in with your plans for your saint."

"She is her own creation, and if you know her, you know that. God cursed her with intelligence and a taste for freedom. A man does not fit in with *her* plans."

"You taught her weaponry. You let her ride into actions and wear men's clothes. You have helped her deny her womanhood."

"It was not for me to stop her. Circumstances let her do it. Demanded she do it. And if she does *not* deny her womanhood, what is left for her? The bed and home of an arranged marriage? Not your bed, I assure you, but someone else's. Picture her thus, embroidering by day and being used by night, and then tell me that I should have been preaching womanly duties to her."

Morvan stretched in front of the hearth, his head resting on an arm slung on the stones above, his body curving around its heat.

"She is so damned ignorant. Oblivious to what she does to me. Oblivious to what awaits her out on the field." He glanced back at Ascanio. "Do you know what she was doing tonight? Planning her surrender if we fail. Practicing negotiation terms and tactics." He laughed bitterly. "Did you see the way Gurwant looked at her? I could read his mind, and I almost killed him then and there."

Ascanio's expression said he had seen too, and not liked it any better. Even priests recognized a desirable woman when they met one. The Gurwants of the world definitely did. Behind those cold blue eyes a mind had been reassessing and anticipating. The armor had not helped delay that, as Morvan had hoped. With the removal of a helmet, the stakes had been raised.

"Did you see the scar on his cheek? She put it there." He told Ascanio about the betrothal night.

"It is only her word against his that he didn't succeed," Ascanio said when he'd finished.

"Do you doubt her?"

"Never. But others might. The proof of her story is her virginity. Another reason . . ." He met Morvan's gaze meaningfully.

He had not thought of that. His body, still half aroused, resented the implications, but his honor knew that a decision had been made for him. For now. "I will not touch her again."

Satisfied, Ascanio turned to leave.

"There is a condition. If we fail, and I live, I would have one night with her before she goes to him. I want her to have memories besides his brutality."

Ascanio smiled sympathetically. "She is not my gift to give or refuse. Besides, with her will, your strength, and my prayers, how can we fail?"

CHAPTER 9

THREE DAYS LATER, two riders approached the gate from Gurwant's field camp. They pushed bundles of blankets off their horses and rode away. Guards carried the bundles in and lowered their burdens to the ground.

Morvan pulled aside the tattered cloths. Freed from their wrappings, arms and legs sprawled out onto the dirt.

They were two females, a woman and a young girl. They bore the signs of carnal abuse, but there was still life in them both.

He saw Anna emerging from the hall. "Go and stop her. I do not want her to see this," he told Gregory.

Several of the young guards stood nearby. "That's Ruth," Louis said. "From the village where we found you, Sir Morvan. And her daughter Marguerite."

"One of you bring the girl."

Morvan knelt down and slid his arms under the woman and slowly rose. The movement brought her to consciousness.

Anna strode forward while Gregory backed up in front of her, entreating her to stop. She came over and eyed the woman in Morvan's arms. She raised the blanket, paled, and turned away. "Bring them to my chamber."

"Anna, let the servants tend them," Morvan entreated her.

"Bring them," she yelled over her shoulder, the command strangled with emotion.

Morvan followed her into the hall and up the stairs, the two of them shouting orders to servants as they went. The woman opened her eyes and stared warily at him. "My baby," she mumbled.

"She is here. She lives. The lady will see to her care and yours. They say she has the angel's touch, you know."

Anna made him lay the woman on her bed and had a pallet brought in for the girl. "Leave us."

"They have been raped, Anna." He doubted she had seen it before.

She looked from the woman to the girl balled up on the pallet. "One of the women will know what to do. Go now, please."

Anna did not spare herself the unpleasantness of washing the battered women. The girl appeared unconscious, but the woman was aware. Broth was brought, and they got Ruth to take some of it. After sheets and blankets had been tucked around her, Anna sat on the edge of the bed. "You were brought to us so that you would tell me what happened. Gurwant wants me to know. When you have rested we will talk."

She rose to go, but Ruth grabbed her arm. "Nay, I will tell you now, for when I sleep I hope never to wake up."

Anna sat down again. "How old is your daughter?"

"But thirteen last summer. Better she die now, I think."

Anna fought for her composure. *Yield and you can save your people.*

"They came this morning right at dawn. We had no warning until they were calling us out. There were ten of them, all on horses, and a big giant of a man leading."

Ruth licked her parched lips. "The big one told us that he was our lord now, and your husband, and that we were his. You could tell he's a man that likes killing. He looked us all over then, and I knew that someone was going to die. He called my man forward. He had one of those big axes the knights use, and as quick as a blink he took his head, my man just standing there one second and dead the next."

Her tears flowed freely, soaking the sheet at her neck. "He said we was to tell you about it. Every day until you yield he'll kill another. When he comes, if one is missing, hiding, he'll kill two." She turned her head and muttered the rest. "He took us back with him. He gave me to his knights. My baby he kept for himself."

Yield and you can save your people. Few lords would respond to this threat, for in truth most offered their people little protection during war and siege. She could sit here in safety and wait him out. But her father would not have done so, nor her brother, and she could not. He was counting on that, counting on her sacrificing herself and the lands to save the many lives that depended on her.

She went to the pallet. The frail girl had not moved, but her breathing came regularly and her skin felt cool.

Within a week you will be in my bed. Gurwant expected her to capitulate as the horrors mounted. But he had gone too far in sending her this child whom he had subjected to her own nightmare.

A servant handed her a cup of wine. She took it, then returned her attention to the girl. "Find Carlos. Send him to me. Then tell the knights that we meet shortly in the hall."

A half hour later she joined her men around the high table. She stood in front of the lord's chair and placed a large scroll on the table.

She told them Ruth's tale. "He is counting on my yielding when he holds true to his threat," she concluded. "It is what one would expect from a noblewoman of any heart."

"Nay, my lady," Fouke replied. "Most would have the sense to stay put. We are strong now and the castle will not fall."

"And while we sit here, what happens to the lands? We have already lost too much to the plague. By the time he tires and gives up there will be little left."

"If you expect to yield, do so now," Haarold said. "You can get better terms."

"I do not intend to yield." Her decision was a rash one, and a tremendous gamble. She'd never expected it to be as difficult to make as it suddenly was. "I have sent Carlos to the town by way of the coast, while the tide is low." She threw open the scroll to reveal a map of the estate. "I have sent word to the English archers that we will attack Gurwant's camp tomorrow at dawn."

There were objections, but no real resistance. These men were warriors, and the idea of a pitched battle carried its own allure. They gathered around the map.

"My father once described how Jeanne de Montfort raised a city's siege. She led the knights out a postern gate, circled behind the enemy camp, and made a surprise attack from behind. We will do the same. We will push Gurwant's force toward the wall, where our archers will aid us. Our main force will charge the camp from here." She indicated a spot directly across from the castle. "Carlos and I and one other will ride with our bows thus at the north end of the field, helping to put down any flanking movement. The English archers will do the same at the south."

Dead silence greeted the end of her explanation. She looked up to find five pairs of male eyes looking at her with shock.

Paul found his voice. "You cannot mean to ride with us, my lady."

"Of course I do. I have before and I will tomorrow."

"We are not so outnumbered as that," Haarold said. "Another will take your place."

"And who will that be? Who else can use a bow as well as I can from a galloping horse? Have you such a man with you, Haarold? Fouke?" She looked at one especially hot pair of eyes. "Morvan? Do any of you disagree with the importance of having archers there?"

"You might be taken," Haarold said.

"Most of the time I will be within range of the wall. And I will be on a fast horse, without armor to weigh it down."

The news that she would be unarmored did nothing for her case. Amidst the objections thrown at her, Ascanio finally spoke. "They too will have archers."

"We will attack before their archers have time to group and deploy. I will wear a hood and not be identified, so my presence will not affect the unfolding of things. But unless you can replace me with an equally skilled man, I will be there."

She left them to plan the details. She spent an hour with Ruth and Marguerite, then went down to the yard for some fresh air. As she crossed to the gatehouse Ascanio fell in step beside her.

"If you've been sent by the others to talk me out of joining you tomorrow, do not waste your breath," she warned.

"Nay, although it was discussed after you left. Haarold is of the opinion that a good beating would make you see sense. Morvan is inclined to agree and feels a certain prerogative in administering the lesson. I wouldn't let him catch you alone tonight. He has more in mind for your rump than last night's caress."

She pictured that and burst out laughing. "I will be on the alert. You came to warn me?"

"Nay, we must speak of something else. Let us go up on the wall where we can be alone."

He led the way to the battlements and found a spot away from the guards. He turned to her with a serious expression. She recognized his priest face. "I will hold mass this evening, so we all can pray before our ordeal. Afterwards, there will be another sacrament. Josce and Catherine will be getting married."

"Married? By whose authority and permission?"

"By their own. They will either do it publicly or privately, but I am the priest and I will witness their vows."

"They cannot marry without the duke's permission. There will be a fee that we can hardly afford—"

"Anna, Catherine is with child. I had suspected, but they finally told me last night."

She stared over the battlements. Besides shock she felt more than a little annoyance. Weren't there enough problems without this? Would it have been so hard for Catherine to have waited just a little while longer? But then she remembered herself in Morvan's arms, and her anger disappeared.

"Poor Ascanio, you leave them with this news and then find me. You must think the women in our family are harlots."

"I think the women in your family are full of life and passion. Actually, there is some gold in this development. If something should happen to you tomorrow, there is nothing to stop Gurwant from turning to Catherine. His plans for you would work just as well with her. But with her married and with child she is safe from him. Even if Josce is gone, she and the estate are secure."

There was great sense in what he said. She had worried about Catherine's future if she died in an attack that failed.

"You should go and see them. They are waiting for you now in the solar."

She headed down from the wall walk, steeling herself for a very awkward conference. It didn't help to know that she had lost her right to moral indignation.

The wedding was a poor affair, with the pall of battle hanging over everyone. Josce and Catherine did not seem to notice. Morvan watched their joy in each other, and a hollow spot thumped in his heart. Even the most hardened man could not but be touched by the way they looked in each other's eyes as they joined in love.

A small attempt was made to mimic a feast at the

evening meal. At the end Anna escorted her sister up-stairs.

Morvan waited for her to return. When the night grew old and still she did not, he went looking for her.

If she thought that he was going to accept her decision to join the battle, she was mistaken. All day he had been plagued by images of her dead on the field. Fouke and Haarold might not care if she died, and Ascanio might assume that angels protected her, but a tight knot in his stomach had convinced Morvan that he would not let her ride tomorrow.

Without looking, he knew that she was not in her chamber. He found her in the solar, sitting in the large, carved chair, gazing into the hearth fire. Her curls were wild about her head, as if she had just risen from a bed in which she could not sleep. A green robe, overlarge like most of her men's garments, wrapped her loosely. She held her sword, its tip resting on the floor, its hilt lax in her hand.

She looked at the flames as if she didn't really see them. He felt her mood as he'd always been able to since that first night. Sadness and resignation emanated from her. Something else too. Confusion?

She did not even look at him when he stepped into the chamber, as if she had known he was coming.

Aye, she *had* known. They were tied to each other in that way. She might not speak of it, might want to deny it, but it was there. Every time he entered her presence, the sense of raw connection sharpened again.

"Contemplating the morning?" he asked.

"I was thinking of Catherine and Josce."

That did not surprise him. If he had felt a twinge of envy, what must she have experienced?

"She appeared so mature, suddenly," she said. "Poised and grown up. And Josce—when did he get so tall and broad? They were children when I returned from the abbey, I'm sure. I find myself wondering how long I have been blind. I am thinking that I live an illusion in believing that I am needed here."

"They are still young, married or not. You are needed."

"Nay. I have been letting the freedom seduce me, but I can feel the truth at the door. It will be over soon."

"Not so soon. Not tomorrow."

It came out too sharply. That pulled her out of her reverie.

She rose, sword still dragging from her hand, and turned a direct gaze at him, as if suddenly aware that his presence here signaled something significant. The loosely tied robe gaped at the neck and over her legs, revealing too much, but she did not notice.

She looked wild and magnificent.

"I have been told that Haarold thinks I should be beaten into changing my mind about the battle. If you have come for that, you had better have brought your blade."

"Nay, I found the notion too arousing, and I have given Ascanio certain promises about you."

She frowned, not understanding. He almost laughed, bitterly. She was so astonishingly ignorant. Unaware of how she affected some men.

Men like him.

She stood there, her very strength a challenge to his most ancient instincts, a denial of all he had been bred to believe and uphold. His reaction was heady and erotic and primitive. The image of that beating *had* aroused him. The thought of her stretched naked over his lap had done wicked things to his blood. It was not the notion of hurting her that stirred him, but of conquering her. Here was a castle worthy of a siege, and a potential submission that would exalt the victor.

His blood had always known it, but seeing Gurwant react the same way had made him recognize its dark power. That a rich estate went with the woman had become secondary, for both her enemy and her protector. And she had no idea of what both men considered the true prize. None.

He was barely able to resist the pounding urge to disarm her and tear the seductive robe from her body. "I think that an intelligent woman will decide on her own against going."

"An intelligent woman will have assessed the odds, and know that every man will be needed tomorrow."

"Aye. Every *man*."

She sighed, disappointed in him. He didn't care. He could not let her do this.

"I thought that you at least would see the rightness of it," she said. "If this was your home, and you were me, would you sit in your bower if you could help? I am not some little hoyden who plays with weapons, Morvan. I am the best archer in this keep."

His mind tried to accept it, but his heart and his very essence rejected her logic. "This is not going to be a hunt, or a minor skirmish against some thieves. Men will die on that field, hacked to pieces in a kind of death that makes the plague look merciful. *You* might die thus."

Her gaze softened, but did not waver. "I know. I am ready."

"Are you? Or do you believe that you truly are a saint, and that angels protect you?"

"I have never believed that. I am all too aware that when God makes women saints, he rarely forms them like me. Now, the morning will come too soon, and we both should rest. I thank you for your concern, but I will fight for my home with the skill and strength given me. Perhaps I was born to be what I am because of this day."

She turned away to face the hearth.

Dismissing him.

A warrior's pride and fury flooded him. His legs took him across the chamber. He grabbed her hand and forced the weapon to clatter to the floor. He swung her around, gripping her shoulders. "You do not understand. You will not ride tomorrow. *You will not do this.*"

Her eyes narrowed and sparked. That only made his blood hotter.

She tried to twist out of his hold. "*You* do not understand. *You do not command me.*"

She glared at him, all challenge and strength, goading his primitive soul.

Words would not make her submit. Nor would hurting her. But there was another way.

Pulling her closer, he imprisoned her in his arms. Shock flashed in her eyes. She turned her head away.

The press of her body sent fire scorching through him. Her vain struggle fed the flames. He grasped her curls and held her gaze to his.

Slowly, her resistance dulled and her curves molded against his embrace. Her lower lip trembled. "I thought that you had given Ascanio promises."

"It is not dishonorable to break them for a good cause." He took that pulsing lip between his teeth. The tremble spread, announcing her vulnerability. It only fueled his heat. He kissed her, pressing her close so that he could feel all of her along his body, her breasts and hips and legs. He demanded more and she did not stop him, but parted her lips.

A chaos of impulses streaked through his fogging sense. Urges to protect and possess and command and conquer spurred his desire. He would bind her to him with passion and pleasure and she would never defy him and wield her weapons on the field.

His hunger turned forceful and hard. He bit down to the hot pulse of her neck, and plunged his hand beneath the parting robe. Softness. Warmth. Her gasping breaths proclaimed his victory. He slid the sagging shoulder of the robe down and tasted her skin. As he caressed her breast, a throaty cry escaped her. The aching pleasure surged in response, saturated with triumph.

She grabbed his hair and pressed her mouth to his ear. "I know what you are about. I know why you do this."

He looked in her eyes while he whisked his fingers over her nipple. Her gaze reflected the pleasure, and his control of it.

"You expect to make me obedient to your will. Docile." Her words came out on broken breaths. Ragged. No longer so strong.

"I think only to give you pleasure, so that we both know some life before we face death." He held her breast and dipped to kiss its hard tip. His tongue swirled. Her whole body moved in response. He used his skill to push her into abandon, and to silence her intruding voice of reason.

"You make my senses half crazed, but I am sane enough still to know the truth," she whispered. Her fight for control of herself could be heard in her voice. "This is not about giving, Morvan. It is not even about desire for me. It is about taking. Not me, but La Roche de Roald itself."

He pulled back and looked in her eyes. They glistened

with passion, but also a fierce belief. He did not remove his hand from her body. He would not give that up until he had to.

"This is not about your estate, Anna."

"You seek only to make me pliant for my safety's sake? I think not, but even so you waste your passion. That might work with your court ladies, but not me. I am made of different stuff. My ignorance makes me weak to you in this, but in nothing else."

Her warmth still enlivened his hand. He imagined knowing all the heat and pulses, the glory of making this complete. But then his mind's eye saw her leaving him, rising from the bed and donning her tunic and lifting her bow to ride out to face the enemy.

The urge to conquer and tame rushed in again, throbbing an order to finish it. The pounding of his hunger joined in. But a deeper understanding admitted the truth. No matter what happened this night, she would fight on the morrow.

He gazed in her eyes and sought some crack in her determination. Only resolve glimmered back. For an instant, no more, he perceived more than he had seen before. A new knowledge of her spirit streamed into him. The revelation did not shock him. It only confirmed that a mere knight in her service could never keep her safe, even if he claimed her this way.

He lowered his head and kissed her breast again, and seared his memory with its softness and her flexing response.

"If I thought that your resolve could be changed, I would take you and not care why you thought I did it. Perhaps I would even beat you as Haarold suggested. You say that you will join us because your skill is needed, but it occurs to me that this is not about that." He released her, and stepped away from the tantalizing closeness. His essence roared with anger at the retreat.

"I am surprised that I did not realize it sooner, Anna, for I know you well. You do not go just because you are needed. I think that you also go because you enjoy it."

He turned away from her stunned expression. He went to prepare for the morning, and to pray that the angels did indeed watch over her.

CHAPTER 10

TWO HOURS BEFORE DAWN Anna entered the low-
est level of the keep and began leading her small
army out of La Roche de Roald. Guards carried torches
to light the way through the foundation maze.

Down some of the blind corridors she could see
doors, their hinges rusted from damp and disuse. She
wondered if any enemies of her ancestors lay interred behind them. The possibility of facing those skeletons kept
her from ever exploring the chambers.

Since Drago's death, she had been the only one who
could guide someone to the cliff stairs. But this morning, as a precaution against the worst, she had passed the
secret on to Catherine.

It had been a short, sleepless night. Thoughts of
the upcoming battle had made her restless, but so had
reflection on Morvan's visit. She had succumbed too

quickly to his flattery and touch. Something inside her, beyond her control, had responded hungrily to his hold on her. Maybe fear of the battle had done that. Perhaps a part of her had wanted him to defeat her, so that she would have an excuse not to stand where she did right now.

His parting words kept running through her mind, suggesting that the part of her that welcomed this was bigger than any fear. Was he right? Did she enjoy it? Had playing the lord become an end in itself? Did she look forward to this battle like a warrior, and not like a woman forced by circumstances to do the unthinkable? Was she, in the end, as unnatural as that? She, who never used mirrors, now had one thrust in front of her soul and she couldn't, for all of her trying, see what was truly reflected there.

She found herself in front of the postern door. She swung it open and the sounds of surf crashed against the granite vaults. Her army followed her to the beach.

The cliff rose ragged and uneven, at places soaring above the beach, at others dipping down to scalable heights. A mile north she turned to a path that led up the jumble of rocks to the forest above.

She heard the soft whinnies before she reached the clearing. Carlos had brought twenty horses from the farm. He pointed her to one tree. Tied there were three magnificent coursers with the lean lines and slender legs that bespoke their strong Saracen heritage. They were the fastest horses and would be the mounts used by Carlos and herself and Louis.

She slid her sword through the leather loops on her saddle's left side. She swung herself up, then bent to attach a quiver near her right leg.

Hands reached out and began tying the lower thongs

to their saddle rings. She gazed at the bright eyes of the man who owned those hands. Morvan looked back, the flickering torchlight making his face appear stern. Memories of last night's intimacies passed silently between them.

He rested one hand on her knee. "Stay close to the wall. Within our archers' range," he commanded roughly.

She would not be effective then. "I will be careful."

"If things go badly, ride back. Gregory will be looking for you. He will get you inside."

She hadn't known that he had given Gregory special orders. She should have guessed that he would.

"If you are in danger, remove your hood. They cannot afford to harm you."

He was telling her to let Gurwant take her alive and unwounded. She had already decided that she would not.

He reached up and pulled her shoulder down. His hand found her head, and he pressed her mouth to his.

Carlos began to lead the men from the clearing. Morvan stepped back to pull on his gauntlets.

"Do not blame yourself for not stopping me. And do not get yourself killed worrying about me," she said. "Carlos will be nearby, and is better at this than you would think. God go with you, Morvan."

"And with you, my lady."

He mounted his bay. It was a fine horse, she reassured herself, with more stamina and speed than a destrier. In an action such as this it might serve him better than a warhorse.

They made their way through the forest. Finally Carlos gestured that they had arrived. The foot soldiers took positions to the right and left and formed their lines. She, Carlos, and Louis moved their horses to the northern edge of the group. Everyone silently waited.

Slowly, the blackness beyond the low fires of Gurwant's camp began to change. Rough shapes emerged that formed into sleeping men and restless horses. The bodies by the central fire grew distinct first, and she saw to her dismay that not all of the men were sleeping. A few, including Gurwant himself, were already up and armored.

Something beyond the camp caught her attention. On the southern field motionless shadows loomed that could only be the English archers from Brest.

Suddenly a silvery gray light spread over the field. The distant shadows grew arms and legs and strode forward together. A whistling sound broke the morning silence as volley after volley of arrows from their longbows flew toward Gurwant's camp.

Anna's own archers ran from the forest and joined the onslaught, aiming as they had been told at the clutch of horses by the forest edge.

Hell broke loose. Battle cries rent the silence. Her knights and men-at-arms charged toward the confusion of Gurwant's camp.

She galloped past the camp with Carlos and Louis close behind. As she dropped her reins and began to let her own arrows fly, she saw Haarold and a small force pour out of the castle gate.

Their surprise attack had at least evened the odds. Many of Gurwant's sleeping soldiers never rose, and most of the others fought on foot, unarmored and unprepared. Gurwant and his knights had managed to get horses, however, and the blond head of her adversary could be seen towering above the battle as he hacked with his ax through the melee.

The battle began spreading out. Controlling her horse with her legs, she galloped along the northern periphery, aiming her bolts carefully, trying to bring down the mounted enemies by hitting the horses that carried them.

Over and over she made her sweeping runs. Her blood coursed with fear and exhilaration. Despite an overwhelming sensation of danger, she had never before felt so gloriously alive and clearheaded.

She galloped toward the castle on another pass, then turned her horse. Her heart jolted. One of Gurwant's knights had broken away from the battle and now charged toward the northern field. He raised his sword as he bore down on young Louis, who didn't see the danger behind him.

She sighted an arrow to bring down the knight's horse, but suddenly Louis was between them and in the way. Slinging her bow onto her saddle, she unsheathed her sword and spurred her horse. The knight had just reached Louis when she ran her mount straight into his, swinging her sword just in time to deflect the death blow aimed at the youth's neck.

The blade grazed Louis's arm. His horse bolted out of the way, but hers and the knight's joined in a tangle of legs that sent them both crashing to the ground.

The impact stole her breath. Pain spread through her hips and legs. As the horses righted themselves, the knight moved laboriously under his armor, pushing himself up. She jumped to her feet and grabbed the reins of her horse, but he skittered nervously and she was not able to mount.

She smelled death behind her. She dropped the reins and turned. The knight had risen. He lowered his visor and faced her.

She grasped her weapon in both hands. The battle suddenly seemed far away, and the field very big.

She heard the knight laugh before he moved toward her.

Morvan knew exactly that moment when the outcome of the battle was decided. As he wielded his sword, forcing his way through the foot soldiers to meet the mounted knights, he noticed the enemy falling back. That meant moving toward the castle wall. The fate of Gurwant's army was sealed with those first steps of retreat.

It was Gurwant himself whom he wanted, and he worked his way toward that towering blond head.

A movement to his left caught his attention. He reared his horse just in time to knock down a swordsman thrusting at the animal's legs. The bay pivoted before settling down and he found himself facing north, where he knew Anna should be riding.

He did not see her. He quickly dispatched a man who challenged him, and looked again. His gaze lit upon two unmounted horses at the northeast corner of the field, and on a slender hooded figure facing off against an armored knight.

His vivid curses came out as a garble. He charged out of the battle, not caring whether he trampled foe or ally. He pushed forward, self-recrimination and fury mixing to a deadly boil. He knew, even as he watched for it, that Anna would not remove the hood and make herself known.

The knight struck. She deflected his sword with her own, twisted quickly, and broke away. It was a good defensive move, but it would not work again. Morvan gritted his teeth and pushed the horse harder. His stomach knotted as he realized that he would not get there in time. He heard himself yell as the knight brought a crashing blow down.

Only Anna's quickness kept her from being clove in two, but the sword connected nonetheless and she fell in a heap to the ground. The knight prepared to finish her.

He did not see Morvan coming. Suddenly the thundering bay was upon him with a sword extended straight out. Under the force of this soaring blade, the knight's head flew from his body.

Despite the armor weighing down his body, Morvan jumped off the horse and strode quickly to Anna's lifeless form. He threw off his gauntlets, sheathed his sword, and dropped to one knee, coldly afraid for the first time in his life. The battle, the field, the sun itself receded as he stared at her inert shape.

He lifted her head and slapped her face hard. A gasp of relief escaped his lips when her eyes fluttered open.

The sound of hooves made him battle-alert again, but it was Carlos bearing down on them, horrified worry on his face.

"She lives," Morvan shouted. "Stay and cover us. I am bringing her in."

Carlos wheeled his horse around to face the fighting, his bow ready. "Take her mount," he yelled. "It will outrun anything on this field."

Morvan grabbed Anna under the arms, forcing her to her feet. Blood flowed freely from her hip. It was a bad wound, but it appeared that no bones had been crushed.

He mounted and pulled her up sideways in front of him, making her cry out. The sound wrenched something deep inside him, but the pain, he knew, had been unavoidable. With his right arm grasping her shoulders, he took the reins in his left. As a last thought he reached up and pulled the hood from her head, and the golden curls tumbled out.

The pain had brought her to full consciousness, and she grabbed on to his armor for support as the horse galloped off. He spared an instant to look down at her. His glance took in the blood soaking her garments and staining the saddle.

The thought of how close she had come to death chilled him. An overpowering anger at her willfulness gripped him.

When they reached the gate they found the drawbridge down. He did not wait for the portcullis to rise completely, but charged in, ducking below its iron edge. He rode over to Gregory and slid Anna into his arms.

"She is sore hurt. Have her brought to Catherine and the women at once." He gave her one last look before he rode back to the battle.

The pain was intense, but Anna felt less weak than at first. "Put me down, Gregory. I am too big for you and I can stand."

He lowered her feet to the ground. She needed to lean against him for support, but her left leg held. "Help me up to the wall."

"You heard him, my lady."

"He is not my lord. I will go to the wall."

He helped her hobble toward the stairs. "There will be hell to pay for this, I tell you. He's not a man what likes being crossed and you're losing a lot of blood."

"Just tell him that I commanded you."

He called for a guard and they managed to get her up

to the battlements. She grabbed hold of both men and surveyed the field. Gurwant's army was being pressed back harder now.

She saw Morvan's helmet and Gurwant's blond head in the thick of it, slowly moving through the fray toward each other. As Gurwant pushed forward his battle-ax fell on one of her guards. Even from a distance she could see blood explode from the skull.

The battle came within range of the castle and the archers on the wall began taking careful aim. As the rear edge of Gurwant's army realized their position, panic set in.

"Get me a crossbow, Gregory."

"My lady, the day is won. Go now and have that wound tended."

She watched cold blue eyes that were fixed on Morvan. "A crossbow."

She had no doubt of Morvan's skill. Yet Gurwant's strength and skill were great too. Morvan could be seriously wounded, perhaps maimed. Even killed. The very thought filled her with a desolation so bleak she couldn't bear it. In that moment she felt that if Morvan fell nothing else would matter, not the battle, not even La Roche de Roald itself. It was foolish, of course. He was but one man and not even kin. He had been bred for this as surely as the destriers that she raised. Still her heart could not, would not, let her risk him.

A guard put a crossbow in her hands. She tried to stand alone as she positioned it, but found her leg too weak. Gregory put his weight under her shoulders and propped her up from the back. She shook off a wave of light-headedness.

If you have to stop a man, go for his neck.

She had never aimed to kill before, but this time she

did, and was coldly aware of her decision. She wondered briefly, absurdly, if the Mother Abbess would take her back if she knew.

She caught Gurwant in her sight and moved it with his slow progress through the melee toward Morvan. When he stopped, face-to-face against her brave knight, in that moment before they raised their weapons, she released her bolt at the blond giant's neck.

She missed. Before the arrow hit its mark, Gurwant raised his ax and his horse stepped back. The bolt imbedded itself in the unarmored underarea of his upper right arm. Morvan immediately looked to the wall, finding her blond curls there. She called for another bow, but Gurwant's arm fell lifelessly to his side and the ax tumbled to the ground.

The bolt must have broken the bone. He pulled his sword from his saddle and threw that to the ground too.

Morvan flipped up his visor. His fury at having his foe surrender was visible all the way to the wall.

"Hell," Gregory muttered. "With all respect, my lady, you'll be laid up all safe as can be in your bower when he gets back in here, and I'll be explaining this on my own."

The world began swirling. She sank into Gregory's arms. "Perhaps you should take me there now."

CHAPTER 11

MORVAN STOOD BY THE GATE watching the prisoners and the wounded being brought into the castle. It had been a bloody few hours, but Gurwant's army had seen the worst of it. Gurwant himself was already resting in the dungeon and others were being led there now.

He walked over to the keep and up to the hall. The wounded from both sides had been laid out there and several of the women servants tended them. He summoned two men to help him remove his armor in his chamber. Finally he threw on a long tunic and went in search of some food.

One long table in the hall had been piled with bread, cheese, and meat. He took some food and poured some ale, then stood near the hearth and ate his meal.

A young servant girl approached. "Pardon, Sir Morvan, but do you know where Father Ascanio is?"

"What do you want him for?"

"Lady Catherine told me to fetch him. It's my lady Anna. Catherine be needing the father for her."

His heart sank. "Lady Anna needs a priest?"

"Oh, it isn't for shriving. Lady Catherine needs his strength with her."

He drained his cup and threw the last of his bread into the fire. "If it is strength she needs, I should do."

As he approached Anna's chamber, he heard an argument within. He made out Catherine's annoyed voice and Anna's low responses.

They did not notice him when he entered. Four women surrounded the bed and Catherine sat beside it with a box of salves at her feet. The women were trying to hold Anna down and she was fending them off with strong arms and stronger threats.

"I say it must be sewn," Catherine said with exasperation.

"And I say it is but a flesh wound. Bind it closed with a bandage and it will heal." Anna landed a sound blow on one of the woman's arms.

They all jumped back from the bed at that, and Morvan was suddenly seen. For a few moments everyone just stared at him, leaving an unobstructed view of Anna lying naked on her stomach. He glimpsed long elegant curves and pale skin, and damp curls falling over her startled face. His mind became branded with the quick sight of her back, more beautiful than any he had ever seen, tapering to her waist. Her bottom rose high and round and firmer than most women's, and her hips and thighs had a lean tension. Her body looked even more glorious than he had imagined it.

The women suddenly found their senses. They jumped in front of the bed like a line of guards.

"Oh dear saints," Anna groaned, burying her face in her folded arms. "Catherine, how could you?"

Catherine walked around to the other side of the bed. A sheet billowed up behind the servants and floated down. "I called for Ascanio." Her tone indicated she was past caring what Anna thought about anything.

"Ascanio is with the dying," Morvan said, advancing on the bed. "What do you require?"

"I require a strong man to hold her down so that I can sew the wound. She is too much for us."

Anna twisted to see her sister. "It needs but a bandage!"

"How would you know? You can't see it. I say if it isn't sewn it might heal amiss and pull at you forever. Furthermore, the scar will be hideous."

"What do I care about damn scars."

Morvan pushed the servants aside. He flipped back the sheet and uncovered her body. The wound was high on her left back flank and formed a ragged thin mountain over a handspan long. The skin had been fairly flayed from her body and at the base of the wound some muscle had torn. A bad bruise was already forming from the sword's impact and her fall. There would soon be many other bruises too.

He glanced over to where a tub stood with damp towels and puddles around it. They had bathed her and she wouldn't feel too stiff now, but tomorrow would be hell.

"My lord," one of the servants admonished as she grabbed the sheet and draped it more modestly around the wound.

"He isn't your lord," Anna said stiffly.

"Aye, if I was the lord the marks on you would be from my hand and not from a sword, and Catherine would not be sewing this warrior's wound. I don't like Haarold and it is hard to admit he was right."

He began unfastening the belt on his hips. Anna rose on her elbows and glared at him. "You wouldn't dare."

"Not while you are abed with wounds, unless you refuse to obey. It will be sewn. This is for your mouth so the pain does not make you bite through your lip."

The servants cast meaningful looks at each other. He regretted his words. He suddenly understood Anna's rebellion. He gestured to the girl who had fetched him. "You stay here. The rest of you go down and tend the men in the hall. There are many wounded there."

With obvious reluctance, the three women obeyed him.

He turned to Catherine. "Let us do it now."

Catherine began lining pillows along her side of the bed. "It will be best if I turn her. I will be able to see the wound better. Face away while I do it."

He touched Anna's shoulder. "They are gone and will not watch you now. Will you obey your sister?"

She nodded, and he turned away. When Catherine finished not only was Anna angled on her back against the pillows, but she had also been gowned in a thin shift. The sheet modestly draped all but her wound. He could see bruises forming on her right shoulder and arm and a slight reddening on her cheek under one eye.

He sat beside her on the bed, then instructed the servant girl. "You are to sit on her legs, just below the knees. Use all of your weight so that she cannot move them."

Anna grimaced when the servant did as she was told. Morvan offered the strap and with a scowl she bit the leather. Then, as gently as he could, for he knew not what other sores she bore, he laid his left arm across her shoulders above her breasts and his right hand on her belly.

"Do it now."

With the first touch of Catherine's fingers Anna bucked hard. He pressed his weight down. Her hands flew up and she grabbed his arms, at first to fight him but then to release the intensity of her pain. He knew each time the needle probed from the way she bit the strap and moved her head.

In his anger he had told himself that she deserved it. If she was going to fight a warrior's battle, she should be ready to take a warrior's pain. But as he watched her small white teeth gritting harder and her eyes brimming with tears, a heartfelt anguish gripped him.

"Can't you be faster?"

"We do this right or there is no point in doing it," Catherine said.

It was true, and since she was sewing a long gash it would not be quick at all. He knew the agony too well. The slow sewing of brutalized tissue created its own special kind of hell.

He bent toward Anna. "Open your eyes. If they are closed you feel it worse. Look at the ceiling, or the weaving of my clothes. Count the threads."

Her eyes fluttered open, and streams flowed down her temples from their corners. Instead of the ceiling or tunic, she chose to look in his eyes. He let her, and tried to absorb some of the pain with his gaze.

"Shall I tell you how I came to have Devil?" he asked. "He was a gift from Edward, for my valor at Crécy. When I asked to be released from the siege at Calais to take service in Gascony, he presented him to me. Devil was one of his own destriers. I have been thinking," he continued, all in an effort to distract her, for in fact he had never thought of it before. "You have admired him, and he comes from good stock. Perhaps we should breed him here with some of your mares. I will take one of the foals in payment. That is customary, nay? Or a palfrey. It is awkward not having one."

She nodded and a smile began to form, but just then Catherine must have probed an especially bad spot, for her mouth flew open and she cried out.

She momentarily looked wild-eyed. He found himself fighting to maintain his composure. "I would take this onto myself if I could, Anna. In God's name I would," he whispered, holding her body more firmly as she rebelled.

The worst must have passed, for she calmed and sought his eyes again. "You know that this must end," he said. "It cannot go on. When you are well you must go to England and see your duke. You must have this settled."

A sad look passed over her before she slowly nodded.

"I know people at the court who will aid you. I will give you letters for them." He tried to ignore the sick feeling the notion of this settlement gave him. He had a vision of her walking away through a gated wall, her brown convent gown flowing gently around her as a door closed forever. But it was preferable to other visions that had plagued him the last few days, of her butchered on the battlefield or frozen in terror under Gurwant's body.

"I am done," Catherine said.

He loosened the pressure but did not move his hand and arms. Anna breathed easier and the strap fell from her mouth, but her hands still clutched his arms.

He looked into blue eyes clearing of pain. "I have held down seasoned knights who were not so brave."

"Before you came they were saying it was a punishment from God that I was wounded. For daring a man's deed. Not Catherine, but the others. I would not let them take their satisfaction in seeing me suffer."

He had suspected as much. It had not occurred to him before that while the men accepted Anna, the women did not. They resented one of their own living as she did. How long had they been waiting for the sign from God that her independence was unacceptable, even for a saint? All the more reason for this to end.

"If you would leave us now, Morvan, I will bind the bandage on. Then she must rest," Catherine said.

Anna dropped her hands. He brushed the damp curls from her face. She grabbed his hand. "Gurwant?"

"He awaits your pleasure. Sleep now. We will talk later of him."

He left her and went outside and down to the door that led to the keep's ground level. Torches lit a narrow passage flanked by prison cells. Even in winter the foundations were damp with the smell of the sea.

He walked to a door and ordered the guard to unlock it. Three knights sat inside on floor pallets.

Gurwant stood, clutching his right arm to his body. His blond head nearly touched the ceiling, as Morvan's did. The cold blue eyes measured him.

Morvan remembered his fury when Anna's arrow had robbed him of the chance to kill this man. His only goal this day had been to free her from Gurwant's threat. Her mercy had not angered him so much as the insinuation that she doubted his skill. The thought still rancored him.

"Someone will come to tend your arm."

"And then?"

"That is for the lady to decide. For my part, I will advise that she hang you."

"She cannot do that. It will bring my whole family here to avenge me."

"Maybe not. They must know what they have in you. A weak offshoot who loses an army to a woman. Even her wound is less than yours."

Gurwant's eyes grew colder. "She was on the field? What kind of men serve her that she must fight for them?"

"Outnumbered men who beat you."

He glanced down at his useless arm. "I am told she is an archer. I think that this work is hers."

"She saved your life."

"Nay, the life she saved was yours. But I think that someday we will find out for sure."

"If you leave here alive and ever come back, I will be waiting for you."

Gurwant smiled. "Who are you, knight, that you protect her so? Kin? I don't think so. Surely you know that you can never have her. She is mine. She has been mine since she was a girl. I put my mark on her then."

"It looks to me that she put her mark on you."

Gurwant's hand stroked the scar on his cheek, and he grinned. "Child's play. She was wilder then, and not too willing. But sweet in the end."

"You lie, but it is not my concern. I serve her, and she does not want you now. She knows that you are still a devil who rapes children."

Gurwant's blank smile twisted into a sneer. "You speak of the peasants. They are nothing."

"Not to her. If she hangs you, it will be for the girl." He turned to the door. "A woman will come and see to your arm. Guards will be with her. If you even look at her, I will tell them to kill you."

* * *

She stirred awake and knew that he was there. At the same moment that she felt the pillow under her face and the tight stiffness in her shoulder, she sensed his presence. It didn't surprise her to find him in this shadowy chamber with her. Even in her dreams she had sensed his arrival.

She reached down with her left hand, startled at the new stiffness in her arm, and pulled a pillow over to her hip. Then she laboriously rolled over onto her back, letting her wounded flank find the pillow's softness. She saw him looking at her.

"It hurts to move. The wound is the least of it."

"That will pass in a few days. Catherine says that you haven't slept much. You must rest."

She was fully awake now and knew that she wouldn't sleep again for a while. All day her body had felt battered and fatigued but her mind had been overly alert. Even when she did doze the rest was fitful and unsatisfying.

Dull noise rumbled through the keep. "What is happening?"

"Some people from the town came to celebrate. The men are in their cups."

"Is everything finished?"

"There will be more burying tomorrow. Fouke and Haarold plan to depart in two days. They will escort the captured soldiers to the estate's border and release them. They are mercenaries and there is no point in holding them."

"And the others?"

He crossed his legs comfortably. "Fouke and Haarold each claim one of the knights as their prize. They will hold them for ransom."

"And Gurwant? What should I do with him?"

It was the first time that she had ever directly asked him for advice. The expression in his eyes showed that he realized it. "What do you want to do with him?"

"I want to kill him."

"It would have been easier to do that on the battlefield. No consequences then. Now it is different."

He was upbraiding her for Gurwant's surrender. What could she say to him? The reason for her interference would infuriate him more than the action itself.

"So what do I do?"

"You do what Fouke and Haarold will do. Hold him for ransom. A high one—the Beaumanoir family can afford it. Include your loss of the serf and the harm to the estate. Send a slow messenger with the demand and let him rot until it comes."

"And then I just release him?"

"Then you just release him. But in those months you go to England. And before he is released you return to Saint Meen."

"I don't want him here."

"Let Haarold take him. It matters not which keep holds him. No one will start a war for him. But they might if you execute him."

His advice was carefully calculated. His desire to kill Gurwant honorably had been thwarted, and he did not want her taking an action that would endanger her further. She would send the monster with Haarold, though. She would not live with him near her.

"Does Sir John live?"

"He lives. He is mine."

She asked the question even though she knew the answer. "And will you ransom him as Fouke does with his man?"

"Nay. He dies, as I warned him he would. I have not

usurped your right of judgment. It will not be an execution. He will be given his sword and we will meet tomorrow in the yard."

"I do not want—"

"It is done."

She nestled down, pulling the covers to her chin. She may even have dozed for a short while, but that odd alertness claimed her again and she struggled to sit.

Morvan reached over to lift her shoulders and place a pillow beneath them. "You are not going to let me get any sleep at all, are you?"

"You are free to sleep. I just find that I cannot. I am very restless, despite my ordeal."

"I would think that you would sleep like the dead."

She pulled at a feather sticking out of the coverlet. "It was like this the last time. Between the two plague outbreaks, some brigands took one of the farmhouses and we had to get them out. Afterwards I couldn't sleep at all. I thought of going riding, but it was night. That's what I felt I needed to do, though. Gallop for miles."

He appeared amused. "Riding a horse. I hadn't thought of that. But the restlessness is common after battle."

"So?"

He looked at her blankly.

"So what do you do about it if you never thought to ride a horse?"

A faint smile played on his lips. "I usually do what your men are doing right now. I take a woman to bed for a few hours."

She felt herself blush. A few *hours*? "Well," she said to hide her embarrassment. "Don't deny yourself on my account. I will be fine alone."

He looked impassively to the hearth. She guessed then that he had not denied himself. He had come to her after his few hours with a woman.

Her pleasure that he had come at all disappeared. A man's base need seemed to take precedence over everything else. But, a few *hours*? What she knew of these things wouldn't take more than a few minutes.

She picked furiously at the feather. She suddenly felt very restless indeed. That and the pressure on her bruised rump made her shift nervously.

"You are angry," he said, fascinated.

"I'm not angry. I'm just uncomfortable. And confused." In her annoyance she blurted out the unspeakable. "I know that I am not worldly, Morvan, but I begin to think that I am unbearably ignorant. I can't imagine what men and woman do that takes a few *hours*."

She shouldn't have said that, she knew, but if he was going to tell her how he'd passed the evening he could hardly be shocked. And she was getting very tired of being stupid about these things. It had become clear that everyone, for example, had known about Catherine and Josce. Except her.

He rose and went to a table where a pitcher stood. He poured some wine and brought the cups over.

"Well?" she demanded as he handed her the cup.

His expression changed. She knew this new look. Its severity had nothing to do with anger. "You can't expect me to explain such things to you. Talk to Catherine. Although for a woman determined to take the veil, you are passingly curious."

She shifted again. It wasn't her bruises making her uncomfortable now. He had gone to his chair, but he hadn't taken his eyes off her. The air in the room changed and she no longer felt annoyed or even very curious, just a bit frightened and a little breathless. She began falling under the spell of those sparkling eyes and quickly shifted her gaze to the poor brutalized feather sticking out of the coverlet.

"Anna."

The quiet resonance of the word took her breath away. She looked over. The chair appeared closer than before. She tried to avoid his eyes, but of course that was impossible. Dark pools full of glittering sparks regarded her.

"Just how restless are you?"

"Not very. In fact, I'm feeling quite sleepy of a sudden."

He took one of her curls in his fingers. The gesture brought him closer. "Ah. Because I could relieve you of it. It is a simple thing."

Something lurched inside her and her whole body tingled. "Under the circumstances, I think it would be very complicated. I *am* wounded, after all. And you said that you made promises to Ascanio." Of course, those promises had not stopped him last night. . . .

He ran a fingertip over her bare shoulder, raising a visible shiver. His gaze seemed to follow the tremor down her covered body to her hips.

"I would not harm your wound or even go near it. I would barely touch you at all. There can be release short of coupling."

She felt her mouth drop open. Her confusion was only partly due to her preoccupation with the pulsing in her body and the way her breasts suddenly felt deliciously sensitive to the fabric of her shift.

He searched her eyes, then sat back, away from her, with a rueful smile. "You don't know what I am talking about, do you?"

She felt so absurdly stupid that she burst out laughing. As she wiped tears from her eyes she saw that he was laughing too.

He tousled her hair as if she were a child. "Hell's teeth, Anna, you undo me. Go to sleep and give me some peace."

When dawn broke, she awoke to his movement. The silvery light seeping through the windows gave a sheen to everything in the room. He touched his hand to her forehead before turning to leave.

"Morvan. Yesterday, I tried to kill him. I missed."

He bent and brushed his lips where his hand had been. "Then it was not God's will that you succeed, for you rarely miss. In my soul I feel that he is mine to kill, anyway. Someday."

She listened to him depart, then raised her hand to her eyes to block out the dawn and the danger that he faced against John this day.

CHAPTER 12

THAT DAY SIR JOHN STOOD to the sword against Morvan in the outer bailey of La Roche de Roald. The entire castle watched, except for the servant who sat with Anna in her chamber and joined her mistress in silent prayer.

An agonizing eternity passed before the crowd's shouts died away. Anna sent the servant to find out what she could.

The door opened, but it was Ascanio who breezed in. "Did you ever have any doubts?"

"Morvan is unwounded?"

"A few scratches. He takes his oath to protect you to heart, and is ruthless with any who threaten you. He would meet Gurwant as he did John if he didn't think it would start a blood feud with the entire Beaumanoir kinship." He patted her hand. "I will be back later. Even John deserves a few words when he is buried."

She sank back into the pillows when he had gone. The exhaustion of yesterday's ordeal had finally claimed her this morning. She'd begun to doze when she heard a soft footfall. She opened her eyes to see a childish face mere inches from hers, peering at her curiously.

She reached out to brush aside the thin brown hair that fell over the girl's face and down her frail body. Little Marguerite looked helplessly small to her. At thirteen years she had been twice as big as this waif.

"I'm glad to see that you are up, Marguerite."

"Don't tell Mama that I came. She says I'm to stay out of sight. But she went to dinner and won't know."

It was the first time the girl had spoken since she had been dumped outside the gate. "You may visit whenever you want. Come, sit on the bed and talk to me."

She hopped up, and lanky legs dangled down from the simple shift that she wore. "Mama says that you got that man. That a great battle was fought to get him."

"Aye. He will harm no one else."

"She says that you saved our lives. That the angels helped you save us."

"Your own strength saved your lives."

"Papa's dead. Mama says she will have to marry someone else so we can eat."

Anna hadn't thought much about Ruth and Marguerite the last two days, except as responsibilities to be avenged. But with the husband gone their situation was precarious. Could Ruth bear going to a new man so soon? Would any man even want her and the girl now?

"Maybe you could stay here. I have no personal servant. Your mother could learn, and you could help her. When I leave, you could serve Lady Catherine."

She was tying ropes on herself that she had always avoided. Ruth and Marguerite would be under her feet, always there, wanting to bathe her and comb her. But they would probably be loyal, and there wasn't anywhere else for them to go.

"I'll talk with your mother. Now, I want you to go down to the hall for dinner. Tell your mother I sent you. Up now. Back straight. Head high. Off with you." The little body marched out. Anna laughed as she saw that she had created a tiny imitation of herself.

The next day Fouke and Haarold visited to take their leave. They brought Morvan and Ascanio with them, and the captured knights whom they would transport back to their castles to await ransom. Anna received them from her bed.

Gurwant's hands were bound and his bare right arm had been splinted and strapped to his chest. He nodded at his hands, indicating his annoyance at the rope. "I have given my parole."

"The rope stays as Haarold has ordered. It is for your own safety, for you will surely try to escape, parole or not, and then my men will have to kill you."

"You insult me, Anna."

"Do not be familiar with me, Gurwant. I see no honorable knight before me, but a common criminal. In another age I would have given you to the villagers to deal with. Sir Haarold will keep you in close confinement until your family sends the ransom. You and I will not meet again. If you ever return to these lands, you will be treated as an outlaw. If it means leaving the abbey to hunt you down, I will do it."

Gurwant glared at her as Haarold led him away. That look spoke more eloquently than any verbal response could have. It made her soul shiver.

Morvan and Ascanio stayed behind after the other

knights left. They faced her together, two halves of one resolve.

"He is your prisoner, but he is not defeated," Ascanio said. "You must settle things with your duke."

"I will write again, at once."

"Aye, write. But if no response arrives, you are going to England," Morvan said. "We will wait until the feast of the Nativity has passed, but no longer. By then your warrior's wound should have healed."

"Surely it is better to sail in warmer months."

He took her chin in his hand and forced her gaze to meet his. "You are going. This is over." He gestured to her covered hip. "*That* does not happen again."

As he strode out of the chamber, she heard the silent words he had not spoken. *It is done.*

Two weeks after the feast of the Nativity, Anna found herself being rowed through Brest's harbor, to the ship that would carry her to England.

Morvan sat beside her. Gregory, and four of Morvan's men who wanted to return home despite the danger of plague, crowded around them.

She had tried to delay this voyage, but Morvan had forced the plans forward. Ascanio had supported his insistence that it be done now, before Gurwant could be ransomed. Ascanio had also suggested that Morvan escort her, since he knew King Edward and the court officials, and could also find her hospitality with his sister.

Taking a free hand, Morvan had arranged the journey to Brest and their passage on the waiting ship. He had neither consulted her nor explained to her. It had simply happened.

She gazed at the ship. She had never been on one before. Aside from traveling to Saint Meen, she had never left her home before. That was one reason she had avoided this means of settling the estate's problems. But this journey had revealed other misgivings in her heart that had no names, and that she could not explain.

"Where are the horses?" She had decided to bring some to sell. Morvan had quizzed her on prices and told her she could get much more for them in England than from the drovers who passed through Brittany.

"In the hold. God willing it will not be a bad voyage, and they will be well."

She glanced back at the receding roofs of Brest. She had wanted to spend the morning walking in the city, but Morvan had insisted that since he had to supervise the boarding of the horses and could not accompany her, she was not to go. He had been giving orders like that since they departed La Roche de Roald. He had begun to treat her as his ward.

"Your trunks are at your berth," he explained. "You will be traveling with a Lady Martha and her servant. You are the only women on board and must stay in the cabin."

"Is that a sea law or something? That women stay in their cabins?"

"It is my law. There will be nothing to see but water and nothing to find but trouble if you don't obey it."

By the time the ship weighed anchor, Anna decided that the cabin would be purgatory. It was tiny and airless, no more than a curtained section of the lower deck, and the berths and pallets and trunks left little room to stand. Lady Martha acted very familiar with her servant, and they passed the time with gossip. Endless gossip. Anna had never been subjected to so much witless talk.

The next morning she woke to several additional dis-
comforting developments. The first was that Lady
Martha spoke too freely of personal things. The second
proceeded from the first, as Anna realized from this chatter that this noblewoman in her fine clothes was a slut.
That might have interested her, since she had never met a
fallen woman of her own class before, but for the final development. Early in the morning she became seasick.

Her situation got worse when they ran into bad winds
that sent them lurching through huge waves. The ship
groaned and creaked and she was sure that she could
hear it coming apart.

It was with great relief that she learned that they were
due to make a stop in Southampton in order to let Lady
Martha and her company debark. As they steered toward
the coast, the waves calmed somewhat.

When Martha had gone, Anna sank onto the bed for
the first peace and quiet in three days. She was falling
asleep when Morvan came to the cabin.

"You have been sick," he said, examining her face.

"I have been dying."

"Then perhaps you won't mind the news. The captain
says that a bad storm is brewing and we were headed
right for it. He plans to sit it out here. We can wait and
then continue with the ship, or go overland."

"Overland."

"The weather is cold and we may have to camp."

"We can be in London in the time we will wait here.
Tell the captain that we debark. I want to get off this
thing."

"Then get some sleep this night and I'll arrange for us
to leave in the morning."

By midday they were on the road. Anna felt better the
moment she set foot on dry land. The familiar sensation

of riding a horse in the fresh air lightened her spirits. Gregory and the other men laughed and jested as they led the horses down the deserted road. They would help get the horses to London and then go their own ways.

"You cannot imagine how horrible it was to be in that cabin with those women," she said as she and Morvan pulled ahead of the others. "They talked without stopping for three days."

"Women are often like that."

"I hope not like this. They spoke about men like they were stud stallions."

He didn't seem at all impressed by this revelation.

"They talked about you, for example."

He colored a bit. "And what did the lady say?"

"I was too sick to catch all of it, and understood even less, but I probably saved your life. They were going to find your berth one night. I'd gathered that Martha's husband told his knights to keep a close watch on her, so I discouraged their little adventure."

"Did you? How?"

She had done it by telling Martha that Morvan was impotent from a war wound. He probably wouldn't like that. "It doesn't matter. Can you imagine the trouble if those knights had found both those women with you?"

"Both?"

"Aren't you listening? I said *they* were going to come. I'll have to get Catherine to explain that to me. But you came close to being in great danger."

"How fortunate for my virtue that you were there," he said dryly. "Actually, if Lady Martha had been so bold she would have had the surprise of finding two of the knights playing draughts with me. They are indeed watching her closely, and the lady faces an unpleasant meeting with her husband. She was supposed to return from Bordeaux by the Nativity."

"I think that she is not a good woman."

"I know that she is not. Her husband's knights know more than the lord himself. The knights in a household always know such things. She has only to bed one and all others, present and future, learn of her availability."

"Indeed? Then Ascanio was right and you were playing loose with my reputation those nights in my chamber."

He opened his mouth to protest, but she cut him off. "Or perhaps it wasn't your intention to bed me at all."

He suddenly looked as if he would prefer to be somewhere else.

"If it was, you also lied." That startled him anew. She was half serious and half teasing, and enjoying his discomfort. "I have learned a thing or two, you see. I took your advice and have asked Catherine about these things. And it seems that when you said that you wouldn't hurt me, you were lying."

A small smile broke. "That was a metaphor. At such moments men are apt to speak thus. Their words have a broader, symbolic meaning. It is a point of rhetoric."

"Rhetoric, no less. I am impressed. But I think that you were lying so that you could seduce me."

"And I think that you have been talking to Catherine too much."

She shrugged. "We had many hours to fill while I was abed with my wound. I am a grown woman and can't help but be curious. Besides, it clearly isn't safe to be as ignorant as I have been." She shot him a look full of meaning.

And saw that it had been a mistake to speak of this,

even in jest. There flashed in his eyes a flame that she hadn't seen since the battle.

She had to meet his gaze, of course. She had never been able not to. How quickly the mood between her and this man could change. One moment merry friendship, and then a word, a gesture, and suddenly the old intimacy tugged, as if he sought to pull out a part of her that no one was ever supposed to know. She had built a wall around her attraction to him, but it was made of wood, not stone, and he could burn it at will with the fire in his eyes.

By the time they stopped to rest, dark clouds filled the sky and the wind bit colder. They sat with the men and planned their stop for the night. Gregory and the others wanted to camp, not trusting any town or abbey to be free of plague.

They approached Winchester before dark. The men set up camp off the road while Morvan took her to see the town. He explained how it had been the capital of the great King Alfred many centuries ago. He described the battles fought by Alfred against the Danes, and how he held on to his kingdom of Wessex even as the other Saxon rulers fell.

Night was falling when they finally left the town and made their way down the road to the camp.

Morvan was glad that Anna had insisted on the overland route. During the nights at sea he had been acutely aware of time slipping by. If King Edward and the duke agreed to Anna's petition, she would be gone soon. On the return journey he would deliver her to Saint Meen. The melancholy he had felt as he contemplated that had surprised him.

He had no trouble picturing her at the abbey, extending her influence as the nuns turned to her for advice and judgment. He could imagine her reorganizing the abbey stores, improving the estate economy, and resolving internal conflicts. Ascanio had been right. These images came more naturally than the others, of her immured in some man's home and submissive in some man's bed.

He had tried to get Ascanio to escort her to England, but it had been a halfhearted effort. He couldn't give up this time with her. He had carefully denied himself her presence since the night after the battle, when, seeing her petulant and restless in her bed, his desire had again vanquished his resolve. The pleasure of this day, of her friendship and confidences, had gone far to dispel the shadow of loss that he saw when he looked at her.

The camp had been set up in a clearing in the trees and a large fire roared in the center. Anna dismounted and went to warm herself.

Gregory approached Morvan to take his horse. "The captain gave us some meat, and we'll be cooking it soon."

Morvan surveyed the camp. "Where are the lady's things?"

Gregory crooked his finger. They walked across the clearing to some bushes and pushed through them. Anna's and his bags rested beside a low fire on the other side.

"We thought that she would like some privacy," Gregory explained. "It wouldn't do for her to be right in with the men, would it, if it can be avoided? They prefer it this way too."

And of course, someone must be there to guard her. He could assign that task to Gregory. It was what he should do, but he knew that he would not.

They ate their meal at the main fire. Anna said little, but she appeared at ease as the soldiers swapped stories of humorous battle mishaps. He watched her hold her own in the company of men, as she always did. When the night wore on and the first head nodded, she rose silently and disappeared through the bushes.

Morvan finished a conversation, then sat for a few minutes more before following her.

She sat by the fire swaddled in her cloak, hugging her knees to her chest. She glanced at him as he came through the bushes. To anyone else it would have appeared a casual look, but he knew her too well. He felt her awareness that it was night and that they were alone and the other camp might as well be miles away.

He took his knife and cut an armful of evergreen boughs, after which he brought them back and made two piles on either side of the fire. Then he opened his bags and pulled out a fur to cover his boughs and a long cloak to use as a blanket. She began to do the same.

"We will reach Windsor tomorrow. The court is probably there, but I think that we should go on to London before trying to see the duke." He spoke casually. Her face betrayed little, but he could feel that she was on her guard. He could sense her fear—but it was a virgin's fear, full of wary expectation. It aroused him, and he knew from the way she avoided looking at him that she was not immune to it either. The night's possibilities hung in the air. "For one thing, we need to get rid of the horses and can stable them at the market there. And I want to see my sister first. She and her husband have a house in Windsor that perhaps you can use."

He built up the fire, then settled himself on the bed he had made. She watched him, as if wanting to be sure that he would stay there.

* * *

The wind woke him. It howled through the clearing and scattered the low embers of the fire. He pulled his cloak to his body and stood up. The storm that had stopped them at Southampton was coming inland, bringing with it a bitter cold that numbed his limbs.

He threw more wood on the fire. It burst into a roaring blaze, but the wind grabbed the warmth and whirled it away. He peered at Anna. She was huddled on her side with her face to the fire and her legs drawn up to her chest. She was shivering in her sleep, and her lips looked pale.

He walked over to the bushes and looked at the other camp. The storm must have woken them too, for new logs crackled. He saw only two large forms near the fire instead of five, since the men had sensibly moved together for additional warmth.

He went to his bag and pulled out a long fur-lined cloak. He picked up the coverings from where he had slept and kicked the boughs around to the other side of the fire, then roughly scattered them near Anna's shivering back. When he had lain down beside her, he spread the fur cloak over them both and waited for her body to stop shaking.

CHAPTER 13

ANNA STIRRED BEFORE DAWN. It was bitter outside the cozy huddle of blankets and furs.

In her waking stupor she gradually became aware of the weight and warmth behind her. She felt the arm wrapped around her from the back, its hand resting peacefully on her bound breast. A lower pressure claimed her attention. Morvan in his sleep had tangled his right leg amidst hers so that she practically sat on his thigh. The warmth of his closeness swept over her lazy senses and she closed her eyes to savor the surprising comfort it gave her.

She couldn't disentangle herself without waking him. She tried to go back to sleep, and when that failed she opened her eyes to await the dawn. At last, the first light began to seep through the trees.

Suddenly his hand and leg pulled away. With a quick

movement, he flipped her. She found herself on her back, looking up into blazing black eyes.

"You are finally awake," she said, beginning to sit.

He pushed her down and moved his body over hers, resting on his forearms with his face mere inches from her own. His thick hair was mussed from sleep and she could read every plane of his handsome face by the light of the embers and early dawn: the firm line of his jaw, the slight hollows of his cheeks, the straight feathering of his brow. His expression looked serious and thoughtful. The fur cloak around his shoulders spread out to cover them both.

"I have been awake awhile." Two of his fingers lifted a strand of her curls to tease his severe mouth. "Imagine my surprise to find that I had embraced you during the night, and that you on wakening had not pushed me away."

Heat began to flush her limbs. "I thought that you were sleeping and didn't want to wake you," she said, making a vain effort to push him away now.

"Even with my hand on your breast and my thigh between yours? You are most considerate." He brushed her mouth with his. "You have been curious about these things of late, Anna. Just how curious are you?"

"You moved yourself here. Do not blame me now for an accident of the night."

"It was cold and you were freezing. Even the soldiers sleep thus at the other fire." He spoke lowly into her ear as his teeth found her lobe. His breath sent shivers through her. She could not hide her reaction. He looked into her eyes and burned away her objections with the flame of his gaze.

The weight of his chest pinned her and his forearms immobilized her. He pulled open her cloak at the neck and lowered his head, finding the pulse with his mouth. He gently bit his way up the side of her neck. Wonderful chills spiraled down her body, creating a throbbing beat low in her belly. His mouth reached hers and he kissed her deeply as he held her head with his hands, his tongue caressing her insistently until a breathless moan escaped her.

"You don't protest. It occurs to me that you never have. It is left to me to act the saint for your saintly sake, but I am not made of stone."

She *should* protest—her mind knew it. But the voice of reason had become a mere whisper, drowned out by triumphant pleasure. The part of her that wanted this, that coiled with tense anticipation, was grateful for her weakness.

He kissed her again, slow and hard, and she accepted it and responded in kind. He shifted off her. Through the fog of pleasure she felt his hand push aside the disheveled layers of her cloak and loosen the ties down the front of her surcotte. He unbuckled her belt and slid his hand down her leg to find the tunic's hem.

"What are you doing?" She lifted her head and shoulders in surprise even as her arm, free now, reached up to encircle his shoulder.

"Hush." He laid her down again. He seductively kissed her cheek, her temple, her throat while his hand worked its way through the layers of clothes that separated them. "Do not worry. I would not take a virgin on a cold winter ground with five others just thirty paces away."

His hand pushed up her tunic and shirt until it found the bare skin of her stomach. He caressed her with rough fingers, and his eyes closed with his own reaction. When they reopened she saw a look which would have made her very worried had she not been on a cold winter ground with five others nearby. But the convulsive shocks of pleasure drove any fear from her mind.

He stroked the silk scarf that bound her breasts. "You make a man work hard." His hand closed on her through the silk. A small sound came from her throat. He traced around and found the tie under her arm. The silk layers loosened and he pushed them away until her breasts were free.

He looked down while he gently stroked around their swells, the thrilling pleasure peaking sharply whenever his hand grazed her nipples. He began playing carefully with those hard points, deliberately summoning helpless sighs from her. Anxious need claimed her. Her body moved without her consent and arched toward his hand.

He lowered his head. She watched wide-eyed as his tongue and lips began to arouse her the way his fingers had. Sharp excitement shot through her again and again. His tongue whisked and grazed her before his mouth took her breast in a more demanding way.

Thundering desire pounded in her. She grabbed at his shoulders in a vain effort to release the mounting madness. A living hollow ached inside her, desperate to be filled. He thrust his knee between her legs, pressing upward, and that only made it worse, more concentrated, a physical yearning that was both torture and delicious pleasure. His kisses and caresses demanded that she crave more, until that primitive hunger was all that mattered.

A moan escaped her and he swallowed the sound in his mouth. His hands abruptly left her. He wrapped his arms around her, his face smothered in her neck and hair. Her body screamed with resentment at the withdrawal of pleasure, but he calmed her with soothing kisses as he pulled her clothes down around her body.

They lay in each other's arms while little arrows of

heat and desire kept piercing her, defeating her attempts to be grateful he had shown restraint. Slowly she became aware of the breaking day around them, and the cold on her face, and the noises from the other camp. The last startled her. She raised her head to glance at the bushes.

He must have heard. That was why he had stopped.

"They are just rising," he reassured her.

"We must rise too," she said reluctantly, not anxious to leave the warmth of his arms. She was embarrassed now, and afraid to look at him.

He stood and helped her up, then draped the long cloak around her. "Go into the trees and right yourself."

A cold drizzle started as the storm finally made its way inland. Huddled under cloaks and oiled canvas capes, they plodded along roads made treacherous by mud and water.

Morvan found himself in a black mood. The lack of fulfillment had provoked a devilish irritation. It was made worse by the presence on the horse beside him of the woman he wanted.

He had no doubt that she would have yielded this morning. He tried not to think about it, but she was right there, reacting to his mood with her damned calm reserve. When he looked at her he saw her beneath him, eyes closed and face flushed with passion, moving herself into his caress, gasping in surprise, joining him in the wondrous pleasure. He knew that the memories were not just with him, but with her also, hanging silently between them, calling for attention. And completion.

At midday they found protection beneath some trees to rest the horses and take some food. Gregory sought him out.

"We can't camp tonight. It will still be raining, and could turn to snow. We should find some shelter."

"Windsor will be crowded if the court is there. We will stop at Reading, just to the west. I know the family at a manor house nearby and they will take the horses and the men. It will only be a barn, but it will be dry."

"And the lady?"

"I will take her into Reading and find her an inn." He looked up and saw Gregory's wary expression. So, his friend had guessed the reason for his mood. "Then I will return and join you."

As the journey continued Anna once again rode alone beside a big, dark cloud of a man.

Except for one warm smile when she'd emerged from the trees this morning, Morvan had been full of nothing but brooding silence. Something dangerous and predatory emanated from him. That she was the source of his mood was all too clear from the looks he gave her. She felt like a sparrow being eyed by a falcon, and she didn't like it.

"You are angry," she said.

"I am not," he replied, but his brittle tone said that he was. "I merely find myself wondering why a woman bound for the convent would tempt a man. I wonder what you want of me."

"Do not be ridiculous. I wouldn't know how to tempt a man."

"You managed well enough this morning for one so innocent. There are limits to what can be expected of me, no matter what my resolve and honor."

He was blaming *her*.

"I did not embrace you. I did not kiss *you* and push *you* down on the ground."

"Nor did you stop me, or make the smallest protest. Do you understand that you would not still be a maid if the others had not woken?"

Did she understand that? Had she believed him when he said that wouldn't happen? She couldn't remember caring too much about it. "I could not stop you."

Her response only darkened his expression. "Do you leave such decisions to the man? If so, the end will always be the same. You have been receiving the wrong education from Catherine. It is just as well that you go to the abbey, or you will end up little better than Lady Martha."

"A man's logic, surely. Seduce a woman and then call her the whore. I thank you for the lesson. Catherine neglected to tell me about the shame men want women to feel." She spit the words at him, then turned her head away.

Silence fell between them. Just the sounds of the wind and their horses' hooves intruded.

"Anna, I did not—"

"Do not speak to me." She kicked her horse and galloped away from the humiliation he had forced on her.

The light was waning when they found the small manor house outside Reading. Morvan knew the knight who lived there and went in to speak with him. Word came for them to enter the barn and make themselves comfortable.

The evening brought colder weather. Morvan sought her out in the barn when he returned from his conversation with the knight and insisted they leave for Reading at once. By the time they found the small inn her anger had grown and she was impatient to get rid of him. She waited on her horse while he inquired about a room.

"The weather has filled them, but since you are a lady the owner will open an extra chamber that they have on the top floor," he said. "Come in and warm yourself. They have to move a bed, and it will take some time."

He brought her into the public room and they sat at a table near the hearth. She studied the people sitting at the other benches while she drank spiced wine and ate some food. She ignored Morvan, whom she felt looking at her the whole time.

Finally the innkeeper's wife led the way up two flights of stairs to a narrow passage under the roof of the building. There was only one chamber there, and from the objects stacked outside it appeared that they normally used it for storage. It was quite small, with one shuttered window on the wall across from the door, but it had a hearth. A big bed took up almost all of the space. She guessed that it was the innkeeper's own and that he and his wife would sleep on straw tonight.

The woman left them, and Morvan made to follow her out.

"Do not leave this chamber, Anna," he said from the threshold. "This inn is sometimes visited at night by young men from Windsor. They gamble and drink in the public room. I will come for you in the morning. Open the door to no one."

When he left, she took a deep breath and exhaled her fury. He kept treating her like a stupid child, and that would have to stop tomorrow. A lot of good his protection afforded her, considering that the only danger she had faced thus far on this journey had come from him.

A bucket of water warmed near the hearth and she stripped off her clothes, laying them on a stool by the fire to dry. She poured some of the water into a crockery bowl atop a small table at the foot of the bed and washed the road off herself. She usually slept naked, but would have been uncomfortable doing so here. She rummaged through a bag Morvan had carried up, pulling out one of her father's shirts and an old pair of her brother's hose.

She rolled the tattered legs of the hose up over her knees. The shirt came down to her thighs and billowed loosely. The garments made her look ridiculous, but they would be warm.

She blew out the one candle and climbed into the bed. The sheets were old but clean, and she snuggled down into their cool scent. It was too early to sleep, but at least she was dry and alone with her thoughts, and not in the rain beside a brooding man with his insults and threatening presence.

Morvan returned to the public room to dry some more before heading into the cold. A group of men from Windsor arrived. He knew two of them and was drawn into a conversation about his travels. It was midnight before he forced himself to leave Reading and the woman in the chamber upstairs.

His black mood had turned into one of regret when he saw how she had taken his thoughtless words to heart. It had been churlish of him to throw his frustration at her in that way, to blame her when she was blameless. Their friendship and his protection gave her every reason to trust him. But probably no one, he mused bitterly, had ever told her that no man could really be trusted in these matters.

A fine icy rain had begun to fall. He turned the horse toward the town gate, trying not to think of Anna, trying not to picture her in that upper chamber now. They would be in London soon, and at his sister's house. He would still see her while she awaited her audience with the King, but not very often, since he would find lodging elsewhere. He doubted that he would be alone with her again. A poignant sense of loss spread through him.

The fault this morning had been all his, but he could not really regret it. There was a purity and freedom in her passion that kept disarming his resolve. Most women used their responses as part of a larger game, but she simply gave without thought and took on the same basis. Her spirit had been with him as well as her body, one wrapping his shoulders and the other his soul. In her inexperience she'd known not where to put her hands, but her heart had been in the right place, as frank and open as that level gaze with which she looked at him. Had he played this game so long that he no longer recognized a girl who didn't even know the rules?

The freezing rain fell harder as the town gate disappeared behind him. Out on the open road the ice clung to his cloak and hair and the mane of his horse. Even in the dark he could see the black reflections telling him that the ice had sheeted the ruts and stones of the road. Finally, his horse lost its footing and scrambled to stay upright.

He stopped, debating with himself. The town was much closer than the manor house. The ice storm looked to be getting worse. It was foolish to risk the horse's breaking a leg.

He turned back to the gate.

As he handed the horse to the groom, as he walked across the yard to the inn, even as he entered the building, he told himself that he would spend the night in the public room with the other travelers stranded by the storm. But as the door closed behind him, his legs took him slowly up the stairs leading to Anna.

* * *

She heard footsteps on the landing stop near her door, and then his voice saying her name.

Even though he did not speak loudly, she could hear him over the sleet pounding the building, could hear him as if he was already standing in the chamber.

She listened to the sharp icy rhythms on the roof and wall. Perhaps something had happened to him, or the horses or one of the men. She climbed off the bed and opened the door.

He stood leaning against the doorjamb. Flicks of ice hung from his hair and cloak. He looked at her, then silently entered, forcing her to back up into the room.

As he pushed past her to the fire, she pressed herself against the wall by the door so that they wouldn't touch. He removed his cloak and gloves and shook out their moisture, then crouched by the hearth's warmth, drying his face with his sleeve. She moved a few steps and found a towel for him. When he took it from her, his fingers briefly closed on hers. The warmth from that brief, firm contact streaked right to her heart.

He stood and turned his back to the blaze. She retreated to the wall beside the door. There was no place else to go. He filled the small space between the bed and the hearth and there was only this strip of floor left to her. Or the bed itself, filling the room, suddenly an insistent obstacle.

His eyes fell on the clothes she had laid on the stool to dry. He fingered the long silk scarf she used to bind her breasts. "The old myths say that there was once a tribe of warrior women called Amazons. They too preferred the bow, and removed one breast so their aim would not be affected. Your solution seems more sensible."

He dominated the chamber, just as he did all of the spaces in which he moved. She became uncomfortably aware of the power streaking out of him as it had last night before they slept, and of the exciting fear he instilled in her whenever he chose. Only tonight, unlike last night, there was nothing reassuring in his manner. A fluttering knot tightened in her stomach.

The heat was drying his hair and clothes. He turned back to the fire and stretched his hands toward it.

"Why did you open the door to me, Anna?"

More blame. "I thought that something might be wrong. It was womanish of me. I see that I was foolish, so if you have warmed yourself you can leave."

"Nay."

She waited for him to say something else, but he simply turned and looked at her.

"I want you to leave." She summoned the anger she had felt all afternoon and pulled it around herself like armor.

"The roads are impassable with ice. I will stay here."

"Then sleep in the public room downstairs."

"Nay." He spoke quietly and firmly, his eyes flaming and commanding her gaze, his face set in its handsome severity. "I am going to sleep here. And I am going to make love to you." He paused a moment. "Come here to me."

He spoke as though the decision had been made, as though the conclusion was inevitable. She gasped at his boldness, and from the flush that passed through her.

His words from the afternoon suddenly burned in her brain, and she desperately threw them back at him. "So that you can use shame against me to your own ends? Nay, Morvan. You said I must make decisions in these things and not leave it to the man. Well, I have decided you will not do this. You are not touching and confusing me now, and I tell you that I am not willing. If you try to force me, I remind you that I have defended myself before."

The fire still flamed in his eyes when he finally turned away. She wondered if he had been measuring her resolve. She hoped not, because her tone and manner were not matched by any internal strength. Secure from her good judgment, separate from it, lived the memory of this morning. If he came to her she did not know what she would do.

"Get into bed and go to sleep, Anna. I have never forced a woman and would never do so with you. I will not touch you if you are unwilling."

He made no movement to leave. She stayed by her wall, watching him warily. It occurred to her that they might stand like this all night.

He bent to her bag, felt through it, and pulled out her dagger. He threw it on the bed. "Sleep with that if you do not trust me."

"I would sleep better if you left."

He shook his head. "Tomorrow I deliver you to my sister and your duke and Edward. I would stay with you this night."

She didn't understand that, but she also knew that he wouldn't go. She climbed on the bed, grabbed the dagger, and huddled under the covers into the dark corner against the wall. She lay there motionlessly, trying to will herself to sleep.

After a while she felt him ease down on the foot of the bed, sitting with his back against the wall, his legs stretched out along the bed's bottom edge. He did not look at her but at the fire. As the minutes passed, she felt her stiff limbs relax.

She did not know if she fell asleep, but when he

moved off the bed she snapped alert, watching from her black corner. Even with her eyes open only a slit she could look down the room and see his movements.

He threw a log on the fire and bent to set the water pail near it. He unstrapped his belt and laid it on the chair, then unlaced his surcotte and pulled it over his shoulders. The tunic and shirt followed, each item of clothing thrown atop hers on the stool.

She didn't move, but she didn't close her half-lidded eyes either. He waited for the water to heat, his naked back visible above the end of the bed. She could see, backlit by the fire, the strong lean muscles of his shoulders and the firm lines of his hips.

He bent for the pail and turned his profile to her, then poured water into a bowl set on the table that was wedged between the hearth wall and the bottom of the bed. The light found the angles and edges of his torso and arms as he took a cloth and began washing.

She remembered doing this for him when he was ill, and almost felt those ridges beneath her own fingers again as her gaze followed the cloth across his chest and down his stomach. A lazy sensuality coursed through her as she watched. Had this started then, when she touched him in his delirium? Or before, when he asked her to stay the night and ease his deathwatch?

He took a long time to wash, his movements slow and studied, his face looking more at the wall than at his body, the lines of his muscles and expression sculpted of stone. She could not take her eyes off him. Even the fingers of his hand as they clutched the cloth fascinated her. He was so beautiful in his male way, and the fire's lights and shadows only made him more so.

He put the cloth down. He turned his head toward her dark corner. Her breath silently caught as his awareness of her became something almost physical. Every part of her froze. She dared not move, even to close her eyes.

He turned away and placed two more logs on the fire. It flared into a huge blaze, increasing the light until even her far corner was penetrated by dancing shadows. The warmth spread throughout the room, almost stifling her under the covers.

She closed her eyes, for if he returned to his place below her he could see her now. And so she was startled when she felt his weight on the bed beside her, stretching out. He had waited for her to be asleep before taking his rest, and she worked hard at looking dead to the world.

"Anna." It wasn't a question. He said it simply and evenly, as if he were giving her a name.

Her heart pounded wildly. Her fingers closed around the dagger under her pillow.

"Anna." His voice was low, with a commanding edge to it. "I know that you do not sleep. I know that you were watching me."

A hand came down on her shoulder.

In a flash she jumped up and away from him, kneeling in a crouch against the wall, facing him like a cornered animal. She clutched the dagger in her hand.

Her sudden movement drew him up too. He knelt upright and tall above her, the body she had been admiring a mere arm's length away.

"Come and lie with me, Anna. After tomorrow I'll not be alone with you again, and it weighs on me. Lie in my arms as you did last night."

"So that you can call me wanton?"

"I was angry, and hungry for you. I did not mean that. Your passion is innocent and beautiful. Come to me. I promise that I'll not take you. You'll leave here a maid, as you entered."

She didn't believe the last part. Twice he had warned her that men say anything at these times. Yet he was making the decision hers, giving her a choice.

As she looked in his eyes she knew that she had long ago made that choice, and made it many times. She had not sent him away from the estate as she should have, but kept him near her. She had not stopped him those times in her room, nor this morning in the forest. She had opened her door to him this night. He had known her choice for what it was. She was the one who pretended otherwise. There was no future to this, but he offered something that she wanted and needed, and she was tired of denying it.

She dropped her dagger and leaned an inch, no more, toward him.

He took the movement for the assent he sought. He reached out for her, pulling her against him, folding his arms around her in a tight embrace that raised her up.

The response of her body was immediate. Pleasure and madness slammed into her as his mouth closed on hers with devouring, insistent kisses. She grabbed at him, found his head and held it to her, taking his tongue greedily and then following his lead with her own. His hands moved and she reveled in their hard pressing touch as he explored her, feeling every inch, moving down to her hips and the back of her thighs.

He pulled at the tie to the neck of her shirt and moved his mouth there, biting her with kisses that covered the skin exposed to him. Her body moved against him in a swaying, primitive rhythm as she gave herself over to the hands and mouth that obliterated her awareness of everything but the feel and scent of his demanding body and the pounding, pulsing insistence of her own.

"Come here." He rocked back on his heels and spread

his knees and guided her down so that she sat on him, riding his thigh. She cried out at the welcome pressure between her legs and the damp feel of her hose. She must have surprised him, because he took her head between his hands and looked into her face as he said her name.

Calmer now, he drew up her shirt and whisked it off and held her breasts as he looked at them. His gaze excited her even more and she pressed against his thigh to find some relief for the aching heat. He kissed her while his fingers stroked her nipples. She cried out again, the sound lost between them, as she leaned into his touch and held on to his shoulders and rocked against his thigh for the hardness that relieved her and drove her to further madness at the same time.

His arms closed around her back and hips tightly and he lifted her up so she knelt slightly above him. He took her breast in his mouth. Her head flew back at the unbelievable sensations as waves of pleasure coursed through her, down her limbs and hips. The need between her legs became excruciating and she rocked in response to the throbbing. He understood, because even as he licked and sucked her breasts he moved one of his arms between her thighs and pressed upward against her damp warmth. It was torture and ecstasy all at once, and she never wanted it to stop.

He pushed away the pillows and the bedcoverings and laid her down, hovering above her with his weight on one arm. He gazed at her as he traced her lines and curves. Her eyes followed his hand's journey, anticipating the excitement of his touch. She felt no shame in the breathless desire she knew he must see in her face. His hand found the tie to her hose and pulled it loose.

He came down over her and took her breasts in his mouth, first one, then the other, drawing gently on them with his lips and arousing her with his tongue, sending her moaning to her heights once more, deliberately pushing her into a frenzy of need. He rose up again as he slowly stroked her thighs.

"Look at me," he said. "I want to see your eyes when I touch you."

She gazed into the dark fires above her. His hand pressed under her hose and down her belly and moved lower until his fingers found the source of the deep pulse that had been torturing her. Everything up until then paled. She closed her eyes as his intimate touch created an exquisite oblivion.

Morvan watched the pleasure overwhelm her and fought the battle of his life against his inclinations. He had told himself with that first kiss that he had made a promise and he would keep it. And so he drew a line and when he crossed it he drew another, and then another, but her passion repeatedly broke his resolve and drove him toward the possession he craved.

She gave herself over with an abandon that made the morning seem tame. There was no defense, no withholding, and every caress brought physical and audible responses. She had come to him already aroused, just as he had come to her, and he took as much pleasure in her inexpert passion as he did in the waves of heat burning his blood.

He fought for control, but the moments of sanity were hard to find, and her cries as he touched the center of her pleasure drove him over the edge of the precipice.

"Look at me," he said again. She forced open her eyes, liquid and dark with desire, and he watched her watch him as his finger found her passage. She tensed against the invasion. He probed deeper, his thumb gently playing at that other point of pleasure.

When he touched the barrier, he was disappointed as well as relieved. He had never really believed Gurwant, but if she hadn't been a virgin it would have made things different.

He gently stroked her, fighting the urge to go on, knowing that she was beyond stopping him if he did. The teasing pleasure turned her wild. She arched against his hand and cried out his name again and spread her legs wide, begging for more.

That did it. His battered resolve crumbled. He pushed down her hose and pulled them off her legs and then she was stretched out naked in front of him as she had so often been in his mind.

She was beautifully proportioned, and her active life had given her muscles firmer and more defined than most women's. There was a tautness to her thighs and shoulders and stomach. Her breasts rose round and high, their light brown nipples tight and their swells hard with her need. Her legs stretched long and slim, with gentle curves. One of his hands returned to the blond hair at the top of her thighs as the other began untying the lace on his hose.

She turned toward his touch, grasping to embrace him. Her movement revealed the side of her hip, so that he could see the edge of the wound on her left flank.

Even as he continued arousing her, even as she cried out and reached frantically for him, a series of unwelcome thoughts pierced his single-minded need.

Gurwant's claim of success and the proof of his

failure . . . *It is about taking. Not me, but La Roche de Roald . . .*
The promise he'd just made to her . . . *You are not touching
and confusing me now and I am not willing. . . .*

Regretting what he was doing even as he did it, angry
that she meant enough to him to require such a sacrifice,
he swung away abruptly and turned from her to sit on
the edge of the bed.

His body yelled in rebellion, and it took a few moments to collect his control.

A hand touched his back like an unspoken question,
and then fell away. He looked over his shoulder. Anna
huddled against the wall, the bedsheet pulled up to her
neck, her face buried in her knees.

He had handled this worse than a green boy might
have. "Anna." He reached toward her.

She held up a hand of warning and reproach.

"Do not blame yourself that it went so far, Anna. It
was my promise to you that was almost broken, and any
fault is mine."

"Then I should count myself fortunate to have been
with a man so capable of restraint." Her voice came low
and muffled, and with a bitter note.

"Anna—"

"Leave. I want you to go."

Anna gave herself over to mortified humiliation. She
stared at the door through which Morvan had entered
and left, staying only long enough to vanquish her, not
even needing the final act to know his victory.

She wanted to hate him, and to blame him as no more
than a predator. But her memories would not let her.
What predator would have stopped when he had?

What man would have?

She pushed down the sheet and looked at her body. It had been the moment he'd seen her like this that he had been repulsed. The sighs and raised eyebrows of her mother and maids, the stares of people, even Gurwant's impotence that night, crowded her thoughts. It was true, then. She really was unnatural and grotesque. It had saved her from rape when she was a girl, but this was different.

She was glad that she was going to Saint Meen. She thanked God that duty and circumstances had not permitted her to waver in that decision. The idea of a life as some man's wife, of being an object of revulsion like this or, worse, of having to submit and endure as some man forced himself to do his duty, sickened her.

A visceral anger toward Morvan pounded through her. She resented him for awakening this side of her. She had been content without it. She had learned to stand proud and straight in her difference, had even turned it to her advantage. She had always known what she lacked, and she didn't need the truth thrown in her face. He may not have intended to insult her, may even have been surprised by his ultimate reaction, but he had cruelly forced her to face her inadequacy all the same.

And as she waited out the night, alone and naked on the large bed, she managed to find some hatred for him after all.

CHAPTER 14

MORVAN, ANNA, AND GREGORY stopped at the end of the long lane leading to the country house. They had ridden in rain all day, and only recently had the clouds broken to permit a bit of sun to shine.

At London Morvan had gone into the city to see if his sister was at her home there, only to learn that she had taken refuge from the plague in Hampstead. So they had circled the city and ridden the five miles to this country lane. On their way, they had stopped at a livestock market and arranged to quarter the horses, and Morvan's four men had finally taken their leave.

The house was wider than a city home and two stories high, with a stone base and a timbered and plastered upper level. Good-sized windows, all of them glazed, dotted the walls, with three side by side on the second floor overlooking the entrance. Two gardens flanked the doorway, planted with roses that would fill the building with fragrance when in bloom.

A servant crossing the yard saw them and hurried inside. A young woman appeared in the doorway, carrying a child in her arms. She cried Morvan's name, handed the child to the servant, and ran to meet him. Morvan trotted his horse forward and swung off to embrace his sister.

She grasped him as if she feared he would disappear. She had matured since he had last seen her, her thin frame having taken on more womanly curves. Her dark hair hung loose down her back and the white skin so envied by the girls at court was flushed with excitement. Her dark, expressive eyes sparkled brightly.

"Almost three years, Morvan. No word since Crécy. I had to learn from others that you even lived. And then the plague ... I will not let you leave quickly now, brother. You had best not be stopping for a meal on your way to somewhere else."

"I will be in England some while, but I know not how long. Do you think David would mind if you gave my friends a place to stay?"

"Of course he would not mind. And you will stay too."

"I will go elsewhere."

"Nay, you will not. I will not be denied. David has been as worried about you as I have. He asks after you of everyone he meets from the Continent."

Morvan doubted that. If his brother-in-law sought information on him it was probably with the hope of learning he was dead.

"He will be here this evening. He will invite you himself. You will see." She looked down the lane. "I am forgetting my duties. Please tell your man and your squire to come. You are all in need of food and warm baths."

Anna sat tall on her horse in her tunic and hose and cloak, the hood over her hair, the sword on her saddle. "That is not my squire, Christiana. It is a lady. Her name is Anna de Leon. I have brought her here from Brittany."

Christiana looked at Anna with new interest. "The sword. Does she use it?"

"She has been known to."

"David will be fascinated."

Morvan waved Anna and Gregory forward. Christiana greeted them warmly. "You must stay here. There is room for all."

She eyed Anna subtly, and as they entered the house she gave Morvan a glance that said she expected full details later.

The front of the house was a good-sized hall with several tables, and Christiana sent for some food and drink. The child was brought, and Christiana placed the year-old boy in Morvan's arms. "His name is Hugh, after Father."

He gazed down at his nephew. The boy had his sister's eyes, but her husband's face. If he were to never have a son of his own, this boy would be the next heir to the lost lands of Harclow. "A fitting name," he said.

Christiana stepped close to take the child from him. "It will be yours, brother. Both David and I are sure of it," she whispered.

The servant carried little Hugh away and they sat to eat. Morvan explained the reason for the visit.

"The court has returned to Windsor," Christiana confirmed. "The King and Queen went to more isolated manors during the worst of the plague, but Windsor seems free of it now. London, however, is still dangerous, and the conditions there are disgusting. Waste fills the streets and there is no one to clean them. David had moved most of his goods outside the city before the sickness struck. Everyone said it would not cross the sea to us, but he thought otherwise. After all, they say it was ships that first brought it to Genoa. This has been devastating to everyone."

Morvan glanced around the attractive room, at the neatly carved chairs and well-made benches. Tiles paved the floor, and a tapestry hung on the wall. David de Abyndon had a Midas touch, and as a young man his sharp wits had led him through some big risks that had made his fortune. Even if the plague stopped his business for a year, Morvan doubted that it would ruin him.

"Why do you seek an audience with the King?" Christiana asked Anna.

Anna had said little all day and nothing after her perfunctory greeting upon their arrival. He had tried to speak with her about that night, but her manner toward him had been cold and forbidding. She had acted ever since as if he were a sword who protected her and nothing more. His initial surprise had turned first to anger, but now it just troubled him.

"It is the young duke whom I need to see. I need him to recognize my father's testament. I also need his blessing on my sister's marriage, and permission for me to take the veil."

Morvan read the burning questions in his sister's eyes. Their cheese and ale finished, Christiana stood up and took Anna's hand. "I am happy that you have come to us. Now, I'm sure that you would like a bath before some rest. The servants have one waiting in your room." She turned to Morvan and Gregory. "My men will show you to yours. Morvan, if you are not too tired, perhaps we can talk after you have refreshed yourself."

* * *

When Anna woke it was almost dark. She rose and stepped from the room. The door to the solar stood open, and she heard low voices coming from within. She entered to see Morvan and Christiana talking by the fire.

He wore garments that she didn't recognize, and she guessed that they must be his own, left with his sister before he went to France. The cut was the fashionable courtly style called the pourpoint, fitted tight about the torso and arms and with loose cloth from the waist to mid-thigh. It showed off a man's physique more obviously than did the old-fashioned tunics and cottes of rural Brittany.

They greeted her, but just then a servant stuck her head in to announce the master's horses coming up the lane. Christiana hurried out of the room. Morvan rose and went to the windows overlooking the entrance. His expression became hard.

"You do not care for this husband of your sister, do you?" Anna said.

"Nay. Nor he for me. He will not be pleased that I am here." He glanced at her, and then trained his eyes out the window again. "My sister was the King's ward, and lived under the Queen's supervision. But there were no lands, no money, no dowry. Somehow this man came to see her. While the King was preparing for war, David offered for her hand. He asked for no dowry, but instead offered to give the King a fortune for her. I objected to the King, but he needed the money and agreed to the match."

The sounds of horses could be heard outside the house now. Anna joined Morvan at the window. Three men approached, and she had no trouble identifying the master of the house. He rode tall on his stallion ahead of the two servants, the thick folds of his cloak floating about his body.

"And your sister. What did she think of all of this?"

"She was young and educated to accept such decisions. She cannot be happy about being married off to a commoner, though."

In the yard below David dismounted. He smiled and opened his arms. Christiana darted into them and he swung her around in a warm embrace and deep kiss. Anna glanced over at Morvan, who looked startled at the display.

"I can see what you mean," she said. "Your sister appears positively miserable."

Christiana spoke to David, then he glanced toward the house. He was a surprisingly handsome man, with regular features, chiseled bones, and a straight nose. His golden brown hair feathered down the sides of his face to his chin. He walked toward the house, his arm still around Christiana.

The sounds of arrival echoed below and then on the steps. David and Christiana entered the room.

There was the slightest pause as David regarded Morvan with blue eyes full of intense inspection. Then he strode across the room, his arms extended.

"Welcome home, brother."

The evening meal was a luxurious affair. They had fowl and venison and fish, all served on silver plates. The wine was excellent, and Anna had a glass more of it than she usually did. She sat herself next to Morvan, but it was just her way of making sure that she didn't have to look at him.

Eventually she would have to speak with him, but not

yet. Her embarrassment still burned. If she didn't ignore him, she feared that she would be undone all over again.

After the meal Gregory excused himself from their company as they all moved their chairs to the fire. Again Anna managed to sit next to Morvan, but in a chair angled toward David, who explained conditions in England.

"Almost a quarter have died in London, and while the worst is over, there are still deaths every day. The cost of everything is bound to rise, and trade ceased last summer and has not resumed. If our King has any ideas of financing another war, I hope that he has magicians at court to conjure up the money."

"Do you go into the city?" Anna asked.

"Only when I have to, and I do not let my servants or apprentices come with me. The city government is ineffective, and crime has increased."

"I would very much like to visit London, if only for a few hours. I haven't seen much of cities."

"You must not, Anna," Morvan said. "Christiana described the conditions to us, and now David says that it isn't safe."

It turned out that Morvan expected no response, for, having announced his will, he now turned the conversation away from the topic. "Is there word that the King is planning another campaign?"

"The treaty with France runs for some years, but Edward has given no indication that he is relinquishing his claims to the French crown."

"Enough of plagues and politics," Christiana said. "David, Anna goes to the court at Windsor. I have told Morvan that she can use our house there. I would like to go with her and stay a short while. It has been a long winter, and I would like to see my friends."

"I should go as well," David said. "If the court is returning, there is business to be done. But I cannot leave for two days. Can you wait and go to Windsor three days hence, my lady?"

"Aye. I have quartered some horses at a market north of the city. Perhaps I can sell them while we wait."

"Charles of Blois will probably be with the King," Christiana said. "High-ranking prisoners usually move with the court. Have you ever seen him?"

Anna had never met the French husband who claimed Brittany's ducal crown through his marriage to Jeanne de Penthièvre. His capture by the English had done little to stop the civil war. His wife continued to organize the fight for their cause.

"Some of your people believe that he is a saint," David said. "He wears sackcloth and rough ropes next to his skin, and does not bathe overmuch. He prays constantly, I am told."

"He is a French butcher. He murdered hundreds at Nantes after it fell. There is nothing saintly about such a man, and if he claims to be meting God's justice, he blasphemes. I hope that I do not see him," Anna said heatedly.

"Well, he hardly attends many feasts, being so ascetic," David said. "I doubt that you will meet."

"I do not think that I will go to such festivities either. I do not go to the court for pleasure."

"You have not taken the veil yet, my lady. Why not enjoy yourself if the occasion arises. Even bishops do so."

How could she explain that not long ago she would have attended such functions with curiosity, but that now she would feel conspicuous, and the object of unkind curiosity herself. A person could stare down just so many raised eyebrows.

She suddenly was furious with herself for feeling this

way. It was as if she no longer knew herself at all, or that she no longer liked what she knew.

She decided that she had done her duty as a guest. Claiming fatigue from the journey, she retired to her chamber.

She had almost entered when she heard a step on the stairs. Morvan's tall form rose into the passageway.

Before she could escape, he took the candle from her hand and pulled her into the solar.

Morvan lit more candles in the solar and then turned to her. She gazed past him, through him. It chilled him to realize how quickly she had created this strangeness between them.

"What troubles you, Anna?"

"Nothing troubles me. I wanted some time alone. I have always liked being alone."

"I do not speak just of this evening, but of the last days. You have not spoken. After what we have shared, it is not—"

"Not natural?"

"Not what I expected. Are you feeling guilt or embarrassment?"

"Embarrassment. Aye, some of that."

He took her hand and raised it to his lips. "You need feel no shyness with me."

She pulled her hand away. "Mostly, however, I am thinking that I need to remember who I am and where I am going."

"Where you are going I cannot change, but who you are includes what passed between us. Even if you regret how far things went that night, do you truly want to build a wall of ice between us now?"

She watched a spot in the chamber ten feet away. She concentrated on a void that did not contain him.

"That night," she repeated, and her expression became hard and immobile.

"Anna, is that what this is about? Are you sorry that you offered yourself to me?"

"Aye, I am sorry. I was weak and foolish and forgot why I am here and where I belong. Worse, I forgot the lessons that you yourself have given me about men. Now, I would not speak of this again. I find myself impatient for this interlude in my life to end, and would return to Saint Meen tomorrow if I could. When we get to Windsor, I ask that you do what you can to help me meet your King as soon as possible."

As she left she glanced back over her shoulder. Her level look met his own gaze directly. It wasn't much, but he suspected that it was all that he would get for a long while.

CHAPTER 15

THEY ARRIVED IN WINDSOR three days later. Anna rode one of Christiana's horses, since she had sold all of hers. They had fetched good prices, and she had arranged to buy grain through David. She drew some contentment from knowing that this journey would at least be good for her estate's economy.

The house in Windsor was a typical craftsman's home. The first level did not hold a shop but instead had been converted to living space. David had purchased the building next door, and that now served as the quarters of his mercer's business.

Two tiny bedchambers filled the second level, along with a solar, and Christiana gave Anna one. The servants and apprentices found cots and pallets in the kitchen and Gregory was sent to the attic above the shop. Morvan planned to find hospitality with one of his court friends, and he left almost immediately upon arrival to do so. A messenger came later to tell Christiana that he would stay with William Montague, the young Earl of Salisbury.

The next morning he arrived early to help Anna write a letter requesting an audience with the King, and took it himself to the castle on the hill overlooking the river. Until she received a summons from the King, she just had to wait.

Christiana dragged her along on visits to the princesses and other friends. Although Anna saw nothing of Morvan for several days, she heard about him. He was a main topic of conversation for the bored courtiers.

Especially among the women.

Everyone expressed interest in his adventures, and relief that he had survived the plague.

Especially the women.

They all seemed very happy to have him with them again.

Especially the women.

Aye, any number of ladies were very excited that Morvan Fitzwaryn was back at court.

Morvan dismounted his horse in front of a prosperous house. An old servant opened the door.

"Good day, Meg. Is your lady here?"

"Aye, she be home. You don't waste much time, Sir Morvan. The last lord be barely cold."

"I never knew the last lord, Meg. I left two husbands ago, so if I don't pay the proper respects I may be forgiven."

"Well, I'll tell her you're here, but there may be a wait. She be abed."

He raised an eyebrow. "Prostrate with grief, I assume."

"She is alone, if that is what you are asking. Go in the hall and I'll have some wine sent. She will be glad to know you are here. She knows that you are back."

He knew the house well, and went to the hall. When the wine came he took a cup to a back window that looked out over a garden. The implications of Meg's words troubled him. He realized that he was a bit sorry to hear that Elizabeth was in bed alone.

He had to come. It would be insulting not to and he did want to see her. But a low buzz of speculation had already begun about whether he would resume his affair with her now that she was free.

He did not think it likely that he would, although he had strong affection for her still. She had been the closest he had ever come to loving. He had wondered at the time if he was in love with her, but had known that the wondering itself meant that he was not.

Still, he might have basked in her warmth again while she sought her next husband, as he had when he was a young knight. Except that he was not so young now, and it had not been Elizabeth who crowded his thoughts these last few days as he renewed old friendships.

A sound made him turn, but it was not Elizabeth behind him. Instead a young man, no more than twenty years old, entered the room.

He was striking-looking, tall, proud, and lean, with the gold spurs of knighthood no doubt very new on his heels. His hair was of an unusual color, dark brown with hints of red. His brooding eyes and dark lashes contrasted with the pale tone of his skin. A beautiful knight. Elizabeth liked them young and beautiful.

"You must be Morvan. She has been waiting for you." Morvan heard a note of disapproval. "My name is Ian. I am Elizabeth's kinsman. Through marriage."

"It is kind of you to attend on her in her time of grief. Elizabeth and I are old friends, and I am glad to meet one of her kinsmen. Through marriage."

"I know all about your friendship. I have been hearing about nothing else at court for days." Ian stood as if he expected some sort of challenge. He reeked of arrogance and pride.

"Ah, well, that was long ago."

Ian was about to reply when, from the doorway, there came a rustle of satin and a scent of roses and a glimmering, ethereal vision.

She was still beautiful. Her hair, white since her middle twenties, rose coiled and braided beneath the silver-flecked veil. Silver jewelry and a white gown completed the effect. Her still youthful face matched a neat little body that never had, and never would, bear the effects of pregnancy. As Morvan walked toward her he knew, however, that if he took up with her again her beauty would have little to do with it. They had moved beyond that years ago. He bent down and gave her an affectionate kiss, and felt the eyes of Ian boring into his back.

Several hours later Morvan escorted Elizabeth into a hall, in which a feast hosted by Princess Isabella was being held. He and Elizabeth had talked for hours, and she then had asked him to bring her here. He really could not refuse, though he knew that her presence beside him would only encourage the gossip.

Ian arrived and was standing close by when Christiana appeared in the doorway. "Your sister, isn't it?" Ian asked, his eyes appraising Christiana in a way Morvan didn't like. He had always resented men's looking at his sister in that way.

And then, behind Christiana, another woman ap-

peared, tall and blond with hair brushed into thick flowing waves around her lovely face. A few rebellious curls
dangled along her cheeks. She wore a plain blue gown
made by Catherine for the journey, and it fit her better
than the brown convent robes. Her simple dress and natural appearance contrasted with the gaudy colors and
jewels of the other women in the hall. She looked fresh as
spring and innocent as a country maid. Morvan hadn't
seen her in days, and his heart lurched.

"Interesting," Ian said. Morvan looked over to find
those brooding eyes studying him. Ian turned his attention back to the doorway. "Stunning, isn't she? The
blond. I haven't seen her before. Do you know who she
is?"

"I know who she is." She *was* stunning. All eyes turned
to her, and the male eyes lingered. A master had been at
work on her appearance, and Morvan guessed who it
was. He would kill David. She appeared oblivious to the
reactions she inspired, and in a crowd of flirting, preen-
ing women that only increased her appeal.

Christiana led the way through the crowd. As they
passed nearby, Anna saw him. Her gaze briefly fell to
where Elizabeth rested her hand on his arm. She glanced
at Elizabeth, put on her face of cool reserve, and looked
away.

Christiana found places for them on benches against
a wall. Two women friends closed in and the four ladies
became involved in conversation.

"Is she the one from Brittany? The heiress who came
with you?"

Damn the court gossips. "Aye. She is convent-bound,
Ian. And you should know that I still protect her."

Ian smiled. It was a smile, Morvan knew, that women

would find devastating. Hell. This was like watching himself at twenty size up his prey. A convent-bound Anna wouldn't have stood a chance.

"Dedicated to God? Well, one never knows. And you can keep your sword sheathed. I have no intention of hurting the girl."

Morvan allowed himself to be drawn into Elizabeth's conversation, but he kept glancing at Anna. A series of young men approached her, but her stiff politeness discouraged them. It was Ian he worried about. The young knight worked his way through the crowd, circling to the wall, chatting as he went, advancing to where the pure flower sat.

His final approach was masterful. He didn't speak to Anna at all, but struck up a conversation with Christiana instead. Morvan watched his sister, who could be unbearably stupid about men sometimes, laugh and make room on the bench beside her. And then, ever so casually, with a word here and a comment there, Ian turned his attention to his real interest and began drawing her out.

He was good at this. Too good.

The crowd flowed to the tables, and with Elizabeth by his side Morvan knew that he would have to sit with her. Several tables away, Ian guided Christiana and Anna to places and sat between them.

Even as he joined the merry group at his own table, Morvan felt a surprisingly sharp anger burning. A single thought repeated like a chant in his mind. *If not me, then no one.* Although he kept forcing himself to look away, his glance always returned to the table where Ian pursued his slow seduction.

That smile came more frequently, and Anna blushed each time. On occasion Ian leaned toward her and spoke lowly in her ear, as if the noise in the hall required it. Soon he had her laughing and coming out of her protective reserve. Finally he lifted a morsel of food to her mouth. She took it self-consciously, but the long fingers strayed in a soft caress on her lips.

Short of dragging her away and creating a spectacle, there was nothing to do, and the blade of jealousy burned hotter in Morvan's head. The feast's wine only fed his quiet fury.

Toward the end of the meal a page came to him and said that the princess wished to speak, and he joined Isabella at the high table. As a member of the household, he had known her since she was a child. He had always found her frivolous and something of a tease, and as he gave her the full attention she was due he decided that the last few years had not improved her on those counts. Except that the way she touched his hand suggested that she had moved beyond teasing. He ignored the subtle signals. He had never had any interest in this girl in that way.

His respectful demeanor began to bore Isabella, and her attention shifted. He quickly turned his head to check on Anna.

Her place and the one beside it were vacant.

Anna knew better than to be flattered, but she felt flattered anyway.

She knew the source of Ian's interest in her. The word had spread that she was an heiress headed for the convent, but an heiress nonetheless.

She had discouraged the young men who approached her, but Ian seemed to know Christiana. Then at dinner Christiana got distracted and it was just the two of them talking. When he complimented her hair, she suddenly realized that she was being wooed for the first time in her life.

He was very handsome, and that flattered her even more. His smile was charming. She felt sure that he knew that, and that he was using it, along with his pretty words, very deliberately in this gentle game he played with her. But the game, she admitted with some surprise, possessed a seductive allure. Even though one knew all was vanity and falsehood, it still felt very nice to be called beautiful by a handsome man.

And Ian did call her beautiful—three times during the meal. A month ago she would have been disgusted at such blatant lies, but she felt clumsy and out of place this evening and she wanted, needed, to hear someone tell such lies.

She could see Morvan from her table. And the woman beside him. Ian noticed her repeatedly glance in their direction.

"She is very beautiful, isn't she?" he said.

"Aye, beautiful." And elegant. And *small*. She looked like everything a lady was supposed to be, and she had stayed beside Morvan the entire evening, with that possessive hand on his arm.

"She is my distant relative through marriage. Her husband passed away not too long ago, but Elizabeth does not mourn her old husbands much. Their deaths leave her free, and by now very wealthy. He was her third, and as with all of them, the marriage contract chartered lands in her name."

Beautiful, small, and wealthy. "Sir Morvan seems to be a devoted friend."

"More than that. It is no secret, and you are bound to hear of it here at court, for with his return it is being discussed frequently. Some years ago, between her first and second old husbands, Morvan was her lover. A great passion, to hear of it. It is assumed they did not marry only because she is barren."

A great passion. A great love. And now he was back, and she was wealthy and free.

Something heavy and sick lodged beneath her heart. At the same time, she knew tremendous relief that she had been saved at Reading. If she had really given herself, only to be abandoned for Elizabeth when they came to Windsor, it would have been humiliating. Yet, even though it hadn't happened that way, she still tasted the devastation as if it had.

To distract herself from Morvan and Elizabeth, she let herself be drawn into Ian's game a bit more intimately. He finally suggested that they take some air in a nearby castle garden.

He slid her away from the table so deftly that even Christiana didn't notice their departure. In the anteroom Ian quickly located his cloak. After he settled it on her shoulders, his arm went around her as he guided her to a door.

The small garden had been laid out for a long stroll between hedges and growings. Stone benches were decked out for the party with cushions, and arbored shelters offered more private seating. Anna could hear soft voices that let her know they were not entirely alone.

Ian kept up a smooth conversation, asking her questions about Brittany. Partway along the garden path he drew her back the way they had come. "I will show you something interesting over here. A hearth wall flanks the garden at this end, and it is quite warm. There is a rosebush there that never dies. Sometimes it even blooms in winter."

She knew that he was luring her toward a secluded spot for reasons besides horticulture. But his flattery had made her feel confident and even a bit bold. When he tugged her to one of the padded benches hidden in an arbor, she let herself follow him.

She expected a brief kiss and some pretty words, so his aggressive assault stunned her. He pulled her down and immobilized her shoulders with his arm. His hand held her head as he lowered his lips to hers.

The kiss was pleasant enough, but she felt oddly removed from it, like an observer watching someone else do this. She was so uninvolved that it wasn't until he stroked her breast that she realized his hand was on her body. His caress evoked surprise, but little else. She waited a moment, contemplating that. Nothing. She might have just brushed against a tree for all she experienced.

She pushed his hand off and whispered a protest. He laughed and pulled her back, holding her tightly as his mouth took hers more demandingly and his hand returned to its explorations.

She could scream, but she didn't want to create a spectacle that would embarrass Christiana. She twisted and pushed. Whenever she could get her mouth free she would protest clearly, but he'd silence her with another kiss. He was acting as if her resistance were merely a courting game.

He leaned his weight into her and laid her back on the cushions, pinning her down with his body. Fingers slid up her leg, lifting her skirt. It appeared that Ian had decided to take the quickest path to La Roche de Roald's wealth.

She sighed with exasperation. She had really tried to be

ladylike here in Windsor. She had worn gowns and acted demure. Her weapons were tucked away, and she even rode her horse with restraint. But right now she had a choice. She could either scream for help, or she could act very unladylike indeed. Whatever had repulsed Morvan probably wouldn't save her in the black night of this arbor, especially with a rich estate as the ultimate prize. In the dark, women were probably all the same to a man with an ulterior goal.

Freeing her right arm so it dangled beside the bench, she forced her mouth from his and made a display of gasping. "Could you move just a little? I can't breathe."

He shifted, just enough. She twice swung her fist with all of her strength, hitting him below the ribs. He jerked to a sitting position, his arm over his stomach.

She jumped up from the bench and ran.

She managed about ten steps before she smacked into a chest that she knew too well.

"Where is he?" Morvan snarled, giving her shoulders a shake.

"He is gone." She could sense Morvan peering into the darkness, but the arbor was pitch black, and if Ian would just sit still . . .

He didn't. He emerged toward them.

All of that trouble to avoid a spectacle, and now this.

"Sir Morvan," Ian said coolly. "Have you decided to take some air too?"

"I warned you."

"She is not harmed."

Morvan grabbed her hand and began dragging her away. "I'll see you later, boy." He pulled the cloak from her shoulders and threw it on the ground.

He hauled her out of the garden like some chastised

child. With each stumbling step, her resentment grew. In the anteroom to the hall, she dug in her heels. "I'll not return like this."

"Nay. You are going home. You are too ignorant for this place. A lamb amidst a pack of wolves would be safer." Still holding her hand, he threw cloaks around. By the time he found hers he had created a tremendous mess. He draped it around her shoulders, then gestured to a page and sent a message of explanation to Christiana. Silently, and with long purposeful strides that had her scampering to keep up, he pulled her toward the castle gate.

She was seething by the time they turned onto the street where Christiana lived. Her hand hurt badly, and the skirt of her gown had been ruined.

She expected him to throw her into the house and then return to Elizabeth, but he followed her and kicked the door closed behind him.

"What happened back there?" His voice was quiet. Too quiet.

He wanted to know how badly to hurt Ian. There was a limit to the damage she would let Morvan do in the name of protecting her. This wasn't Gurwant, after all.

She swept past him toward the stairs. "It is none of your concern."

A hand grabbed her shoulder. She flew backwards, landing against the wall, pinned there by his forearm. With his other hand resting on the wall near her head, he leaned over her.

"What happened back there?"

"*Nothing.*"

"Nothing? He was after you all evening. He took you into that garden, to that arbor, and didn't even try to kiss you? It is the only reason that damn garden was even built."

She struggled against his hold, but in vain. "Aye, he kissed me. Is your curiosity satisfied now?"

Something dark flashed in his eyes. She smelt the wine on his breath. Too much of that, she knew, could turn men either stupid or mean. Just her luck that with him it was the latter.

His head came down to hers, and his mouth found her ear. "Did you like it? Did you lose yourself in it like you do with me?"

Icy fury spilled through her. This had nothing to do with her at all. It wasn't some threat to her safety or even her virtue that made him like this, but only his stupid male pride. He didn't want her in this way, but God forbid someone else bested him at it anyway.

She gritted her teeth against the maddening emotions that pounded through her. "Well, Morvan, it wasn't waves crashing against the rocks, but the tide came in all the same."

His head jerked back. The dim light picked up a dangerous sparkle in his eyes. Despite her smug satisfaction at his reaction, she knew that she had made a mistake.

He brought his hand over and held her chin. She knew what he was going to do. Furiously, she struggled against him. This was ludicrous, pointless. It had nothing to do with desire or lust and everything to do with power and pride. She didn't intend to be some chess pawn in a game of male competition.

He ignored her protests and lowered his mouth to hers, then pressed a kiss on her that deepened quickly.

She expected to feel nothing, as with Ian. But she found to her horror that despite everything, despite even the appalling way he was using her, Morvan was not Ian. Her body began betraying her. She beat back her response, pushed it away, just as she continued to try and push away his body. But he only kissed her harder, hungrier, and then turned his mouth to her neck. He moved his restraining arm down and slid it over so that his hand closed on one breast.

It was cruel mockery, and she would not let him do it. She grabbed his hair and yanked. "Nay, you *will not*. I have been manhandled enough for one night."

He froze. She had never seen anyone so furious in her life.

"You let him touch you."

"Aye, damn you, but then I fought him as I'm fighting you."

She swung her fist, but he was too quick. He caught it and slammed it up onto the wall. Livid beyond reason, she pounded his shoulder with her other clenched hand. That ended up high above the other side of her head. He took both her hands in one of his and repinned them to the wall above her. Then he kissed her again.

She fought it. She gritted her teeth against the sensations. Furious with her weakness, she tightened her body against showing any reaction. But when he forced his knee high between her legs, her whole body flexed.

"Are you contented now?" She glared at him through tears of rage. "Your reputation as the greatest lover in England is safe. Even unnatural women respond to you. Are you satisfied? Will you leave now?"

"Nay. I am not and I will not." He lifted her away from the wall and moved to close his arms around her.

It was her chance, and she took it. She kicked and pummeled and broke free. "Go to hell, Morvan!" She flew toward the stairs, barely escaping the hand reaching to grab her.

Near the top landing she ran straight into David, heading down. His clothes looked as if he had thrown them on, and he was blinking sleep from his eyes.

He looked at her, then to where Morvan followed just steps behind.

"*Damn*." He pushed her behind him and up the stairs. "Go to your chamber and bar the door."

"Get out of the way, David," Morvan said.

"Nay. You will not do this in this house. You are drunk."

"At worst only half so."

"It is the half that governs your judgment. Is this how you protect women?"

"She is in no danger from me."

"Are you sure? I am not. She doesn't want you this night. Leave."

"You are wrong, David. He will not threaten me in that way," Anna said.

"*Go to your chamber.*"

Startled by his severe tone, she backed away.

Morvan laughed. "Hell, David, I am impressed. I think this is the first time that she has obeyed a man without an argument since I met her."

She hurried to her chamber and heard no more.

Morvan had his anger under control by the time he returned to the hall. He knew that Ian was still there, but he forced himself not to look for him. He would deal with Ian later. And then he would deal with what he had done to Anna this night.

Musicians played, and he took Elizabeth's hand and led her to the floor. The dancing calmed him enough that he felt almost normal when he finally escorted

Elizabeth back to her house. She turned to him once they were inside, her lovely skin looking translucent in the warm glow of the candles.

"Are you staying?" she asked.

He remembered his first night with her. He had come here bent on a grand seduction, but she had drawn him into a companionable evening of laughter and conversation. And then, late in the night, she had simply risen and announced she was going to bed, and asked this same question. Without flirtation, without words, he had followed her up the stairs.

"Seeking another interlude, Elizabeth? Before the next old husband?"

"I am thinking that I have done this backwards. The marriages are too long, and the interludes too short. I am thinking that I have had enough *old* husbands."

The insinuation astonished him. She was beautiful and landed and wealthy. He did not doubt that whatever those old men had given her had grown tenfold under her steady hand. Along with the gold and emerald necklace, it might be enough to support his fight for Harclow. He did not need his own son for an heir—Christiana's would do as well.

He should grab the prize; only a fool would not. Perhaps if he did not care for her at all, he could do it. But he knew something of what was in her heart, and she deserved more of him than he could give.

Also, she was not the woman he wanted.

"If you tire of old husbands, you should find a young one. But I am not he, and not because you are barren. There is someone else in my head and my heart, and until she is gone it would not be fair to you."

"I saw you watching her. I hear that she goes to an abbey. When she is gone, will she be out of your heart?"

It was a painful question. Coming from Elizabeth, it carried significant implications. She was saying that she would wait for him if the answer might be yes.

"I do not know. In truth, I fear not."

"Then you are right. If I seek a young husband, you are not he."

He kissed her for what would surely be the last time, and she turned away.

He did not leave at once. He waited for the house's other occupant. When the door finally opened, he grabbed the young man and slammed him against the wall with a grip at his neck. Briefly stunned, Ian quickly composed himself and stared coolly over the hand threatening to strangle him.

Morvan wasn't nearly as interested in killing this knight as he had been two hours ago. He had spent the worst of his fury on the wrong person and in the wrong way. Still, he gripped the neck a little harder.

"Lady Anna. She is not for you, boy."

Ian looked back confidently, fearlessly, placidly. Lids lowered over his brooding dark eyes. "And Lady Elizabeth is not for you."

So that was how it was.

"A fair bargain," Morvan said as he let his arm drop. And it was. He was trading a woman that he had rejected for one that he would never have.

He stepped through the open door.

"Morvan," Ian said, stopping him. "You should know that she fought me from the first. I have the bruises to prove it. She uses her fists like a man."

He suspected that Ian was lying, but doing so to protect Anna. Though he had used her in a dangerous game, he was at least showing some honor now.

Well, one good turn deserved another.

He glanced up at the second level of the house. "And you should know that she is aware that you want her, because most men do. If I were you, I would go to her now. If she opens her door to you, it is done."

He walked away, hoping for Elizabeth's sake that the boy's finish was as good as his start.

CHAPTER 16

THE SUMMONS FROM THE KING came early the next morning.

Christiana accompanied Anna to the castle. A dozen other people already waited for an audience, even though tierce had not yet rung. Anna brought all of the documents relating to her petition. She tried to ignore the coiling tension that had claimed her since she had woken.

She smoothed the light brown wool of her skirt, and felt the simple veil hiding her pinned hair. She tried to empty her mind of all thoughts except the upcoming meeting, but to no avail. Memories of last night forced themselves on her.

She had come a long way since she was twelve years old, but then she had planned it that way. After the attack of Gurwant and his father, she had sworn to learn to protect herself so that she would never be a man's victim. Last night she had proven the value of that vow.

What had happened with Ian was, she suspected, a common thing for most women. Her only regret was that she hadn't hit him sooner. Morvan, on the other hand, had surprised and disappointed her. His treatment had been an act of anger, and she had done nothing to deserve that except challenge his pride. For most men, though, perhaps that was enough.

It was not thinking about Morvan that pained her, but rather remembering her own reactions to him. The idea that she had let anyone develop that kind of power over her was daunting.

She found some solace in the knowledge that Morvan would never want to use it again. Last night had not been about desire. He had acted as if he were teaching her a lesson, although for the life of her she couldn't imagine what the lesson was supposed to have been.

Her thoughts were distracted by the approach of a man. He was of hearty build and thick-legged and had hair a color much like her own. She judged him to be about thirty-five years old.

"You are Anna de Leon?" he asked.

"I am."

"I am your kinsman, Harvé. I saw you once at La Roche de Roald when you were a small child."

Anna had no recollection of the visit. Harvé was, if she remembered correctly, a third cousin to her father and had lived most of his life in England.

"Edward asked me to attend this morning. He thought it best to have a member of the family present to aid you."

The King thought it best to have a *man* from the family present was what he meant, even if that man was a total stranger.

"Edward is a good man with sound judgment, cousin," he said. "But he is very busy, so don't expect any lengthy discussions."

"Is there anything I should know?" she asked, hoping that blood counted for something.

"The continuing strife in Brittany worries him. He hoped that the capture of Charles de Blois would end things. He cannot commit too heavily to Brittany, and wants to hold what the young duke has at a minimal cost."

"Then he should be glad of my solution for my father's estate."

"When we go in, do not speak unless you are asked to. Edward does not care for clever women. Put yourself in his hands and he will be generous with you."

Not speak? Then was Harvé, the kinsman who was more English than Breton, to speak for her? The notion rankled her.

The door to the King's chamber opened and a page announced that the King would see them.

Harvé guided her into the noisy chamber, where the King sat behind a square table strewn with parchment documents. At a long table nearby three men passed papers and mumbled to each other. Another very officious-looking man went to the clerks and gave them instructions of some sort, pointing to pages here and there.

Two chairs faced the King, and Anna took a position behind one, her eyes carefully lowered. Harvé stood beside her.

"Please seat yourself, my lady." She glanced up. She

had been addressed by the officious man—the King's secretary, she surmised. But her glance also took in the King himself. He was an attractive man in his middle thirties. Long brown hair framed his face and a mustache hung along the edges of his mouth and chin.

Anna sat on the chair's edge with her hands folded on her lap. She prayed that she looked suitably demure and not at all clever.

A young boy with blond hair, dressed very sumptuously, walked in and sat in a chair beside the King's table. It was the young Duke Jean. He had a piece of parchment in his hands that interested him more than anyone in the room did. He proceeded to turn his attention to it, folding it this way and that.

"This is Lady Anna de Leon, daughter of Roald and sister of Drago, both deceased," the secretary explained. The boy glanced over to her and nodded.

The King finally spoke. To Harvé. "We received the lady's letters after her brother's death, and regret that affairs kept us from replying. We would have spared her this journey if we could have. However, it is well that she has come to us."

"She asks only for your judgment in this, for the situation at the estate is precarious. The Beaumanoir family is pursuing a spurious claim."

"We are well aware of that. They have appealed to us, through the French king no less. There was brief mention of it in our last communication with France. You hold one Gurwant de Beaumanoir, I am told."

They all looked at her. She was going to be allowed to speak. "He was taken in battle after he laid siege to us. I hold him for ransom as is customary."

"He claims betrothal to you."

She handed over the papal annulment. "It is no forgery. My brother himself procured it in Avignon."

King Edward examined the document. "Your brother never swore fealty to the duke."

"He died soon after my father, and without testament or heir. My father's will still stands. I ask that the line of inheritance dictated in it be recognized."

"With your brother's death, that makes you heir."

"Aye, but I plan to take the veil, and so it would fall to my sister Catherine, and through her to her husband."

"But as long as you lived, the estate could still be claimed through you."

"I will be in an abbey. If my duke recognizes my sister's rights, there can be no claim through me."

"Another king may choose not to recognize her rights. And then the estate is still yours."

"Are you suggesting that I would leave the abbey and deliver La Roche de Roald to the Penthièvres and their French alliance? After all that I have done to save it for Brittany, as my father wanted?"

"I am suggesting that someone could take you from the abbey and effect the same thing."

A nervous pounding began throbbing inside her. She did not like this. Not at all.

The king gestured to Harvé, who rose and went to him. King, kinsman, and secretary huddled together around the table and spoke in low mumbles. The pounding grew. She felt as though she were standing at the very edge of a rocky cliff.

The arrow of parchment landed at her feet. She reached down and picked it up as the young duke came forward.

"It is a falcon," he explained, reaching for it.

"It is very clever," Anna said as she handed the parchment to him. He was an attractive boy. He possessed a wiry energy that spoke well for the future. Would he ever become his own man if he was raised under King Edward's influence like this? Could Brittany ever be independent again?

He showed her how it was folded. He was still there when Harvé retook his seat beside her. The duke whispered in her ear. "The King's lieutenant in Brittany wrote about you. He said that you fight in battles and wear armor and have the heart of a man."

Her stomach sank. So much for the demure nun. The King was letting her play her role, but he knew the truth.

He whispered again. "My mother wore armor, too. They say she is mad, but I see her sometimes and she doesn't act so with me. You don't look mad either." He went back to his chair, absorbed again in his game.

Either. It felt as though the cliff had gotten higher.

"Lady Anna," the King said. "If not for the Penthièvre claim on the ducal crown, and their French alliance, your requests would be a simple thing to grant. But under the circumstances we cannot allow it. La Roche de Roald is too close to Brest, and its cove could hide ships that would harass our shipping routes."

The edge of the cliff began shaking.

"We cannot assume that your defeat of Gurwant de Beaumanoir, complete though it was, will end things. And there may be other adventurers. Even in the abbey you would not be secure, for in the last years in Brittany these scurrilous knights, some of whom I am ashamed to say are English, have not been deterred by sanctified ground."

The cliff edge was crumbling, falling away. She thought that she was going to be sick.

"In order to hold the estate for the duke, we must see that you are safe. It is obvious that you must marry."

She was falling, falling. The room was gone, the chair, the very substance of herself. Far away she heard the King's voice continue. "We will find a suitable husband for you forthwith."

Space righted itself and her wits cleared. She raised her gaze on this English king.

He didn't like clever women. Well, she no longer had anything to lose. "My lord, I claim my father's testamentary rights according to the Assize of Rachat."

Edward looked at her, startled.

"In return for the freedom to execute the testament as written, the estate will pay the duke one year's income from the estate," she continued. "The right was agreed upon by Duke Jean II and the Breton lords in 1276. My father's will clearly states that I am to enter the abbey if I so choose, and even sets aside a dowry for that purpose."

"She is right, cousin," a young voice said. "I know the Assize of Rachat. It was so agreed."

"Get me this testament," Edward said icily to the secretary.

Anna calmly handed over the copy she carried. Edward read the whole thing.

"You have misinterpreted your father's will," he said. "Let me read the clause to you. 'To my daughter Anna I give the properties at Rennes, to follow her to the Abbey of Saint Meen or to her husband as she so chooses.' There is no assumption there that you will go to the abbey, and indeed a husband is mentioned." He dropped the parchment. "I will find a suitable husband for you who will protect the estate for your duke. You will be betrothed while you are here." His tone communicated dismissal. Harvé began rising.

She would not be used in this way. She would at least salvage something and show this English king what Breton women were made of.

"Excuse me, but those last words must mean something. If that clause does not give me the choice between the abbey or a husband, it must reserve to me the choice of the husband himself."

Edward's eyes fell on the document, still beneath his hand.

The duke looked up from his paper falcon. "I think she is right."

The King glanced coldly at the child, but Anna could have kissed him.

"Whom do you choose?" Edward asked, his eyes boring into her.

"I will need a day or so to think about it. This is not what I expected."

"Listen to me. You will choose a man known to me as faithful to your duke's cause, and I must approve him as such. I will draw up a list of suitable nobles who have shown themselves worthy of your estate and send it to you. You will make your choice in one day, and be betrothed in the castle chapel this Saturday after mass. Your kinsman here will negotiate the marriage contract for you, and advise you on your duties in this matter."

He looked away, and Harvé took her arm. As she turned to go, young Duke Jean gave her a conspiratorial wink.

Perhaps Brittany had a future after all. Her own, however, had just become a disaster.

Morvan slept long into the day, the wine and the fury of the night before taking a toll worse than a battle could have. In mid-afternoon he finally dragged himself out of the merciful oblivion that obscured the memory of what had happened with Anna.

He was disgusted with himself. He had never forced his attentions on a woman before and was dismayed that he had done so with her. She was driving him mad—that was all there was to it. He could not blame it on the wine, much as he would have liked to. Raw jealousy had provoked his darker reactions to her, and the desire to conquer had driven him. He ruefully admitted that he had enjoyed their little battle too much.

He undoubtedly had insulted her beyond forgiveness. And so, when Salisbury mentioned that a message requesting his presence had come from Anna, he was surprised but not very hopeful.

As he approached David's house he saw several men whom he knew lounging in the lane. They were all unmarried and dressed up like popinjays. Anna had made even a bigger impression at the feast than he'd thought. Suitors, undeterred by rumors of the abbey, were literally lined up to woo her.

Christiana sat with two more men in the hall. She jumped up when she saw Morvan and pulled him aside.

"Where have you been?" she asked, smacking him in the chest with exasperation.

"Sleeping."

She studied his face. He studied hers. Nay, she didn't know about his behavior last night. He owed David a debt for that.

"You haven't heard then. It would appear you are the only one who hasn't." She rolled her eyes in the direction of the hall.

"What has happened?"

"Let Anna tell you. She is hiding in the solar."

Perplexed and curious, Morvan mounted the stairs.

Anna sat on a stool staring into the fire, her hands folded on her lap, her back as straight as ever. She wore the brown gown with the lacing at the neck. She had her right hand placed over the left.

He knelt on one knee and uncovered the hiding hand. An ugly bruise showed where his grip had crushed her. It was the least of what he had done, but he lifted the hand and kissed it.

"Can you forgive me for this?"

She was startled out of her daze, and looked down at her hand. "Oh, that," she said absently. "It doesn't matter."

He saw a veil of worry on her face. Something was very wrong. He was reminded of the days after she had learned that Gurwant was coming.

"I have been to see your King," she said. "This morning. My kinsman Harvé was there. Your English king has decided that I must marry. He has drawn up a list from which I can choose."

He stood so that she wouldn't see his reaction. Tucking her away at Saint Meen was one thing. Watching her marry was another. His reaction to seeing her with Ian had taught him that much.

"Do you want my advice on these men?" he asked, even though giving her such advice would be hell itself. "Let me see the list. I probably know most of them."

She looked up with an expression of determination stronger than he had ever seen before. She rose and walked to the desk. She returned with a sheet of paper in her hand, handed it to him, and retook her seat on the stool.

The paper contained no names, just three numbers. He glanced at her in question.

"That is the income from my family's estates. The first

is the income reported to the duke and King. The higher figure is the true income. They do not know the real size of the stud farm. The third figure is the coin on hand at the castle. My father always believed that one could never have enough coin. But the plague was costly. Still, it is more than most estates hold."

Morvan looked again at the figures. The income was sizable, even the false one. The estate must be bigger than he thought. He had never ridden over its entirety. She was a very wealthy heiress. No wonder the men lined up.

"Why do you show me this?"

"Although one year's income must now go to the duke, there is enough there to support a small army very shortly. An army that could cross a sea and fight to reclaim a family's lost honor. It appears that I am in need of a husband. Are you willing to consider it?"

"Are you saying that I am on the King's list?"

"Nay, but I was not specifically limited to the list. Though it was your King's intention, I have witnesses who heard what he in fact said. He set conditions, but you appear to meet them." She told him the gist of her conversation with the King. "Will you consider this? If not, Christiana tells me there are some men waiting to make my acquaintance."

Something inside him tried to break free and soar, but an instinctive wariness made him halt its flight. He brought a chair to the fire and settled into it, facing her. "Aye, my lady. I will consider it. Who will speak for you?"

"I will speak for myself, and I will speak now. I have less than one day to resolve this—your King insists on a quick betrothal. My kinsman Harvé is charged with negotiating this contract, but I will give him a completed bargain."

She was wounded and angry, and he couldn't blame her. After last night he could hardly expect her to throw herself into his arms. Still, her distant manner pricked his caution.

"Well then, Anna, perhaps you should tell me your terms."

Anna lowered her gaze to her bruised hand. She looked at it while she began the litany of conditions she had rehearsed. "The written contract will be straightforward. All of the lands will be yours, except the property near Rennes that was to be my dowry to the abbey. I want that put in my name."

"As dower lands? In the event you are widowed?"

"Chartered in my name, the income to be mine from the start." She looked at him. "Like Lady Elizabeth."

She saw a flash in his eyes, but continued. "The inheritance of the estate will revert to my family if you die without an heir by me. It will go to Catherine and Josce or their children. It will go to Bretons. Of course, your own testament can dispose of any additional lands added to the estate or reclaimed by you any way that you wish, and La Roche de Roald will be yours while you live."

"An unusual provision, but not unheard of," Morvan said. "Is there anything else? I have no objection to this."

Anna stroked her skirt. She was a little surprised to be giving her performance. A part of her had expected him to refuse outright. But marriages were practical arrangements. She was counting on his being very practical.

"Those are the terms of the written contract, the terms that I will give Harvé. But I also want an unwritten agreement between us, bound by your honor, and the terms of that are more extensive."

He contemplated her in silence. She began to feel uncomfortable under his scrutiny and rose from the stool and paced as she spoke.

"I want you to give Josce and Catherine some property. As it is they will have little. Her dowry lands, as you will see when you read my father's testament, are small."

"I would have done so anyway. I know that your marriage will be a disappointment to them."

"Carlos and Ascanio are to be allowed to stay. As long as they want."

"If they are loyal to me, why would I ask them to leave?"

Because they belong to *me,* she thought. There was loyalty and then there was loyalty. "The serf girl Marguerite must never be married against her will."

"Don't you trust me to find a good man for her? I know what she has endured."

"She may not want to marry at all."

"As you do not?"

"She suffered far worse than me, Morvan. I know that."

"And what of you, my lady? Do you negotiate nothing for yourself?"

"There is quite a lot I want for myself."

"Somehow I thought so. Unlike with Gurwant, you will bargain hard with me."

"Unlike Gurwant, I know that you are honorable and will keep your word. It is one of the reasons that we are talking at all."

"And what are the other reasons, Anna?"

She had planned to lay down the terms and be done

with this. She hadn't expected such a question. "There is affection and friendship between us. You are not a stranger. And my estate is more valuable to you since you are landless."

"And so you can press your advantage," he said coolly. "Continue, then. Let us hear it."

His quiet voice did not hide his increasing rancor, and she knew it wasn't going to get any better. But she did have the advantage now, and she never would again. *Ever.*

"The income from the lands I receive is to be mine, to use as I choose without interference."

"And how will you use it?"

"That is to be my business alone."

He waited silently.

"After three years, if I choose, you are to let me retire to Saint Meen."

"*Nay.*"

"It is all or nothing, Morvan."

"No man will agree to these things. No other will give them to you."

"I may not be able to get this from another man, but if you do not agree La Roche de Roald will still not be yours. Should I finish?"

He responded with a cold silence.

"You will have no rights over me. I will not interfere with your authority, but I am too old to be told what to do every minute. Even without any rights you have been too overbearing, and I will not be commanded by you."

"You go too far, Anna—"

"There is one more thing."

"What more could there be?"

She realized she probably shouldn't have saved this point for last. Part of it would be easy to accept, but the consequences would infuriate him. She went over to the desk and stood behind it, to form a barrier. "La Roche de Roald will eventually revert to Catherine and her children. You will have no heirs by me."

Hot anger would have been preferable to the cold fury that strode through the room and faced her from across the desk.

"Do you have reason to think that you are barren?"

"Nay."

"Do you know some woman's tricks to stop pregnancy?"

"Nay."

"Then I can assume that you are insisting on a chaste marriage."

"I do not expect you to be a monk. You can continue as you always have. You can even have children by your women, and they can inherit your lands near Scotland. A bishop can be found who will legitimize them. Regaining Harclow is the main reason for this marriage anyway. If you want to bring a woman into the castle I will not object. And your children can be raised there." She spoke lightly, as if these things were of no consequence, when in fact they would be a form of hell.

"You are most generous."

"I know that you would not need my permission. I am simply saying that I would not make life hard for them."

He moved around the desk. She fought the urge to retreat.

"You would deny me in marriage what you once offered in sin?"

"I would deny you under obligation what I once offered freely. You are making too much of this, Morvan. It is, as you say, a simple thing."

"You call refusing me children a simple thing? Is this

about last night? Are you so angry that it is your goal to see me unmanned?"

"This has nothing to do with last night. And it is my goal to see my father's lands remain Breton and not English." She paused and added quietly, "And it is my goal to never see you unmanned."

But he had already walked away when she said that. "I will send you my answer in the morning, Anna. But if I were you, I would see if there is a bigger fool than me waiting downstairs."

CHAPTER 17

MORVAN STORMED INTO the castle practice yard, borrowed weapons from the armory, and joined the knights practicing with swords and axes. He threw himself into the game with a black ferocity.

When the day waned and his partners deserted him, he headed toward the poorer section of town where the common laborers dwelled, and found a rude tavern with strong ale.

Settling into a dark corner, he was dismayed to find that all of the afternoon's exertions hadn't dimmed his outrage in the least.

He forced himself to consider Anna's proposal. He understood all too well its value. Rich lands, at least during his lifetime, and the chance to fulfill his destiny were there for the taking. She was giving him the opportunity to change his life, to avenge his family, and to amount to more than a hired sword. She was offering a way out of obscurity.

Yet, just as clearly he saw what she would not give. The income would permit her to leave at will and would provide a degree of independence unheard of for most women. The provision to retire to Saint Meen did the same, and meant the marriage would simply be a temporary delay in the future she had chosen for herself. And even while she lived with him, he would not be her husband in truth. Her terms denied him her dependence, her body, her spirit, and her submission. She was refusing to give him herself.

It was late at night when he finally stepped from the tavern into the deserted street. Thumps and scurries caught his attention as he walked through the dark. He was being followed. No doubt some other patrons at the tavern had noticed his garments and purse and decided he would be an easy job.

Good. He was in the mood to break a few heads.

Darting down a side street, he pressed against a wall and waited. The moon was out, and as his pursuers turned the corner he could see their forms before the dark shadows swallowed them. He tensed for the attack.

"How many are there?"

Morvan swerved with his fist halfway to its mark before he recognized the voice. "What are you doing here, David?"

"Your sister made it clear that I either find you or I sleep alone. She has been worried since you left so ungraciously and suspects that you are looking for trouble. So how many are there?"

"At least three. Perhaps four."

"I have my sword. Let's just brandish it a bit and be done with this," David said.

"Nay. They are unarmed, I'm sure. Have you gotten any good with it?" Sounds indicated that the footpads were approaching, and Morvan and David backed down the narrow lane.

"I have kept up my lessons. I'm about as skilled as you were at sixteen."

"I am impressed."

"Conceited bastard. So we don't use our swords, and I presume it is ignoble to simply run."

"Highly ignoble. And no fun at all."

They had reached the end of the lane. The only way out was along a short dead-end alley. "You are in luck, brother. I am much better with my fists than a sword anyway. While you were tilting at the quintain as a lad, I was surviving in the alleys of London. This brings back old times."

"On your left, David."

"I see him. Just one question. If there are four of them, and we are in danger of being beaten to bloody deaths, are we then allowed to use our swords?"

"Aye."

Shadows darted in and out of the moonlight.

"Here they come," David muttered. "Damn, Morvan, you are too drunk to count. I see six. Hell."

A half hour later they were back in the tavern, sitting on a bench against the wall, soaking their fists in pitchers of warm water that David had charmed out of the serving woman.

Morvan looked over at his brother-in-law's bruised cheek and cut chin. It had been an exhilarating and harmless brawl, and the footpads had eventually scurried off without any swords being drawn. He decided that

David wasn't such a bad companion to have along in a fight.

He unsheathed David's sword and admired it. "For someone who barely knows how to use the weapon, you pay for the best."

"It is from Damascus. They forge steel differently there. Lighter in weight, which I find useful, but very strong."

Morvan tested its balance and heft and decided the lighter weight would not be a disadvantage.

David pulled his fist out of the pitcher and examined it. "Is there any particular reason why you are trying to get yourself killed tonight?" he asked casually.

Morvan set the sword down, leaned against the wall, and closed his eyes. He still felt sufficiently full of battle camaraderie to answer.

"Anna de Leon, daughter of Roald and heiress of La Roche de Roald, Breton amazon and saint—you don't know about the saint part, do you?—proposed marriage to me this afternoon."

"Well, that is certainly something to die over. Christiana had hoped that was why Anna sent for you, but when you left as you did . . . I assume that you accepted and have been out mourning your carefree life."

"Nay."

"Don't tell me that you refused."

"Not yet."

"In terms of property, you are unlikely to ever get a better offer."

He knew that. *She* knew that.

"Forgive me for prying, Morvan, but you make no sense. She is beautiful and rich and how you feel about her is written all over your face when you look at her. None of your usual cold calculation."

"Her terms are unacceptable."

David shrugged. "So change the terms."

"It is all or nothing."

"The hell it is. People always say that and never mean it. This isn't one of your sieges where the choice is yield or die. This is commerce. Everything is negotiable. Speak with her. Work from your strengths—give where you can and take where you must. It is very simple if you don't let your pride rule you. If you want, I will do it for you."

Don't let pride rule. Easier said than done.

"It is in her interests to marry you too," David said. "Edward thinks to give her to Sir Giles, to repay a debt. She will not have the choice of the man like she thinks, unless she chooses another one to whom Edward is also in debt. Like you."

"You seem to know a lot about this."

"One hears things."

Aye, Morvan reflected, but David de Abyndon always managed to hear more than most. "Have you been planting ideas in the King's head, David? Is your hand behind this?"

"You flatter me. I am only a merchant who sells the King silks."

"Like hell. If you have interfered, you are playing a dangerous game."

"Only if the knight fails to check the king, and lets some pawn cut him off."

"The danger I speak of comes from treating the knight like a pawn."

"Is that a threat, Morvan? No one is manipulating you. The move is yours to make or not. Stay put if you prefer."

"And what of what the woman prefers?"

"You mean the abbey? She cannot have it. Edward

decided that on his own. Marriage is the best of the options he debated, I assure you, and he is still considering the others. Besides, she would not have been content there. She is neither pious nor obedient. If ever a woman would have been wasted in such a life, it is your lady."

David set aside his pitcher. "Let us go home and allow Christiana and Anna to fuss over our wounds and scold us for our bad behavior."

"I will go back to Salisbury's."

"Why not come back and settle it now?"

"I have to even the odds before I reopen negotiations. I have seen this woman plan a battle strategy better than most barons, and get half again their value for her Breton horses. Nay, David, only a fool would go unprepared to bargain with Anna de Leon."

Morvan was ushered into the King's chambers soon after dawn. There had been no waiting in the anteroom with the other petitioners. The message he had sent to the castle had gotten Edward's immediate attention.

No secretaries or clerks attended the King. This would be a private audience. That was a good sign. Morvan made his greetings, then followed Edward's gesture to sit.

"I am sorry that I was unable to see you before this, but matters of state have distracted me," Edward said. "I received your earlier note, however, and made time for Lady Anna as you requested."

"That was generous of you, but I do not come today to speak on her behalf."

"Nay, you come to speak for yourself. Your note made that clear, signed as it was 'Morvan Fitzwaryn, Lord of Harclow.'" He did not speak with annoyance, but his discomfort was palpable.

Morvan was glad to see the King's ill ease. It meant that Edward had not forgotten, despite the passing years. "I have decided that it is time to go north and regain my father's honor. I have come to ask for your permission and your help."

A veil came down over Edward's eyes. Morvan suspected that the King was seeing himself fourteen years ago in a tent on the Scottish border, swearing an oath to avenge the death of Hugh Fitzwaryn. Was his memory as clear as Morvan's own? Did he also see the trusting eyes of the sick and broken woman before him, and the awestruck boy who stood by her side?

"Your father was a good friend," Edward said. "He was one of the first to stand beside me when I went against the usurper Mortimer. He was a strong voice on my behalf with the border lords. I will never forgive myself that I could not relieve him at Harclow."

Morvan waited.

"I understand your resolve to regain your family's honor, but it is not a propitious time. The French question must be settled first, and the situation with Scotland is precarious. I cannot spare an army, and would not have a family matter disrupt the peace we have there. In a few years, perhaps . . ."

Morvan had known for some years that Edward would never spare an army for such an expedition, but it was just as well that the King didn't admit as much to himself.

"I would not plan an action without your approval, of course, and am willing to wait a few years if that is necessary. But not much longer, I hope. I would have my father rest finally in his grave."

Edward nodded in a way that looked oddly grateful for a king.

"As to the army, I have thought of a way to take care of that. If you agree to it, I would need much less help from you."

"Have you indeed? Let us hear it."

"I have learned that you commanded Anna de Leon to marry. Give her to me."

Edward frowned. "I had intended those lands for Sir Giles. . . ."

"She will not accept him, and believes the choice is hers to make. Find Sir Giles a different estate."

"If she does not accept my will, there are other ways to deal with her." A steely look accompanied the statement.

"Let me deal with her."

The King considered it. "Damn Bretons," he muttered. "They are an irascible race. They will eat each other alive in this war of theirs. The men are bad enough, but these women . . . Do you understand what you would get in her? The lands may be rich, but the woman goes with them. I know all about her, and I wonder if she is not half mad, or a witch."

There it was, explicitly. The thin line that she walked. The other ways of interpreting her behavior. Anna might have Breton law on her side, but this was an English king who would see the worst if it suited his purpose.

"Her people think that she is a saint."

"Oh, aye, and that is worse. I do not need a saint in Brittany. If the forces loose there gather around her, who knows what will transpire. I cannot afford such trouble. The ports are too important to our trade and war plans. Best if I keep her here. I have debated it since I met with her and saw how she does not know her place. If she won't accept my choice of husband, I will confine her with that other Breton madwoman."

"Give her to me. I am known by her people, and by

her. A virgin warrior might be the stuff of saintly legends, but a married woman is not. If you command her to marry me, you will be spared the worry of her, and know the loyalty of the man who holds that coastal fortress." He paused, then added, "And you will have fulfilled your oath, to my mind."

Edward's gaze sharpened. "Would you trade Harclow for La Roche de Roald? Would you trade an army for a woman?"

"Aye." Except that he traded nothing. If Edward consented to this, *all* of it would one day be his. He was bargaining for the means to fulfill his destiny, and Anna was not merely the path to do so—she was part of that destiny. His soul knew that with certainty.

"You are so sure that you can get her to accept *you*?"

"I am sure."

"She must be controlled. Nay, the more I think of it, the more I am convinced that confining her here—"

"I will control her."

The King studied him, then rose and walked to a table. After dipping a quill, he scratched some words on a piece of parchment. "The day may come when you do not thank your King for approving this. Still, I will permit it if you agree to wait on Harclow. Give her this, and let her know my displeasure. If she still insists that choosing another is her right, we will know for certain that she is mad."

"I will handle her. She will not deny your will."

The King handed over the parchment.

Morvan took it and left the chamber. He paused in the passage beyond, and leaned against the cool stones of its wall.

That thing inside him that had tried to soar yesterday finally burst free of its restraints.

* * *

Christiana and David were breaking their fast in the hall when Morvan arrived at their house. He sat down to join them.

"No popinjays here yet?" he asked.

Christiana rolled her eyes. "Seven in all came yesterday. Like locusts they descend. I expect it to be worse today."

He ate some bread and washed it down with ale. "Where is she?"

"Still asleep. She waited up with me for David to come home and is probably exhausted from yesterday."

"Aye. So many suitors. It must be tiring."

"Morvan—"

"It is all right, sister." He got to his feet. "Well, off to battle."

"Aye, and I see that you plan to give no quarter. The red pourpoint was a good choice. Draws attention to those damn eyes of yours," David said.

"I thought so."

"Do you want us to leave and clear the servants from the house so that you can seduce her in peace?"

"David!" Christiana gasped.

"I trust it won't come to that, but if so I will be discreet. You might stay off the second level."

"Morvan!"

He gave his sister's wide-eyed face a little pat before leaving the room.

He mounted the stairs and opened the door to her chamber. In the dim light from the shuttered window he saw her sleeping on the bed, the covers pulled up to her chin. He reached down and gently pushed away a curl that hung over her nose.

Within an hour she would be his. He had no doubt how

this morning would end. It had been fated from that first day when she opened the door to the longhouse and appeared to him in the halo of the afternoon sun. He had been led to her and she had been waiting for him, and they had both been spared from the plague so that they would have each other. Perhaps angels had been involved after all.

She was an unusual woman, and he admired her. She had briefly managed to create and lead the life that she wanted, and that was something even few men achieved. Yesterday she had fought to save that life. But it could not go on. The King had made that clear this morning. As Ascanio had once said, unique circumstances had permitted it, demanded it. In a world torn apart by war and plague, she had found herself. But it had been, in her own words, an interlude.

A part of him regretted that he would be the agent that ended that interlude, but she was better off with him than with someone else. Another man would either break her or be ruled by her. In either case, she would be in danger.

She would not have the strength this morning to be as cold as yesterday, he was certain. It was not in her nature and not in their bond, and, after all, one could only wear such heavy armor so long. Eventually she would submit to his reasoning, would accept his bargain, and she would never know that if she had stood firm he would have given her everything she asked for. Except Saint Meen. Once she was his, he would never let her leave him.

He shook her shoulder. "Awake, Anna. Come into the solar. We will speak now."

She waited until he had gone before rising from the bed and wrapping the robe around her. Dragging her fingers through her snarled curls, she looked down at her long body wrapped in the overlarge green garment. So much for the lessons in negotiation he had once given her. Well, if any man knew what he was getting in her, it was Morvan.

She did not expect an outright rejection. He probably would not have come himself for that. He planned to bargain.

When he had left yesterday, she'd realized that any chance of getting all she wanted went out the door with him. If victory were to be hers, it would have come immediately. In a matter of hours, she had lost the advantage.

He stood by the window behind the desk, wearing a red pourpoint and high boots and looking beautiful in the sun's morning light. Her heart lurched at the sight of him, and she remembered the reassurance she had given Ascanio that night he found them together. *I will not live out my life in some foolish jongleur's song, pining for a man who does not want me.* Yet that was exactly what she was asking for now, was it not? At Saint Meen there would have been time and distance to heal the pain, but in marriage it would be a scar reopened daily.

She padded her bare feet over to the chair by the fire, sat with her legs drawn up under her, and waited. He picked up the King's list from the desk and came over to her.

"There are five names. Have you met any of them?"

"Several. One seemed quite decent."

"Most of these men are well known for various scandals. There is no choice here, Anna. The King sought to beat you at your game. Only Sir Giles is suitable. Edward expected you to be told this."

"Perhaps the King is wiser than I thought. Perhaps his choice should be mine."

"Aye, it should be, and not Sir Giles. Edward has

changed his mind." He tossed the list into the fire. The flames jumped and quickly consumed it. "There is a new list. A very short one." He handed her the new parchment.

She read the King's firm statement of command, and the name of the man he had chosen. "Only you this time."

"Only me."

"You went to him. You asked for this, to place me at a disadvantage. Why did he agree?"

"He has a debt to me."

"So I have been bartered and made powerless in order to repay a debt. And to salve your pride. My horses are left with more dignity. Yesterday I offered to share my bread with you, but you have found a way to gobble it all. I will not agree to this. I will tell the King that I accept Sir Giles if necessary. If your King changed his mind once, he will change it again." She turned her gaze away. "You may go. I am done speaking of this with you."

He was in front of her suddenly, lifting her chin with his hand, forcing her to look up at him. "Hear me well, Anna. That is the *last* time that you will dismiss me."

"Aye, because if I have my way, this will be the last time that I *see* you."

"You will not have your way. You will marry the man of Edward's choosing, or he will deal harshly with you. Be glad that man is me."

"I cannot imagine why that news should hearten me."

"Because I know that you are not a saint, or a witch, or mad. And because I am willing to bargain with you, despite the King's command."

"I doubt that the terms will be generous."

"Generous enough, but if you insist on being willful, we can marry without them. Because we will marry, Anna, or the King will put you away with the duke's mother."

Her throat tightened. She searched his expression for a sign that the threat was an idle one, but saw only stern honesty.

"I suppose I should at least hear these terms," she muttered.

He moved another chair and sat beside her. "I offer you something that you did not ask for yesterday. Brittany herself. Sir Giles holds lands in England. Not only will he not negotiate with you at all, but he will just appoint a seneschal to your lands. You may never see your home again. If you refuse to marry at all, you can be sure that you will not."

"And if you someday once again have lands in England?"

"If I return here, it will be your choice whether to come."

She had not thought to ask for this concession. She wondered what she would have to lose to pay for it.

"I am also willing to accept the written contract as you described it, and your provisions for Catherine and Josce and the others on the estate."

Now they were down to it. "And the rest?"

He crossed his arms over his chest. "The lands near Rennes will be yours, but the income derives to me until you are widowed. I will hold it for you, and give it to you as you request unless I think your judgment ill advised. And the choice of retiring to Saint Meen while I live will not be yours. However, if after six years you are still set on it, we will talk."

Six years. It was a long time, but she had expected complete refusal on this point; it was embarrassing for a man to have his wife leave him thus. Still, for six years she would have to watch him go to his women.

"You must know that your last two conditions are unacceptable. The issue of children is up to God, but a marriage that is not consummated can be challenged. I will not risk that."

"People fake the proof, I am told."

He looked amused at that. "To hide a woman's previous experience. But a fowl's blood on the sheets will not suffice in your case. You are still a virgin."

"Who would know? You have my word—"

"If there are no children, it might be suspected. A simple examination would confirm it. Josce could decide to challenge the marriage. Gurwant could abduct you and learn the truth." He looked to the fire. "You might meet another man and try to end the marriage yourself. Of course, I would kill him before it got to that."

A heavy knot formed in her stomach. She would have to suffer the humiliation of Reading all over again, only this time with him determined to surmount his reaction while she knew what he truly felt. Perhaps, if the room was very dark, like the garden arbor . . .

"And after the marriage is consummated? After there is sufficient proof?"

"If you are determined not to have children I will not thwart you. If you refuse me, I will never force you."

She had his word now. Giving up the prospect of children couldn't be easy for him, she knew, no matter how dutiful he would find the process of making them with her.

"Well," she said dully, "I suppose I can manage one night."

"Aye. I think I can get us through that. But, Anna, that is the only right as your husband that I will compromise. There can be only one lord on the estate. I cannot have you wild and free, separate from my control, undermining my authority."

"As you undermined mine."

"I cannot be worrying about your safety every day."

She glared at him. "I told you when we first met that I would not change myself to please a husband."

"And I told you once never to look at a man thus while you negotiated with him," he replied. "You must accept me as your lord and submit to me as such. Do you accept that?"

The very word "submit" rankled her. She need not give in on this. She could spurn him and petition the King to find another. In time, without any negotiations, she might have all that she wanted.

He rose and bent over her, then turned her face to him, until her eyes had to meet his. She would not close them and give him the satisfaction of knowing his effect, but meeting his sparkling gaze was its own defeat, and the familiar mesmerization dazed her.

His lips touched hers in a kiss that managed to be gentle and possessive at the same time, a kiss that despite her defenses and her hurt, despite his arrogance of two nights before, wrapped her spirit in invisible arms.

"Our talk has been all of land and rights, Anna, but there is another reason for you to make this marriage. You know me as you will never know another man. What we shared in that shelter was a rare thing." He kissed her again—a chaste kiss, but full of his will and power and the intimacy that he spoke of. She was, as always, defenseless against it.

He had been using that spell against her from the start, with this end in mind. She believed that, but still fell under his power once more.

"Come to the desk and write to the King," he said, lifting her by the hand. He slid his arm around her shoulders and guided her toward the table. "I will deliver your acceptance myself."

Morvan carried Anna's letter back to the King. Edward, no doubt feeling relieved of the burden of his old oath, insisted they share some wine and even related a few stories about Morvan's father. Finally taking his leave, Morvan made his way back to Anna.

He found her in the small garden behind the house, surrounded by the bare branches and gnarled stumps of winter. The only green was a vine that ran along the ground and up a stark trunk, and she was crouched down examining it, her fingers poking in the dirt to see how it grew. She rose as he approached, dusting the dirt from her hands.

Smudges of soil dotted her nose. Her golden curls, longer now than when they first met, fell with their wild abandon about her shoulders. He felt an exhilarating joy at knowing that she belonged to him now. He doubted that possessing Harclow again would affect him as powerfully.

He gazed at her lovely face, drawn with worry. Reaching out, he brushed the smudge from her nose.

"It is done."

CHAPTER 18

THREE MEN LUGGED IN the heavy round tub and placed it by the fire. Other servants began bringing in buckets of hot water. Anna watched from a stool by the hearth, pulled her big robe around her more tightly, and wiped the sleep from her eyes.

Over on her bed a group of women chatted and caught up on news and gossip. Ruth and Catherine entered with the wedding gown and laid it out amongst them. They all fell to examining the green velvet and fashionable cut that had been designed and started in England and completed by her own servants.

They filled the castle, these strangers, these wives of lords and vassals. She hadn't seen most of them since her mother died, and before that they had been adult guests of little interest to a child. But now they were suddenly her friends and confidants, immersing themselves in the wedding preparations, getting underfoot, descending on her repeatedly as they had moments ago, this time to raise her from her sleep to begin the long procedure of bathing and dressing for the ceremony.

Four weeks gone in the snap of a finger. Four weeks, first of travel and then of hard work and preparation, of cleaning and supervising and planning. One week now of strangers everywhere, first the vassals and their households and then the long processions as the neighboring lords arrived with their retinues.

She watched the last of the buckets of hot water being brought in for her bath. She had carefully ignored the reason for all of the preparation. She had avoided thinking about the upcoming wedding.

But now it was here, an imminent reality. She had been forced to face it squarely yesterday morning when Ascanio came to discuss the ceremony. In his most priestly manner he had described what she was to do. When he had finished with the vows, he had recommended an additional gesture on her part that was not required or expected.

He had advised her to kneel before her new husband.

The suggestion had raised her ire. "Did Morvan ask you to request this?"

"He doesn't even know that I speak of it."

"It is no longer done in these parts, Ascanio."

"Sometimes it is. Anna, there is some resentment among the people over this marriage. A saint should be pure, to their minds, and they think an English king has forced you to debasement. And while the vassals and lords like Morvan, and are inclined to accept him, they watch you closely. The ones with the distant fiefs, Baldwin and Gaultier, do so especially. They are wondering if you marry against your will. One of them may decide that the daughter of Roald de Leon will welcome the chance to be free of this English husband soon."

She hadn't noticed anyone looking at her at all, let alone watching her closely. But Ascanio, in his quiet way, would have seen all.

"I cannot make this decision now."

"When the time comes, do what you will."

Anna stood up and walked to the tub. It would kill her to do as Ascanio had asked, but she did not want it thought the marriage had been forced on her. She may not have welcomed it, but that was different. In the interests of harmony she would kneel, but she would also explain why to Morvan, so he did not misinterpret it as submission.

She glanced at Catherine and then at the women on the bed. Catherine understood and made some excuse for the ladies to accompany her down to the hall.

Lady Gervaise, Haarold's wife, disengaged herself from the group and came over to where Anna was lowering herself into the tub. She moved a stool and sat herself down.

Lady Gervaise was a thin-faced, purse-lipped woman of middle years. She had taken an unwelcomed supervisory role since she had arrived, making it obvious that she thought Catherine and Anna were too young to be trusted to do everything properly.

"You know, your mother and I were great friends," she said.

Anna busied herself washing her hair.

"Since your poor mother isn't here, and you have no older women kin, I think it best if you and I had a little talk. It is important that you understand your duties."

"I know my duties."

"Do you? My husband has told me of your life here."

"I know my duties, Gervaise."

Gervaise paused at her tone, but only paused. Too bad. Anna had meant to silence her permanently.

"Do you understand what is expected of you tonight? You were raised in that abbey—"

"I know all about it. Do not trouble yourself. I know what to expect." Saints, did she ever. The sick knot twisting inside her never forgot.

"That is well. However, Haarold has expressed some concern that you will know your place once you are married. It is important that you honor your husband's rights."

"Oh, my lady, I was taught that at great length at the abbey. In fact, we had to memorize it as a lesson and recite it daily, for most of the abbey's wards would eventually leave to marry."

"Memorize it? Of what do you speak?"

"The Holy Writ of Woman's Duties, of course. It was chiseled on the back of the Ten Commandments that God gave Moses, was it not?" She began reciting. "Thy husband is thy lord and over thee in all things. Remember to honor thy husband and be abjectly grateful for any generosity. Thy body and person belong to thy husband to do with as he will, even to beat or kill. Thou hast nothing, but all that is thine is thy husband's first. . . ."

First Gervaise looked confused, but as she realized that Anna was making this up, she became shocked. When the list continued, her eyes turned devilish and her pursed mouth twitched.

"Thy husband need not explain anything, but thou shalt answer his questions promptly," Gervaise interrupted with a giggle.

"Thou shalt offer thy husband no counsel, for as a woman thou art by nature a fool."

"Thou shalt remain pure to thy husband, but he may whore about at will and thou shalt not upbraid him for it."

They continued on, topping each other as they expanded the Holy Writ. Lady Gervaise gasped with laughter and put a bony hand on Anna's arm. "Child, I think that you will do just fine. Is there anything that you want to ask me?"

There were a lot of things she wouldn't have minded learning from an older woman, but Lady Gervaise was not the one to ask, even if they had shared this little rebellion together.

"I expect that I will learn as I go along, like most women."

"Then I will leave you to your bath. It is known that you are overly modest and do not like others present. The abbey's influence, no doubt. Although that will have to end tonight." She raised her eyebrows. "At least Sir Morvan is a handsome man, and seems to know what he is about with women. And you are not a child. In that you are luckier than most."

The door closed behind her.

Grateful for the respite of privacy, Anna sank lower in the warm water.

Tonight. She had managed not to think of that for four weeks, but a good deal of last night had been spent worrying about nothing else. She was resigned and prepared, but not convinced that Morvan was.

She had seen little of him since the betrothal. A week after they returned from England, he had made another journey to Brest, not returning until the morning that the vassals began arriving. He brought back two jongleurs to entertain, and the news that he had recruited three knights and five men-at-arms who would soon come into service for him.

It had been a productive journey, but an unnecessary one. She suspected he had made it in order to avoid her.

He had said that he could get them through this, but last night she had concluded that he would need a little help. She had a plan in place to make things easier for both of them.

"Master Phillipe," Anna exclaimed, taking his hands in her own. "I had not seen you in here." She had nursed Phillipe during the plague, and had tasted with him that intimacy that she had also known with Morvan and Ascanio.

"I am honored to be here, my lady," he said in the formal way he always spoke to her. "Your husband was kind enough to invite me."

Phillipe politely offered his good wishes and then drifted away. The merchant still acted very awkward around her. He probably always would.

She looked to the distant wall, where Morvan spoke with Ascanio. Her new husband had a very black look on his face. Something was wrong.

Her mind turned to Phillipe again, and for the first time she paid careful attention to the people feasting at the wedding in the hall. It was very crowded, full of the normal castle folk and also the servants and retainers of their guests. Most of the town's people and the estate's workers celebrated out in the yards.

She surveyed a sea of faces and noticed other people whom she hadn't expected in the hall besides Phillipe. Her eyes moved quickly, picking out a face here and there.

The butcher's young son. The forester's wife. Even the babe, not yet two years old. They were all here, all of the people who had survived while she nursed them. She hadn't even noticed.

Morvan retook the lord's chair to her left.

"Is something amiss?" she asked.

"A simple thing. Ascanio will see to it."

"Not so simple, Morvan, if he told you of it."

"Some of your people are praying in the field for your saintly virtue, asking the angels to deliver you from me. Perhaps you would like to join them."

She pushed back her chair. "Nay, but I will go speak with them."

He grabbed her arm. "You will not."

"One word from me and they will leave."

"One look at the expression that your face has held this last hour and they will know that you welcome their prayers."

"That is not true," she lied. She had felt so gay until the sun went down, but in truth *had* offered a few prayers for deliverance since.

"Do you think that you can hide such things from me? I can feel your moods more clearly than I feel this velvet. I do not know what is in your head, but I remember well the terms that you first offered me. Yet know this, Anna. You are mine now."

He glanced down the table and beckoned Catherine. She hurried over. "Soon," he ordered sharply.

Anna stared at the silver plate in front of her. Along the polished edges she could see her reflection. She had removed the veil, and her curls fell on either side of a pale face. She gazed at the distant look in her eyes. He was right. She had not been playing her role well this last hour.

She tilted the plate to see better. An emerald necklace glittered back. She remembered seeing it in Morvan's bags while he was ill, and had been surprised when it arrived as his wedding gift. He had explained that it had been given to him by a woman in Caen after he helped save her family from the English army when the city fell.

She touched the stones hanging from their gold chains. One emerald would have been a sufficient gift. He might be taking all that she had, but he had given her everything of his in return.

She rested her hand on his. "They are all here, aren't they? The ones who survived like us? Master Phillipe said that you invited them to sit here with the favored guests."

"I thought that you might want them here."

His thoughtfulness moved her. She raised his hand and kissed it.

Hoots and shouts along the table distracted her. The ladies came to her chair. Catherine touched her arm. "Come, sister."

Morvan released her hand. His eyes flashed into hers before the women hustled her away.

In her chamber, she stood numbly as the women twittered around her, preparing her for bed. Lady Gervaise pulled back the new coverings and sprinkled some scented oil. Two of the others began getting her out of her gown.

Finally she was naked, and they pushed her to the bed. She climbed in and they tucked the covers over her so that her breasts showed. That horrible twisting began again in her belly.

She caught Catherine's gown. "Get them out of here *now*. And go down slowly to the hall. I need some time."

As soon as Catherine herded the ladies from the

chamber, Anna jumped out of the bed and went to her trunk. She grabbed a long woolen shift and slid it over her head. She blew out the two night candles, then untied the bed curtains. She peered inside at the total darkness that she had created.

Those lords, those strangers, would probably insist on bringing Morvan up here. They might even come into the chamber. She could not, would not, be lying here if they did.

Grabbing her robe, she scurried over to the gallery door. Let them tease Morvan about the skittish virgin if they came in and found her gone. After all, she *was* a skittish virgin.

Morvan tried to hide his impatience.

How long could it take nine women to undress one girl? They were probably sitting around telling stories of their own wedding nights. He glanced down the table at frowning Haarold and bland Fouke. God, he hoped not. He'd be lucky if Anna didn't jump into the sea.

He had been very restrained this month. Avoiding her had helped, and visiting Brest had yielded practical benefits. But the days since his return had been a slow torture of anticipation.

Even as he sat beside her at meals and joined conversations, a part of his mind relived that night at Reading. Expanded it. Completed it. His mental lovemaking had gotten much more creative than it would be this night. She was frightened enough already. About what? He didn't know for sure.

A noisy commotion from the stairs claimed his attention. He was out of his chair as soon as Catherine appeared, and a roar of laughter swept the hall. Baldwin

and Gaultier and several of the younger lords fell in behind him. Ascanio, carrying a vial, appeared at his side.

His companions amused themselves all the way up
the stairs. They made innuendos about her skill at arms
and recommendations on the use of his own weapon.
They voiced concerns that she might be too much for
one man and offered to help. He parried the jests, but in
truth he wasn't really listening. His spirit was already in
the chamber with her.

At the door he raised a hand. "Only the priest, to bless
the bed." A chorus of complaints greeted that, but he
stood firm until they drifted away.

"She will appreciate your sparing her dignity,"
Ascanio said.

"Sparing *our* dignity. Enough is enough."

He opened the door.

She was not there. The bed curtains had been drawn,
but he knew she did not lie within them.

He glimpsed an instant of profound relief flash on
Ascanio's face. Well, whatever she was up to, she had
spared one man a moment of hell.

He lit a rush and bent the flame to the candles flanking the bed. Then he tied back the curtains while Ascanio
sprinkled the holy water and said his blessing.

Ascanio turned raised eyebrows to him. Morvan gestured to the gallery door, which stood ajar.

"I imagine she is afraid," Ascanio said.

"Aye. Though about what I have yet to learn."

Ascanio shrugged. "It is normal. She is still a child in
these things."

Morvan looked at the bed and thought a moment.
"Not entirely."

Ascanio laughed. "Since all has turned out well, I will
not upbraid you for that." He headed to the door.

"If you were not a priest, it might have been you," Morvan found himself saying.

"But I am a priest, and so it is you."

Morvan listened to Ascanio's footsteps grow dim.

Then he turned to the gallery door.

CHAPTER 19

ANNA HEARD THE LOW MUMBLE of voices in the chamber, and then silence. She crossed her arms more tightly over her body to contain the unsettled emotions that churned inside her.

She had made a terrible mistake in turning to Morvan. It would have been easier if it had been a stranger for whom she felt nothing.

She felt Morvan's presence as she always did, and tonight it quickly filled the small gallery, sending an unwelcome, expectant thrill through her. She turned her gaze from the sea to the doorway, where he leaned against the threshold watching her. The dim light leaking from the chamber found the sparkle of eyes that glinted like the stars dotting the sky above.

"Will I need my sword?" he asked.

She turned back to the sea. "They are gone?"

"It was only Ascanio, blessing the bed. You should have known that I would not let the others in."

He stayed at the doorway, but she felt him all around her, as if something dangerous that he normally restrained had been let loose. It had been like this that first night in the shelter. It was why she had wanted to leave.

She couldn't leave now.

"I find that I am not ready for this," she said.

"Perhaps you never would be. It is time nonetheless."

Inevitable. Now. She felt horribly vulnerable in the confined dimensions of the gallery, but even the infinity of the sky and sea wouldn't be space enough to hide.

"You will come inside now, Anna." His voice was soft, but she recognized the edge in it.

She glanced back at the doorway, and he was gone. She steeled herself and moved.

She stepped into the chamber and closed the door behind her. Morvan stood by the fire, watching its flames. Waiting for her. He had relit the candles by the bed and retied the curtains. She frowned at that. Surely he must know that the dark could only help.

"I have decided that you were wrong, Morvan. We don't have to do this. We will fake the evidence and I will swear an oath to you never to reveal the truth."

He turned to face her. His lids lowered, but they could not hide the flashing sparks.

The silence became crushing. She kept her back straight and her gaze level, but could feel her determination retreating before the force emanating from him.

"You do not know me well, if you think that I will agree to that," he said. "The ceremony and ritual have unsettled you, that is all. Come to the fire. Warm yourself and drink some wine."

He filled a goblet and carried it back to the hearth. She dared not move.

"Stop acting like some terrified and untouched child bride, Anna. Come here now."

The rebuke and command had their effect. She strode over to him, took the goblet, and then claimed the only chair. She drank a good swallow of the wine.

"I thought that you do not force women."

"Perhaps that is only because I have never had to. You, for example, have been willing enough every time that I touched you. You will be again."

She stared at this bold statement of his power over her. Stared with annoyance even as her traitorous body tingled. That invisible presence of his was something he used at his whim, and now it surged out and surrounded her.

"Do not think to pursue this, Anna. I warned you down below not to try. This night ends only one way. This is not Reading, and I do not give you a choice. You are mine and I will take you."

Her heart began pounding in a confused, panicky beat. He came toward her.

Her awareness of his closeness grew anxious and fretful. She stared hard at the goblet. "Then put out the candles, Morvan, and let us get this over with quickly."

She sensed his hand reach toward her even before his fingers touched her curls.

"I am not inclined to do anything very quickly—I might hurt you more than I had to. And I prefer the candles lit. I would see you and have you see me. I would have you remember the man who claims you."

His slow strokes through her hair made her scalp and neck tingle. So that was how it was to be. He would continue the lie he began that first night in this room. He would pretend desire and she was supposed to pretend she believed it. She could not go through with that. She did not want her own passion for him used in that way. She did not care if he had to hurt her.

What her mind wanted was very different from what her body needed, however. His fingers traced along her neck and around the edge of her robe, slowly pushing the fabric down her shoulders. Shivering tremors shook her, and the knot in her belly began untying to make room for a different, more compelling fullness.

He pushed her hair aside. Bending low, he kissed the exposed nape. She closed her eyes to the exquisite chills. Mixed with the pleasure, however, was confusion and a profound sense of danger.

She bolted from the chair and sought the relative sanctuary of the hearth.

A protracted silence filled the chamber. She didn't turn to look at him.

"There is nowhere to go, Anna. Come back to me now. There is nothing to fear with me."

There is everything to fear.

The force of her reaction stunned her. "Fear" was the word he had given this, not her, and she was very, very sure it was not fear. That would make no sense.

She faced him. She would be blunt and at least be spared the mockery of a seduction.

"I am not afraid. I just find that I don't much like being some man's duty in such things. I know that you lied about Reading and why you left. I have always known that I am not the kind of woman that men want in that way. Not even you in the end."

A series of reactions quickly passed on his face. Surprise. Amusement. Long thoughtfulness.

"So that is where you found the rocks to repair your breached walls," he said. "I cannot speak for other men, but I have wanted you since that first day. I have been mad with the want of you. But it does not matter if you believe me. You will find the proof of it soon enough."

But the proof burned in his eyes even as he spoke, for he permitted the firm control to drop. She quickly turned away from the onslaught of male desire that surged across the space to her.

Strong hands came to rest on her waist. He was behind her. She felt the heat of him all along her back, and heard her heart beating too loudly and too hard.

He nuzzled her ear. "You have been deceiving yourself, Anna, and that isn't like you. Perhaps at first you thought thus about that night, but you knew that I spoke the truth when I explained that I stopped because of my promise. Your heart knew. Yet it was easier to go to your abbey believing otherwise, I think."

He kissed her hair and bent his head so his lips could reach her neck. She fought the mounting fullness in her belly and the hollow ache between her legs, and recoiled from the shocking recognition of the truth in his words.

"That night surprised you in other ways, I think," he said. "Your fear tonight is not the usual one, is it? You are not afraid of a virgin's pain or a man's taking. It is a woman's giving that terrifies you."

The fire's flames suddenly grew and danced around her, as if magically reflected a hundred times in mirrors of polished metal. But the only mirror present was his devastating knowledge of her. Even as she sought the argument to refute him, his last words echoed through her, down to the depths of her heart, and the terror itself responded *Aye, aye.*

A stranger. Easier with a stranger. No giving. No loss. No power.

He reached around and slowly untied the sash of her robe. "But you will give yourself to me now," he commanded gently. "It will be a simple thing, for your soul made the choice long ago."

Something in her tried to rebel, but the robe fell open and his hands found her body through the shift. A rush of exquisite sensation crushed the resistance.

He stroked the length of her, sliding the robe off and letting it fall in a pool at their feet. He stayed behind her, kissing her shoulders and neck, his arms surrounding and turning her a little so that his lips could also reach her face. She pressed against his warmth while his hands caressed her, coming up to stroke her breasts, causing pleasurable shocks to quake through her. She moaned and arched, and he caught her hips with one arm and pressed her to him while the other hand continued its slow arousal.

"I have wanted you too long." He held her, his fingers circling and stroking her nipples, his warm breath enflaming her skin, his kisses biting her. The wonderful madness rose through her.

He pushed at the shoulders of her shift and the soft wool fluttered down her arms and hips, following the robe to the floor. She trembled at the sudden vulnerability of her nakedness. He stepped away as his hands stroked over her back to her hips and bottom. His invisible gaze felt warmer than the heat from the hearth, more arousing than the caress of his hands.

He turned her to him. His fingers drifted, feathering over her. "You are beautiful." He held her breasts as he looked at them. She gasped as his thumbs grazed her nipples.

"Beautiful. All of you. Your spirit and your strength and your body. I have never told you that, have I? They were words I had used too often before, and they felt too cheap for you." He let his gaze and caress do their worst, and by the time he pulled her back to him her body was crying with desire.

His controlled passion broke loose. He abruptly lifted her in an embrace that raised her breasts to his mouth. "Did you really think that I would let you deny what waits for us this night?" he said, his ragged voice smothered against her skin.

It felt so good. Too good. It always had. She abandoned herself to the flows and peaks of passion as he drew on her breasts and his lips and teeth pressed along her neck and chest. Through the fog, in the distance, she heard her own sighs.

He lowered her and moved away from the hearth, his arm on her shoulders and his hand on her breast. "Come to bed now."

Somehow she found her legs and went with him. She climbed into the bed and watched the emergence of his beautiful hard body as he stripped his clothes off. She ached impatiently for him, but the waiting and watching brought its own tantalizing pleasure.

He stood beside the bed a moment, his eyes slowly moving up the length of her, their bright flames of desire burning hotly. She let her own gaze linger on that handsome face for a moment, and then drift lower to his chiseled chest and shoulders, then lower still. He came down beside her.

The feel of his skin and warmth along her body intoxicated her. She wrapped her arms around him to hold on to the sensation. He gave her a consuming kiss as his hand sought her breasts. She moved into his caress, instantly as excited as she had been moments before.

His head turned and he watched her body react to his touch. He traced around her breasts' swells, teasing her, before his fingers tantalized her nipples. She turned her head to the arm on which he rested and pressed her mouth to its warmth, tasting where her mouth could reach.

Her body and her skin were alert and waiting every inch of the way for the rough pressure of his fingers as he caressed down her body. Long before his mouth drifted to her breasts and his hand lowered to her thighs, she was frantic.

The pleasure felt so delicious that she thought she would scream or die. She knew no space or time anymore, just a small world of flickering light and incredible sensation.

As he brought her dazed passion higher and higher, she became aware of his caresses moving over her stomach and thighs. All of her body's attention focused on that hand that ventured so close to her crying need. When he slid his hand between her thighs, her hips rose anxiously to meet his touch.

He looked at her, watching first her body as her legs opened to accept him, and then her face as his fingers stroked, sending her into a need that mounted and grew until it totally undid her. Nothing existed anymore but the incredible pleasure he gave her, a pleasure so intense that the rest of her body didn't exist either, a pleasure filled with wonderful, shivering anguish.

"Your passion is beautiful, Anna. Glorious. Give me all of it. Come to me now."

He kept touching her gently but insistently, sending her to a wonderful, horrible place. Invisible walls closed in on her slowly, containing the sensation into a smaller and smaller spot, increasing its intensity as they compressed it. Everything in her wanted to break through those walls, and the need became excruciating.

"Come to me," he said. "It is but a small step."

The walls shattered. The intensity coursed out from its center through all of her. For an instant she wasn't alive at all, but existing only in a dark point of perfect pleasure. It continued to flow through her in slower waves. While she floated in the sensation, Morvan eased on top of her.

She wanted the closeness and the fullness and even the pain seemed a part of that and so she didn't mind. She held on to him as his careful but relentless press claimed her to an intimacy that would be his alone. She knew when the virgin tear was coming from the way he paused and captured her gaze with his own. She knew that he did it to brand both of their minds with the memory, but also to distract her. Even so it was a burning tear, and he stopped, buried inside her.

Morvan closed his eyes to the overwhelming pleasure and fought a brief battle for control. She was beautiful. Beautiful in her abandon, in the silent scream of her ecstasy. In her eyes, still dark and liquid with her passion, he saw the desire that he filled even as her body wanted to rebel against this invasion.

He briefly lost himself in the soft warmth, and felt her sheathing him tightly, accepting him slowly, opening to him. Her fingertips lightly stroked his back and his breath caught in his throat.

"Is it done then?" she whispered.

It was easy to forget how little she knew of these things. "I will finish quickly. I know that I have hurt you." He rose up on his arms and moved carefully inside her.

She smiled at the sensation, drew a hand between them and placed it on his chest. "I am not one of your delicate court ladies, Morvan. Stay with me."

The request surprised and disarmed him, since he knew that she must be sore. An unfamiliar emotion poured through him, and his chest clenched. He slid his hand down and closed on her leg. "Then bend your knees up like this, Anna."

He moved in her accepting body again, deeper now, and the well-known pleasure flooded him. But that new emotion joined it, transforming it, making it something stronger and more than physical. He felt as raw and exposed as he had that first night with her, and the connection spread like a river undammed. He looked in her eyes and saw her awareness of the intimacy claiming them. He also sensed her fear of it. With the thrusts of his body and the gaze of his eyes he commanded her to accept this other thing, this total joining that had been waiting for them since that desperate November night.

He knew when she succumbed to it, when the power vanquished her guarded separateness, when she gave herself to him. He felt the walls crumble, sensed the sweetness flow through her and into him, saw the wonder of it in her eyes. In the small world where they joined, nothing existed but the two of them wholly together.

He reached down between them to bring her with him to the end. Soon her frenzy began forcing him to fulfillment. She clawed at his shoulders as the release climaxed through her again. She screamed this time, pulling him into her and crying his name. In the echoes and eddies of her ecstasy he came to her hard, the profound emotions splitting his mind, the intensity making his soul shake.

"Aye, my love," he said, breathing out the last of his passion.

Anna held him, her arms and legs wrapped around his body. She was afraid to let him go, afraid that the feeling would go with him and never return. And she was terrified of the emotion itself, and of the vulnerability it contained.

He had been waiting for this, she realized, since that first night. It was what he had offered her in the shelter, what she had refused. It was why he had stayed, why he protected her, why his will kept reaching out to her in that almost physical way.

He had called her "My love." Did he know that he had? Perhaps in the space and time of this bed he had meant it. But he had no doubt known this before with other women, and probably better and stronger. It was something that he controlled, and accepted or rejected at will.

What now? He had used their bond to bring her to this. She had felt his spirit demanding it, absorbing her into him, forcing her to acknowledge her love for him. Was that love supposed to change everything? Change her? Would refusing such unity be the ultimate unnatural act?

He took her face in his hand. His gaze met hers, and she knew that he read every thought. "Do not be afraid. I have always known that this would be the easiest part of our marriage." He pushed some pillows against the board, then rolled over to them. "Come and lie with me now. Sleep in my arms."

Unaccustomed as she was to sharing a bed, she woke after a few hours. The candles still burned, and she raised her head to look at him propped on the pillows. She could imagine that handsome face as it had been as a child and a youth and a newly dubbed knight.

Her gaze dropped to his chest. It was bared by the sheet crumpled at his waist, and she traced the angles of his muscles with invisible fingers.

He took her hand in his. He raised it to his mouth and kissed it, and then placed it on his body. "You can touch me if you want. I am yours as you are mine."

"I thought that you were asleep. Do you always know when I look at you?"

"Always. I feel you just as you have felt me."

She let her fingers drift over his chest. He might not, Anna realized, be in love with her the way he had been, and perhaps still was, with his Elizabeth. But he did love her. Their bond gave them that. And the desire, for as long as it lasted, was undeniable.

She gave him a kiss as her fingers found the ridges of his abdomen. His hand closed over hers and held it still. He had not opened his eyes. "I should warn you that this is going to get you into trouble," he said, smiling.

She laughed and raised up on her elbow and deliberately stroked him again. She watched the subtle signs in his face and muscles which told her that the power did not just go one way in these things.

He took her hand again. "If you are determined to seduce a man, you must show some courage, Anna." He guided her hand lower.

She was fascinated by the controlled but distinct reactions she was able to get from him. A lighthearted inspiration struck.

"Look at me," she whispered. "I want to see your eyes when I touch you."

His eyes flashed open in shock at hearing his own love words spoken back to him. Laughing, he threw her down on her back. "Another time you can play at controlling me," he said as he came over her. "I will even teach you how. But this night is mine."

CHAPTER 20

FOR THREE DAYS ANNA LIVED an idyll of pleasure. Morvan kept her close to him during the revelry and feasts celebrating the marriage. She lived in a state of barely dormant arousal, waiting for the changes in his touch or look that said he wanted her.

He didn't always wait for the night, and their delight in each other became the object of friendly jokes whenever he led her to the stairs on impulse and spirited her up to the chamber. She didn't care about the teasing, but only about the furious excitement he gave and showed her in the dusty afternoon light filtering through her southern windows.

Three nights of flickering flames and passion. Three days of bright colors and tournaments. A paradise of pleasure and laughter.

On the fourth day the lords and vassals departed with

their wives and retainers. Anna and Morvan bid them farewell and watched the long lines file out the castle gate.

The household yawned and found its natural rhythms. Servants removed the extra pallets from the chambers and returned the looms and stools to the sewing room since it would no longer be needed for sleeping. Everyone took their old places at the tables. Carlos left before dinner to work at the horse farm. Catherine resumed her duties managing the women.

Life became normal again. For everyone but Anna.

After the crushing activity of the last month, she found herself suddenly with nothing to do. The abrupt contrast left her restless. In the afternoon Morvan took a much-needed nap. In her bed. In her bower. She called for Shadow, deciding that a good ride would shake the boredom that nagged her.

Her horse arrived at the same time as three mounted guards. "Where are you off to?" she asked as she swung up and fixed her stupid skirt around her legs.

"We go with you, my lady," one of them said.

"The groom made a mistake. I will return shortly."

"It is my lord's order, my lady. You aren't to ride alone."

She stared at them. The one who spoke was Morvan's man, but the other two were her own guards who had obeyed her command for months.

"I need no guard. I am going for a brief ride."

"It is Sir Morvan's will, my lady. He informed us and the grooms some days ago."

His words were like a splash of water waking her from a played-out dream.

She could easily outdistance these men and lose them, she knew. Instead she swung her leg and dropped from the saddle. She marched into the keep and spent the afternoon pacing the upper battlements.

At the evening meal she told Morvan what had happened.

"Aye, I want a guard with you when you leave. It is only for your protection."

"I do not need them."

"You do need them. It is no more than most ladies have for their safety, especially in these times."

"I am not most ladies, and Shadow can outrun any brigand's horse. I prefer to ride alone."

"You will get used to it. Ignore them. It is how it will be, for I will not risk you. And until Gurwant is long gone and that matter settled, I do not want you leaving the castle at all unless I know."

Another splash of water. "I do not accept this."

He smiled, but his eyes narrowed. "Accept it. It is for your protection. It is done."

Morvan's chests and clothes had been put in her chamber while the guests attended, but had not been removed during the day's rearrangements. That night as he fell asleep, peaceful and sated with their lovemaking, she admitted that he probably never intended to move out. She looked at the handsome face half buried in its pillow just inches from her head. Would he do that, too? Deny her this sanctuary?

He had negotiated with her too well that day in David's house. He had used her ignorance and misunderstanding against her. He had given up very little in the concessions he made, for he'd never expected her to want them in the end. If they kept up like this he would have his pleasure at his will, and even his heir in good time. He planned to tie her to him with passion and a family so that after six years she would never want to go to Saint Meen.

Did he expect her to capitulate on all points? If she could maintain an illusion that he was in love with her, maybe she would. But he had known this magic before with other women, and most likely would again. He desired her and had called her "My love." But there was love and then there was love.

After all, Ascanio and Carlos and Josce loved her. She felt sure that Morvan did not face the vulnerability that really being in love held, or the ache that racked her now as she faced her choices. Perhaps he had felt it with Elizabeth, but not with Anna de Leon. Yet he knew love's power with women. He expected her to be absorbed and made docile by it, much as he had tried the night before the battle.

She had not bargained for this. If she let love do this to her, there might be nothing left of her when he eventually turned away from her to desire someone else.

The next day she stayed in the keep, noticing how irrelevant she had become in this household run so smoothly by Catherine and commanded by Morvan. He had married the wrong sister. Catherine was the kind of woman men wanted.

She reminded herself why she had struck the bargain with him. It was time to hold him to it.

When she rose to retire after the evening meal, he came with her. She stopped him at the door to the lord's solar.

"I have had your things moved in here," she said. "I will sleep alone tonight."

He looked at her hard, as if trying to probe her mind. "You are serious."

"Aye."

"I don't believe this."

"Believe it."

He pulled her to him with one arm while the other hand took her face. "You will not deny me and what we have shared." He grazed her mouth with his. "I have only to touch you and you want me. In this you are mine."

It was a bold assertion of the naked truth, but it only stiffened her back. "I don't deny what we have shared, but I will not be a slave to it."

"You speak nonsense. I do not treat you like a slave."

She felt the heat of his anger, and his desire. His arm gripped her more closely. She remembered that night after Isabella's dinner when he had been like this.

"That remains to be seen, doesn't it?" she said quietly.

That checked him. The dangerous fire dimmed. He released her. "This is madness. Go to your sacred bower. I can see that it is time I recalled the exact details of our agreement."

She walked away from him and entered her chamber. She dismissed Ruth, and prepared for bed alone. Then she laid out her garments for the morning.

A tunic and hose, and boots for riding.

Morvan waited patiently for the groom to saddle the bay courser.

He had always expected trouble with Anna, but not this soon and not this boldly expressed. And especially not coming on the heels of last night's rejection.

He had underestimated her. The average woman would be besotted still—but then, she had never been the average woman. He probably wouldn't have wanted her if she had been, but that didn't make this blatant challenge any less significant.

He lounged against the stable wall, forcing a fragile control on his anger. Ascanio and Gregory hustled across the yard. "About an hour ago," Gregory said. "The guards thought she had permission."

Short of announcing that she was a prisoner, Morvan knew, it would be hard to keep her from having the gate opened. She was the lady, and had some authority. She was also a lot smarter than any of the guards. He wondered what ruse she had used.

"Perhaps I should come with you," Ascanio offered.

"Do I look that dangerous?"

"Fit to kill, actually."

"Then my face shows more than I feel. I will not hurt her over this. I assume that she has gone to the horse farm."

Ascanio shrugged. "It is her joy and her life."

"I have not forbidden her that."

"Not yet."

The groom led out the courser and Morvan swung into the saddle. He looked down at Ascanio, and the anger he barely held in check surged. "Do you disapprove of how I'm handling my wife, priest?"

"Since you ask, I will say this. Remember what makes her who she is. Especially since it is clear that *she* will never forget, no matter how much pleasure you give her."

He would have struck down a different man. Instead he pivoted the bay and headed to the gate.

He looked straight ahead, his eyes on the rising portcullis, but he could sense the guards and servants turning to watch him pass. They all knew that she had defied him, and that he was going after her. Her rebellion delighted some of them, the ones none too happy to be given an English lord at the command of an English king.

He galloped across the field. He wanted to separate this from last night, but it was not a thing apart. Never in his life had a woman refused him like that, and now his wife, *who belonged to him*, had dared it. His control of women had always been complete after he bedded them, and with Anna it had not just been pleasure that he gave when he touched her.

He did not care why she had turned away from that. He only knew that, bargain or not, he would not tolerate it. He would not permit her to deny him that temporary but complete unity.

He had thought to make the changes in her life gradual so that she might not mind them too much, but she was too smart for that. She had seen the pattern and knew where it led.

Well, so much for subtlety. He had tried passion. Now he would use reasoning. And if that failed . . .

He slowed the bay when he found the forest path leading to the farm. The direction of his thoughts made him pause. He stopped the horse and forced reason on his chaotic reactions.

He knew how he was supposed to handle this. He had seen lords use their belts or rods on wives or daughters. But he had never been one of the heads nodding approval, nor had he ever hurt a woman with his strength. The idea of punishing Anna sickened him, especially when he began considering the implications of it, of what it would do to both of them, and of what it might destroy.

His distracted gaze fell to the ground. His blood chilled.

He had noted Shadow's fresh prints on sandy patches as he crossed the field. On the main path they had covered earlier tracks, probably made by Carlos. But now, mixed among them, were the prints of two, maybe three, other animals.

Any sympathy that he felt for her, any inclination toward understanding, disappeared as the cold fear he had known when she was wounded claimed him again. He moved his bay to a trot, his gaze never wavering from the confusion of marks passing below him.

Her damn stubborn will would get her killed if he let it. He had been too careful of her pride. He would lock her up if he had to.

Finally Shadow's marks disappeared into the brush, heading toward the farm, but the others continued along the path. Only then did the horrible foreboding lift. All that was left then was a cold resolve born of protective possession.

Anna charged the black mare across the pasture. She was a spirited animal, young and willful, and would need a lot of work before she would be suitable for the tasks for which she had been bred. A workhorse, that meant, since she was female. She was strong and fast, and would make a fine courser. But knights would never ride coursers that were mares.

The ride exalted her. It had been weeks. *Weeks.* She reveled in the speed and danger and power. She wished she hadn't saddled the mare so she could stand on her back like she sometimes did with Shadow.

Alone and free. It would be short-lived and she would pay for it, but by God, how her spirit soared. *I think that you do it because you enjoy it.* Aye, Morvan, you saw more clearly than I. Do not make me choose between you and this, because I don't know how it will go. Don't ask me to choose between you and myself.

She aimed the mare toward the farmhouse, then reined her in when they arrived. She jumped down and handed her over to Louis, whose turn it was to guard the farm. She darted into a shed and emerged just as Carlos came around the building.

"Work with me, Carlos." She held up the two practice swords.

"Nay. He will have my head."

"He hasn't forbidden this."

"I don't need to be told not to jump into the sea in order to know I should stay away from the cliff's edge," Carlos said. "Do you? When he was only a knight in your service you knew he did not approve."

"I didn't think you'd be afraid of him."

"Only a fool wouldn't be. And it is for you that I fear. You have worked with the horses. Go practice with the bow. Let that be enough."

She stood her ground. This morning would cost her dearly, and she wanted her value's worth. For a brief while at least, she wanted her life back.

She saw Louis watching over by the corral. He would do it for her. He was one of several guards who were not pleased about the new lord's displacing her. His eyes sparkled now, delighted at seeing her back to normal. But he was no match for Morvan, and she had not included the protection of him in her bargain as she had Carlos and Ascanio.

"Then I will practice on my own and at least rebuild my strength. I have become a weakling this last month."

Carlos sighed and shook his head. "There are ways for

women to handle men like him, Anna. You go about this all wrong."

She ignored him and dropped one of the swords.

He started to walk away, then saw something and muttered, "Oh, hell."

Anna followed the line of his gaze. The rigid form of a knight on horseback stood on top of the hill that over-looked the farm and pasture. He was dressed all in black, and the set of his body spoke his mood.

"He knew that you were coming, didn't he?"

Anna didn't reply. Morvan hadn't moved.

"Oh, hell," Carlos said again. He stepped in front of her. "He is your husband and I cannot help you in this, Anna. But hand me the sword now."

The horse began to walk down the hill. She slipped Carlos the sword. He picked up the other and strode to the fence, where he slid them behind the water trough.

"Do not bother. He saw them." She followed the bay courser's progress. Morvan was coming slowly on pur-pose. He wanted to scare her. It was working.

"At least they are not in your hand and at your feet," Carlos replied, returning to her side. "Try being very sweet to him."

"You expect me to just give in?" The taste of freedom had quickened her will, not salved it. She was in no mood to be sweet. She wasn't even sure what that meant. Docile? Pleading? Such manipulation would make her sick with herself. It was one thing to be conquered, and another to grovel for mercy.

"You have already lost," Carlos said. "You lost the day you married him."

Morvan was close enough for them to see the sparks in his eyes and the severity of his expression.

"Holy saints, girl, what have you done?"

"I came here, that is all." *And denied him my bed.* How much of his anger came from that, she wondered, and how much from this morning's defiance? "He is just being overbearing. As usual. You had better go."

"Nay. I had better stay. For all the good it will do you."

The bay courser trotted into the yard. Morvan sat there a while glaring at her before swinging down.

He strode over to her, stopping an arm's span away.

A terrible stillness throbbed. Straightening her shoulders, she raised her head and met his hot gaze with a level one of her own.

Fury at her insolence hardened his expression. He stepped forward, bent, and rose. She found herself slung over his left shoulder, her legs pinned by his arm, her face to his back.

"Put me down," she hissed.

"Have her horse ready," he ordered Carlos.

From her humiliating position, she saw Carlos move toward Louis and made out the stunned looks on their faces. Furious, she pummeled Morvan's back. He didn't seem to notice.

He began taking her to the farmhouse. She struggled vainly against his hold. She would not be treated like some child. She leveraged her body up against his shoulder. Grasping her hands together, she raised her arms as high as she could. Then she let her weight fall, bringing the fist down with all of her might on his back.

He sucked in his breath and stopped in mid-stride. "Thank you," he said, tightly. His right hand swung into view and then landed hard on her bottom.

Shock took her breath away. He continued walking. Rage and humiliation clouded her mind. Gritting her teeth, she tried to kick her legs free. He swung again. Out of the corner of her eye she saw Louis step toward them and Carlos throw out an arm to block him.

Morvan kicked open the door of the farmhouse. "Out," he ordered. With a scurry of feet the other guard flew past them. Morvan dropped her onto a bench by the hearth. She started to rise.

He pressed her back down. "Do not move. Do not speak."

She seethed silently beneath his restraining hand. He stood in front of her like some threat out of hell.

"Do not move," he said again. "Do not, or I may well do you violence."

She let him know that she wouldn't challenge him. He released his hold. He didn't move for several long, tense minutes. She looked only at the floor, but knew the exact moment that he regained control.

"You go too far, Anna. You said that you would not undermine my authority."

"I meant with the others. I never accepted these rights you use. I cannot break rules that don't exist." She almost said "stupid rules," but caught herself.

"I am in no mood to argue with you now. We will talk of that later."

He walked over to the table. The guard had been breaking his fast when they arrived, and Morvan picked up some bread and stood by the fire eating it.

She shifted uncomfortably. It hurt a bit where she sat. She thought resentfully about Carlos and Louis's seeing him humiliate her that way. On the other hand, she had hurt him first with her fist.

Morvan sank onto one of the stools at the table, his back against the table's edge, his legs extended. His anger had only partly abated.

"What are we doing here?" she asked.

"Waiting for enough time to pass."

That made no sense. She began to get up.

"Do not move," he said quietly. Too quietly.

"Enough time for what?" she asked, exasperated.

"For me to punish you. Right now Carlos and the others assume that I am either beating you or taking you with violence. Probably the latter, since you are not screaming."

Rebellious anger burned again. He was right. And the guards would talk about it, and by tomorrow the whole estate would know that the lord had lessoned his lady.

She wouldn't give him such an easy victory. She stood abruptly and walked to the door.

His voice followed her to the threshold. "Do not force me to a public punishment, Anna. My hold on the people here is too new and partly unwelcome. I cannot let any challenge of my authority pass, especially one coming from you. Go out that door and I will do what I am expected to do."

"Do you really think that will change anything?"

"Nay. But Carlos and Louis will try to help you, and then there will be hell to pay for your willfulness, won't there?"

Her hand fell from the door, and she returned to the bench.

A long while later he brought her outside. Carlos led the horses over. He gave Morvan an unfriendly look. The ruse had succeeded magnificently.

"You will ride back on my horse, in front of me," Morvan said.

"I have not ridden thus since I was a child. I will not—"

"You will do it, either seated like a lady, or slung face-down with my hand on your back."

He meant it. Swallowing her insulted pride, she mounted his horse.

He did not speak to her as they rode, but his black mood draped them both like a coarse wool cloak. It reminded her uncomfortably of that day when he had ridden to Reading like a relentless threat beside her. The same aura of unfinished business hung in the air between them now, and the same predatory sensuality.

He stopped his horse outside the gate. "When we go in, I want you to look subdued. Do not raise your eyes. The slightest smile and it will go badly for you. Go up to your chamber and wait for me there."

He was repairing his authority at no real cost to her, she realized. Most other lords would just whip their wives in the hall for all to see. Pretending a docility that she hardly felt, she followed his instructions.

She was deciding that the morning had been a draw at worst when she opened the door to her chamber.

His chests were back. Boots and shoes stood lined up beside them, and several of his weapons rested in the corner.

Her own sword was gone.

He must have given orders for this as soon as he woke, probably before he knew that she had left.

She looked to where her sword should be. She lifted the lid of one of her own chests and saw the void where once her tunics had lain.

"You don't need them anymore," Morvan said from behind her. "You told me yourself that you only wore them because you did men's work. That is over."

Over. "Who will train the horses?"

"Carlos will teach one of the grooms to help him. Or I will hire someone."

"My sword?"

"It is in my solar. No more men's garments, Anna, or men's weapons. You can use your bow when you join a hunt."

He was stripping her of everything. She had known that the cost of this morning would be high, but not this high.

"Why don't you just lock me in here and be done with it."

"It has occurred to me."

"This is because of last night, isn't it?"

"This is for your protection. Last night and this morning just make it easier."

Morvan unfastened the brooch on his cloak and let the long garment fall to the floor. He walked over to the bed and sat on its edge. "You say that you didn't agree to my rights. Well, I didn't concede them, and anything that I didn't concede belongs to me. Aside from my responsibility to protect you, and aside from the fact that you belong to me and will do as I bid, there is another reason why I can't have you living thus."

He bent down and pulled off one boot and then the other. "Soon, new knights will be arriving here. They will have never known you as the lord or the devoted nurse or the abbey-bound saint. They will know you only as my lady. Some of them will desire you. Some may truly love you. It is not a bad thing in itself. A knight's chivalrous love for a lady can bind him closer to a lord. But if it appears that you are independent of me and that I don't control you, very soon one of those knights will misunderstand. I won't be killing men because you are too ignorant to realize the encouragement that your freedom is sending to them."

She wanted to tell him that she didn't care. She almost explained that she intended to have nothing to do with his knights. But he had removed his belt and was unlacing the front of his pourpoint, and along with the anger she saw a flame in his eyes that she knew too well. That damned, dazed breathlessness descended on her. "So I am to be kept in close confinement, with you here watching my every move?"

He slid off the pourpoint. "I did not move back to keep a watch on you. You are my wife and I will share your bed."

He pulled off his shirt and came toward her. Black leather hugged the hard muscles of his hips and legs. The planes of his torso created a pattern of shadows in the morning light. She closed her eyes to him.

He would share her bed. Their bargain gave her the right to deny him her body, but not her bed. He had carefully chosen the words of his concession to create this gaping trap. It was one thing to refuse him outside his solar door. It would be another to turn away from his touch during the night.

"So. You refused me last night and I permitted it," he said quietly. "Are you content now? Are you satisfied that I will honor my word?"

His hand cupped her breast and caressed her through the layers of fabric. Her teeth bared at the pleasure. She opened her eyes.

There was still anger in his face, but it began lifting like a slowly rising veil. He pulled her into his arms and kissed her furiously. The pulsing excitement instantly began its commanding beat.

He unstrapped her belt and threw it to the ground. He grabbed at the shoulder of her tunic and tore the garment off.

He looked down at the silk scarf binding her breasts,

tantalizing her by playing at its folds and creases. "I may actually miss this." His hand found the knot and loosened it, then stripped it away.

Lifting her up, he bent her into his body as he sought her throat and breasts with his mouth. He drew on her, taking her erect nipples between his teeth. His breath flowed hotly on her skin.

He was deliberately showing her how helpless she was to the pleasure, but she didn't care now. She gasped at the welcome pressure as his hand moved up between her thighs and cupped the damp heat already torturing her.

"Our bargain still stands," he said. "You have only to say nay."

She had become incapable of saying anything at all, least of all that.

Reality slowly lifted her from the sensual dream.

This lovemaking had begun as a display of power, but it had not ended that way. His anger was gone by the time they reached the bed, and it had been as if last night and this morning had never happened. But the lesson had been learned anyway. It was hopeless to fight him on this. Unless she proved barren, La Roche de Roald would eventually have a Fitzwaryn heir.

It was not taking Morvan long to make their bargain meaningless.

"So," she said, breaking the beautiful stillness. "If I am no longer to work with the horses, and I can no longer leave the castle, what am I supposed to do?"

"I did not say you couldn't leave the castle."

"Nay. I need your permission, though."

"Until Gurwant is dead."

Gurwant gone and Gurwant dead were two different things. "That could take years."

"It will be soon, I think."

She didn't want to think about what he meant. "In the meantime, what am I to do? I can't just pace about. I need to *do* something."

He shifted to his side and looked at her while his fingers played with her hair. "Do whatever it is women do."

"Weave? Embroider?"

"Whatever."

"Perhaps you are right. I think that I will take charge of your garments. I will do all of the repairs and embroidery."

"That would be fine. And you have the whole household to manage."

"Catherine does that."

"She won't be here forever, Anna, and even now grows heavy with child. It is your place, and you should claim it."

"You don't think she will resent my displacing her?"

"Catherine is very sensible. She will understand."

"So you will take my place and I will take Catherine's," she mused. "I can keep myself busy administering the household."

"Exactly."

Small lights of triumph flickered in his eyes. He appeared well contented with the evidence that he had won the war.

She smiled at him. Sweetly.

CHAPTER 21

A WEEK LATER THE THREE KNIGHTS whom Morvan had recruited in Brest before the wedding arrived at La Roche de Roald. He had chosen them because they impressed him as both skilled and honorable. Their decision to take service proved the last point. They could have gotten rich if they had joined one of the free companies that floated through Brittany, pillaging with abandon.

Two were English. That did not sit well with some on the estate. Resentments still simmered about his marriage to Anna. No challenge came, nothing was said, but Morvan could feel the mood. An English alliance was one thing, but an English lord another. There were also those who believed their saint had been corrupted by taking any husband at all. It would be a long time before he held this land and these people securely.

Any more rebellions by Anna would only delay that

hold. None came. Morvan was relieved to see her take up her new duties and busy herself with the household. He decided that he had handled that last episode very well, and that she had accepted the reasoning behind the changes. She even began addressing him as "My lord," something he had never demanded. True, she said it in a peculiar way, as if on two low drumbeats, but she always smiled very sweetly when she said it, and he concluded she did not intend to sound quite as sarcastic as she did on occasion.

The day after the new men arrived, a messenger came from Gurwant's cousin, Robert de Beaumanoir, to say that the ransom would be delivered the week after Easter. The news meant that Gurwant would remain confined for another month at least.

Then, unexpectedly, young Louis disappeared. On the last day of one of his rotations at the horse farm, Carlos sent him home early, giving him one of their best palfreys to bring back to the castle. The next morning it was discovered that he had never arrived. Morvan rode out with five men to search, but no sign of Louis or the two horses could be found.

"He has run away, Anna. And taken two horses with him," he said that evening in bed.

"Louis is not a thief."

"It appears that he is. If he had been hurt, we would have found the horses. Or his body. It is clear what has happened."

"It is not clear to me. Why would he leave? He had a place here."

"He was no longer contented."

"He would have eventually accepted an English lord."

"Aye. But he could not accept your marriage. He was in love with you."

She gaped at him, and laughed. "That is preposterous."

"He worshiped you."

She laughed again. "You flatter me too much, Morvan, and sound like a suspicious, jealous husband. Next you will tell me that Carlos, Ascanio, and Gregory are in love with me." She gave him a playful nudge.

He pulled her more tightly into his embrace. Still ignorant. Still oblivious. It amazed him that she had not realized the truth. Perhaps she assumed that his own desire was just a result of that deathwatch.

He had finally given her a mirror, after debating if he really wanted her to know. He needn't have worried. Even gazing at herself, she had not seen. The image reflected back to her was still that of an awkward twelve-year-old girl.

The next day he began a circuit of the estate. He did this frequently so he would become a familiar presence, but it also provided an opportunity to orient the recent arrivals to the properties. During the next six days he rode out early and returned late and saw little of the daily workings of the castle.

They toured the closest properties last, and on the final day they arrived back at the castle several hours before nightfall. Morvan led the men into the hall and called for some ale, and they stood around one of the tables talking.

His gaze caught the sight of several white veils poking out of the weaving room. Suddenly ten women emerged from the chamber and formed a phalanx.

They marched toward him with a grim determination. The woman in front was stout and middle-aged. He remembered that she had worked on the wedding garments and that her name was Eva.

"My lord, we would speak with you," she said.

He gestured for the men to leave. They strolled out of the hall slowly, sorry to miss what promised to be a small spectacle.

"What is it?"

"It regards Lady Anna, my lord. She has taken charge of the household. On your orders, she says."

"It is her right." He let his voice get stern.

Eva licked her lips and faltered. A young woman behind her piped up. "She is changing things, my lord."

Eva regained her valor. "Aye. Changing things what don't need changing. She has moved all of the looms into rows so we can't talk to each other. Says we will produce more that way."

"And she has all of the embroidery threads in one place, sorted by color," another woman offered. "We used to have our own baskets, arranged as we liked."

"And she's been working alongside us," a third voice threw in. "Working on *your clothes,* my lord." Several pairs of eyes rolled at that. They all looked at him meaningfully, as if this point obviously deserved attention.

"Show me."

The cluster opened to admit him. He was carried along in a sea of bobbing veils to the weaving room. Indeed, all of the looms had been set up in rows, one behind the other. The stools for the sewers and embroiderers had been arranged the same way. Private gossip would be nigh impossible. On the corner wall the threads hung in neat precision from wooden pegs.

In theory it would be more productive, but the women would not produce if they were unhappy. Only a stupid person would change the work routine thus, he thought.

Anna wasn't stupid. A breeze of wariness wafted through him.

"Look at this, my lord," Eva said. She handed him one

of his pourpoints. Someone had worked an embroidery pattern up the sleeves. It was a brown garment that he didn't favor too much. Good thing. The embroidery skewed unevenly off line. The stitching was frankly horrible.

"All week she has worked on this. Twice I've had to spend hours pulling it all out. The garment will be ruined soon if we keep this up."

"It is well known that she is the worst needlewoman in Brittany," another woman said. "We were shocked to learn that she intended to take care of *your* garments, my lord."

"What says Lady Catherine to this?"

"She refuses to hear us. She says Lady Anna is mistress now and must be obeyed."

It was a conspiracy.

"I will speak with them." With a smile that he hoped looked reassuring, he backed out of the room to a chorus of additional complaints.

Escaping into the hall, he found a scullery maid standing by the table that held his ale cup. "My lord, the cook noticed that you are back early today," she said.

"Aye. We were not expected. Will that cause a problem?"

"Nay, my lord. But the cooks would like to speak with you."

He followed the maid out of the keep and across the yard to the kitchens.

Steam and heat and pandemonium greeted him as he entered. When he was noticed an eerie silence descended as all activity ceased. Out of the dark corners three figures floated toward him like ghosts. Two men and a woman lined up in front of him and literally dug in their heels.

In the center stood a short, bald man with round indignant eyes. Blood stained his clothes. He still held a large butcher's knife.

"My lord Morvan, I am Pierre, the head cook," he announced imperiously. "I have served this family for twenty years. I have fed armies. I have fed great lords and dukes. I cooked during the plague. My servants and assistants dropped like flies around me, but did I leave? Nay. I fed them all, sick and healthy." The knife pointed accusingly. "Are you unhappy with my food, my lord?"

"Not at all. It is excellent."

The knife began jabbing the air. "I am freeborn! I do not have to stay here. I will not take such insults!"

Morvan leaned against a worktable. "Why don't you tell me what has happened?"

"Five days ago, she comes here," Pierre began with a dangerous squint. Morvan didn't have to ask who "she" was. "She sits. She watches. I think, fine. The lady is interested, or maybe bored. Her husband has taken away her toys, and she needs something to do until she has a child. It happens. Sometimes ladies even want to cook a bit. But not her. She sits. She watches. She asks a few questions." The round eyes flared. The knife grew agitated. "Two days ago she arrives and calls us together. She has decided that we will be more efficient if we divide the work. One does baking. One does fish. One does pottage. Forever. The same thing, day in and day out. And!" The knife came down with emphasis, stabbing point-first into a slab of wood inches from Morvan's arm. "And, we are to share our secrets. I am to give this idiot here my recipe for fish soup." Pierre gestured to the man on his left, then folded his arms over his chest. "No one makes Pierre's fish soup but Pierre."

The two assistant cooks hadn't said a word, but stood there nodding their support, even when Pierre had called one of them an idiot.

Morvan rubbed his forehead and began his retreat. "I will speak with her."

"Give her back her toys," the bald cook shouted. "Get her out of my hair."

He should have known. She was going to be the death of him.

Gregory intercepted him on his way back to the hall and fell in step. "You returned early today."

"Aye. I wish I had camped on the road."

Gregory's eyes twinkled. "You had better come with me. There is something you need to see."

"Oh, God help me. Where now?"

Gregory pointed up to the top of the keep. Morvan's spirits lifted. Battlements. Defenses. A decent problem.

He followed Gregory to the roof. Gregory fixed him with a big smile, then threw open the door and gestured grandly. Morvan stepped outside.

On the roof, in an intricate circle, stood a variety of dirt-filled wooden casks and tubs. Additional small tubs dotted the wall walk.

"What the hell is this?"

"This," Gregory announced with a flourish of his arm, "is a garden."

"*A garden?*"

"Aye. There are to be roses in these casks come spring. You can imagine how excited the men are at the prospect. Their enthusiasm as they helped carry the dirt up all of those steps was something to behold." He chortled and shook his head. "Did you know that between the soldiers and servants, this castle knows how to curse in seven different languages?"

"A rose garden." Morvan glanced around, feeling utterly and totally defeated.

She was incredible. Relentless.

"I am going to my solar, Gregory." He paused and glanced back suspiciously. "Is there anything else that I should see or know?"

"Well, except for the plans to paint the castle white, and a general insurrection among the servants, I wouldn't say there is anything else of interest going on."

"*Paint the castle white?*"

"It seems that it is often done in France and England."

"Only when the stone is poor, and you know it. This is good granite." He sighed. "I don't need to ask whose idea this was, do I?"

"I seriously doubt it."

"Are you enjoying this sufficiently, Gregory?"

"Me? I am insulted that you think I would take amusement at your expense. Father Ascanio, on the other hand, is having a wonderful time."

"No doubt."

"And the head groom Carlos has eagerly awaited the completion of your circuit."

"Indeed."

"And the Lady Anna, my lord, has been in wonderful spirits. It has been a pleasure to see her thus."

"I can imagine." He hustled down the stairs to the sanctuary of his solar before any more of his wife's subversions waylaid him.

Damn it. He had underestimated her again.

"You are doing this on purpose," he said to her when they were alone that night. He waited until after they had made love before raising the servants' complaints.

"Whatever do you mean, my lord?"

He heard the two drumbeats. He looked at her suspiciously. She smiled sweetly.

"You know what I mean."

"I only do as you wished, Morvan. Are you going to tell me how to manage the household now?"

He was on slippery ground. If he interfered, they would start coming to him with every little complaint. If he didn't, there could be chaos. Wherever you walked in the castle you heard a low buzz of complaint. On the other hand, they no longer grumbled about the English lord.

"It won't work, Anna."

"I'm sure that you are right, Morvan, whatever it is that you are referring to." She spoke like a docile and submissive girl. He wasn't fooled in the least.

"You must fix things with the servants."

She hit him with that level gaze. "I am only doing your bidding. You told me to occupy myself with women's work. Are you saying now that I am no good at it? Should I perhaps be doing something else?"

The trap gaped in front of him. "Nay, dear wife, I would never suggest such a thing. You do as you think best. I have complete confidence in your skills." Inspiration struck. "Indeed, I am so confident that I have decided to make a visit to Sir Baldwin. It is time that I examined the distant fiefs, and would do so before Gurwant is released."

Her face fell, and he smiled smugly. He'd let her boil in her own stew.

"How long will you be gone?"

"A week at least, I should think."

"A week," she repeated thoughtfully.

"At least. I will take Josce and four others with me. All should be safe here. But you are to stay within the walls."

She didn't react at all to that. She smiled very sweetly and stretched to plant a kiss on his lips. "I will miss you, my lord."

Two drumbeats again. It was deliberate, he was quite sure now.

Anna went about her duties for four days with smiles and cheer. The only alteration in her schedule, now that Morvan had left, was that periodically she went into the lord's solar and studied the gatehouse across the yard. On Morvan's orders the portcullis stayed down and the drawbridge up.

All of the guards had been informed by Morvan that the women were to stay in the castle. That meant she would be unable to slip through among some servants. He had anticipated her defiance once his back was turned, and seen to it that she could not leave. But leave she would, she'd vowed. It had become a matter of honor.

On the fourth day, she noticed a pattern. Gregory kept assigning the new men to the gatehouse during the afternoon hours. She made her plans, and went back to disrupting the household.

That night at the evening meal she measured the knights sitting at her table. Her gaze came to rest on Sir Walter. He was one of the new men, and had been left behind to help Ascanio defend the keep.

She dallied at her food until the others began to disperse. Once Ascanio had left his place by her side, she gestured to Sir Walter to come and sit next to her.

Surprised by this honor, he carried his wine cup down the table.

He was about Morvan's age, and a very nice man. His face was a bit thin and his brown hair a bit shaggy, but his eyes looked kind and his expression earnest. She felt a pang of guilt at how she intended to use him.

She engaged him in conversation as the hall emptied and the servants cleared the tables. Finally, when they were alone, she said, "I realize that I have not seen to my duties properly with the new knights, Sir Walter."

"You have made us most welcome, my lady."

"Nay, nay, you are too generous. I have left all of you to fend for yourselves settling in, and I know that it is awkward at first getting help from strange servants."

His expression looked very earnest indeed. "I assure you that none have complaints."

"Still, we must remedy the situation. For example, have any of the women seen to your garments? Have they been examined to see about repairs and things of that sort? Nay? Well, let us do it at once." She rose from her chair. "You were given my husband's old chamber, I believe?"

She breezed across the hall and opened the door to the chamber. "Just as I thought. You have not even been provided with a chest." She clucked her tongue and descended on the stack of clothes on the bed. She began examining them. For the most part she found them in depressingly good condition.

"My lady, I do not think . . ."

"Come, come. Sit down. Is it not my duty to see to the comforts of my husband's men?" With relief she found a shirt in need of washing and a cotte with a tear. She reached for the hose.

Sir Walter hadn't answered her, or sat down, or even moved. She absently threw a smile and a glance over her shoulder at him. She returned her attention to the hose, but something nagged at her. Sir Walter had simply been watching her, leaning with his back against the wall near the almost closed door, his arms folded over his chest. What was it? His eyes. Aye, that was it. There had been a strange glint in those kind eyes, rather like . . .

Oh dear.

She fussed furiously with the clothes, setting aside the ones she wanted. As she did so she thought of Sir Walter's earnest expressions when he looked at her, and then of young Paul's. She suddenly comprehended some of the reactions she had received in Windsor. There flashed in her memory the look Gurwant had given her during her parlay.

Some will desire you. Some may truly love you.

Well, well.

Reflection would have to wait for later. Right now she had to deal with the immediate implications of this stunning revelation.

She grasped the clothes to her chest and turned to Sir Walter with a neutral and, she hoped, thoroughly discouraging smile. "I will have these tended and returned to you," she said, stretching for the door and throwing it open.

"Will you honor me by tending them yourself, my lady?" He looked slightly awestruck. The way Louis used to.

Oh dear.

"In truth, Sir Walter, be glad if I don't. You may have heard of the botch I made with my husband's things."

"I'm sure that whatever your lovely hands do is magnificent, good lady."

She barely managed not to gape at him. Surely nice Sir Walter would not make a lewd reference.

Trying to look authoritative and untouchable and very much the lady of the manor, she stumbled out of the chamber and hurried through the hall.

Anna slowed her horse to a walk once she reached the cover of the trees. It wasn't Shadow beneath her. Someone would have recognized Shadow. She had arranged a diversion at the stable and saddled a palfrey instead while the grooms were distracted.

It had been easy, almost too easy. She had simply called for the gate to open and ridden out. The new guards had never seen her in men's garments, and had not recognized her.

She emerged from the trees on the hill overlooking the horse farm. Exhilaration swept through her as she surveyed her favorite place in the world.

And then her whole body tensed. Her heart and her blood began pounding. Her legs instinctively gave a signal and the horse backed up into the cover of the trees.

Two bodies lay on the ground in front of the farmhouse.

Strange horses were tied to the fence. As she counted the mounts, the door opened and a man stepped out of the house. In the shadows by the corner of the structure she saw another man standing guard.

Cold terror replaced her shock. Carlos and two others should have been here today. Was there a third body as well, out of sight behind a fence or water trough? She sent up a prayer that they were not all dead, that one had survived at least.

She turned her horse and sped back up the trail. Glancing down she saw the rough marks that indicated many horses had come through here. She had been so full of herself and her stupid victory over Morvan that she hadn't noticed them when she rode in.

Fifty yards up the path, she reined in her horse. Out of the corner of her eye, she had seen something move.

The brush rustled again. She made out a dark form hidden by undergrowth. Drawing her dagger, she dropped from the horse. Halfway there she recognized the tunic and the black hair and beard.

She fell to her knees beside the motionless body. Very gently she raised Carlos's head to her lap. An indescribable grief, such as she hadn't felt since the first days of the plague, numbed her.

An arrow lodged deeply in his side and another in his leg. A trail of blood streaked off into the brush and a small pool had formed beneath him.

His mouth moved in a grimace of pain. The black eyes fluttered open.

"You live," she said, gratefully.

"Aye. Barely, I think," he muttered. "They came right after midday. Poured down the hill like devils out of hell. When the two guards fell, I slipped away, but their bolts caught me on the hill. I managed to climb up here, but they came looking. I must have appeared dead to them too, eh?"

"These are bad wounds, Carlos."

"Are the thieves still there?"

"Aye."

"They must plan to move the horses out in the morning." He grasped her hand. "Go and get help. Tell Ascanio that there are at least ten of them."

"I will not leave you thus."

"If these bolts were meant to kill me, I would be dead already. Go. This is no time for the daughter of Roald de Leon to suddenly get womanish."

She pulled off her cloak and tucked it around him. "I will be back with help soon."

"Nay. Let the knights and soldiers handle this."

"You sound like Morvan. I will see you soon."

She charged her horse along the path, guiding it with one hand while the other pulled out the pins that held up her hair. Let them see from a distance that it was their lady and not a strange man who approached. Let no time be wasted with explanations and the slow rise of the portcullis.

Halfway across the field she began waving and yelling for the gate to open. By the time she clamored across the ditch the way was clear, and she bolted into the yard.

She had already yelled twice for Ascanio before she reared the palfrey to a stop at the keep stairs. She yelled again and ran up to the hall.

She slammed into a man's chest. Morvan's strong hands gripped her shoulders and almost lifted her off her feet.

"Thank God you are back," she said, gasping for breath.

His dark gaze turned hot as he took in the forbidden clothes. Something else mixed with the anger, however, when he saw the blood staining her hem and hose. The men who had ridden with him closed in. Ascanio ran into the hall, alerted by her yells.

"Thieves have taken the farmhouse," she said. "The two guards are dead, I think, and Carlos lies off the trail with mortal wounds."

"How many?" Morvan asked, his hands still gripping her.

"Carlos counted ten. He thinks they will wait until morning to take the horses."

"Everyone goes armored," he ordered the men. "Ascanio, tell Gregory to take two men at once and find Carlos. He and four others will then stay at the gate-house. For the rest, we ride in one hour."

The men peeled away. Morvan strode toward the stairs, a firm hand on her arm. "Josce, find a servant to help you armor me," he snapped over his shoulder.

He pulled her up the stairs and into the lord's solar, then threw her into the chair and began pulling off his pourpoint to prepare for his armor.

"You defied me again."

"A good thing too, or Carlos would die and the horses would be gone. For the sake of God, Morvan, men have been killed and the estate threatened, and you are angry because your wife has been naughty."

"I am angry because my willful, disobedient wife is covered in blood and could well be dead."

"I was never in any danger."

"Because fortune has spared you this time you think that makes this acceptable?" He cupped her chin in his hand. "Tell me, wife, if I had not been here when you returned, what would you have done?"

"Sent Ascanio and the others to clear the thieves out."

"While you sat here and embroidered? I think not."

Scratches at the door indicated that Josce and the servant had arrived. Morvan harshly bid them enter, but continued holding her face. "I will deal with you later, Anna. But know this. Do not think, do not even *think,* of involving yourself in this action."

He released her and stepped back so that Josce and the servant could begin their work. She rose and went to the door.

"Anna," he said, his voice quieter now but somehow

more dangerous. "When we discuss this defiance, you can explain how you came to be wearing Sir Walter's clothes."

"I took them to repair. I am not one of your noble whores, Morvan. In this my vows were honest. God go with you, husband."

When the armor was finished, Morvan dismissed the servant and sent Josce down to prepare Devil. Alone in the solar, he stood thoughtfully for a moment, and then went to a large chest. Opening it, he removed a sword, and a bow and quiver, then closed the chest and placed them on top of it in clear view.

He would not have her unarmed, or using unfamiliar weapons, if she disobeyed him.

He looked long at the weapons and they were, as always, a symbol of her repudiation of any man's right to her. Of his protection and his command. Of him. He noticed the wear on the bow where her hand had gripped it over the years.

He could order her confined by the servants. He could tie her to a chair.

He left the weapons on top of the chest.

CHAPTER 22

S HE MOVED SHADOW INTO THE TREES that edged the hill overlooking the farm. Readjusting the bow and quiver on her back, she peered at the scene below.

Morvan stood in front of the farmhouse, his armor gleaming in the light of the low-lying sun. The other knights formed a line curving along the front of the building. The rest of the men had been deployed around the building's front and sides.

The mares crowded nervously at the far end of their corral. A fire had been started near the water trough; if it came to it, Morvan was prepared to burn the building.

She was in no danger, so she really had not disobeyed Morvan, she told herself. He had forbid her to involve herself in the action, and she would not. But she could not just wait for word. Her horses were at risk, as was Morvan himself.

The retaking of the farmhouse appeared to be at an impasse. But the early evening light had begun to wane, and whatever was going to happen had to happen soon.

She surveyed the scene again. Something was missing. She realized what it was. The thieves' horses were no longer tied up in front.

She moved along the edge of the forest until she flanked the side of the farmhouse. From there she could see the horses behind the building, still saddled.

None of the castle men-at-arms were back there. The enclosed pasture behind the building where the stallions roamed had no way out, backing as it did against the precipitous hill into which the end of the valley cut. That hill formed a natural barrier to the horses, and would hold these thieves as well.

Suddenly, she saw two movements. They occurred simultaneously, each catching one of her eyes.

At the front of the building, Morvan shifted his position and turned to face her. He looked directly at the spot where she sat on Shadow, as if he sensed her hidden presence.

At the back of the building, visible only to her, a dark figure fell from a window and crouched toward the saddled horses. One thief had decided to make a run for freedom.

Once on the horse, the man did not charge around the building as she expected. Instead he bolted into the back pasture. As he did, another man fell from the window.

She looked down at Morvan and the other men. She was too far away to yell and warn them in time.

A third man eased toward the tethered horses. The first man streaked toward the stallions. He was going to stampede them, and in the confusion the thieves would ride away.

Her blood pounded at the thought of the horses surging down the valley, spreading up into the hills and forest, lost in this desperate bid for escape.

She turned Shadow onto the path that snaked along the top of the hill. She gave the signal for a gallop just as the roar of stampeding hooves rose up from the pasture.

She pulled off her bow and quiver and dropped it to the ground. She released the reins and unbuckled her belt. The sword slid away, leaving her light and mobile. Turning Shadow, she flew down the hill.

A daunting scene pressed toward her. Cramped along one side of the valley stream, the massive warhorses and coursers poured forward, all fiery eyes and bulging muscles. In their lead ran a huge white brute of a horse. Dotted amidst them she could see the heads of the thieves and, one hundred yards behind, the vanguard of the remounted knights and men-at-arms bearing down hard.

The lead stallion led the storm directly at her. She turned Shadow and rode in the same direction. She prayed that her plan would work. If not, the horses would go up over the lower hill at this end of the valley and disperse into the trees.

She felt the breath of the stallion on her leg and paced her speed so that he could draw even with her. She forced the two horses to run side by side, even though she could feel the stallion's rage and Shadow's quivering fear. Bringing up her legs, she crouched on Shadow's back, then jumped over to the stallion. Her legs grabbed his sides, and she held on to his mane for dear life.

She clutched at his head and twisted it. Using her arms and legs, she signaled the stallion to turn left, toward the stream. He went airborne to jump it.

The other horses followed. Again she pressed and pulled, doing with her arms what a rein should do. He followed her command, and they began heading back down the valley toward the farm at the same thundering pace.

The thieves, caught in the confusion of the turning herd, saw her coming back along the stream. Two of them pulled their horses out of the fray and crossed the water.

The setting sun reflected off the steel of an upraised sword. The orange glint mesmerized her as it began its deadly, downward curve. As a result, she wasn't prepared for the other, less entrancing danger when the other thief reached over and dragged her from her animal.

She held on to the mane as long as possible, and managed to slide to the blur of ground instead of falling hard. She found the sense to roll toward the safety of the stream. It was merely luck that the two closest horses in the herd jumped her instead of trampling her underfoot.

Her face sank underwater. Cold liquid seeped into her clothes, shocking her. She floated, dazed and helpless, for a small eternity. Then a steel hand grabbed the neck of her garments and set her on her feet at the stream's edge.

She wiped her eyes. Morvan, his armor streaked with red from the setting sun, shielded her with his body as his knights and soldiers came up to clash with the thieves.

He kept between her and the action, and his sword fell on any thief who thought to escape across the stream or who dared challenge the horseless knight and lady.

The closeness of the death blows staggered her. The spreading carnage raised bile to her mouth. Morvan's visor was up, and she could see the fires that burned in his eyes as he anticipated the moves of man and horse. The herd, long gone, milled in the distant pasture.

Suddenly, it was over. Six dead men and three wounded horses lay sprawled on the ground. Four of the thieves and a few stallions had disappeared up the hill into the forest.

Morvan gripped her arm and pushed her toward Ascanio. "Take her back to the farm and have her dry by the fire. Then get her to the castle."

Ascanio's eyes appeared harder and hotter than she had ever seen them. He pulled off his gauntlet and extended an arm to her. Grasping it, she swung up behind him.

They were silent on the way back to the farmhouse. He dropped her next to the fire and went to help the guards herd the stallions into the back pasture. He finally returned with another horse in tow.

"Are you angry with me too, Ascanio?" she asked as they threaded their way through the forest.

"Aye. And if my heart stops when you come within a hair's span of death, imagine how your husband feels."

"I was not in so much danger as that."

"We saw you go down beneath the herd. We saw the sword raised on you. He was beside me. I heard the yell that came from him. I saw his face."

"If I had not done it, the horses would be gone, scattered. At best we would have rounded up half, for in a day they could reach our borders and then there would be no retrieving them."

"Do you think that I give a damn about that? Do you think that he does? He has been willing to die for you from the start, Anna. How do you think he measures a herd of horses against your safety?"

He should value it very highly. The horses were the true treasure of La Roche de Roald. Without them this marriage would benefit him little.

And yet, even as she reasoned this out, she knew that the logic would carry little weight with Morvan. Too much existed on the other side of the scale. His oath of protection. His authority, and her defiance.

"Anna, when there were but a handful of us it was one thing. Yet even then I died a little each time that you rode into danger. And your going was no insult to me as it is to him. Your games of rebellion are one thing. This was another."

They rode into the yard together. A sick void opened inside her as Ascanio's words repeated in her head.

She felt Morvan's gauntlet pulling her from the icy water, and saw his armored body standing between her and death. She had felt no real danger because he was there. In an awful moment of truth, she admitted that she had been enjoying the security of his protection even as she defied the protection itself.

She wondered how long it would be before he returned, or if he would even come back this night. As she went up the steps to her chamber, she hoped desperately that he would. She had the terrible feeling that if he did not come to her tonight, in anger if nothing else, a part of him would never return to her again at all.

Morvan stayed at the farmhouse late into the night, directing the burial of the dead thieves. The activity cooled his blood a little.

Finally, all was done. He told two extra guards to stay at the farmhouse. In the morning they were to ride to Fouke and Haarold and bid the two vassals to be alert for the escaped thieves. He considered staying the night at the farmhouse himself, but he found himself mounting

Devil even though he hadn't made the conscious decision to do so.

He entered a hall filled with raucous noise and general good cheer. He felt little of that cheer himself. It
must have shown, because a pall fell on the assembly
when he was noticed.

His gaze went to Ascanio with a silent question. The
priest glanced to the ceiling to tell him that Anna had
gone to her chamber.

He paused at one of the tables and drank some ale.
The calm that he showed was an illusion. During these
last hours his thoughts had not been far from Anna and
they had not been calm at all. Only blocking out the details of her danger had kept him even superficially composed.

He drank another cup of ale, as if to emphasize to
himself that he was not dangerous. Then he gestured to
Josce and went to the solar to have his armor removed.

He walked toward Anna's chamber and knew with each
stride that he should not see her. It was the only sane
thought in a head exploding with a fury still colored by
the battle's bloodlust. He knew that he should not go,
but he went anyway because there would be no peace
tonight unless he did.

He threw open the chamber door harder than he
planned, but then all of his actions came stronger when
he was like this. It flew wide and crashed against the wall
behind it.

Anna sat on the edge of the bed while Ruth combed
out her hair. The servant's face paled.

"Leave us," he said.

Ruth hesitated, and Anna placed a reassuring hand on her shoulder and nodded. As Ruth ran out, the child Marguerite suddenly appeared in her wake. Braver than her mother, she cast him an accusing stare. It was all he could do not to bring his hand down on her small back.

He closed the door and faced his wife. She had removed the cotte and hose, and had wrapped on her robe. He could tell that she had already washed. Her hair fell in riotous curls around her face. She gave him a long look that contained neither apology nor pleading.

She gestured vaguely, and the movement covered everything. His anger and her defiance, their past and their future, the violence that he barely kept in check. "If it will make you feel better, go ahead," she said. "I will not hold it against you. I cannot even blame you."

Anything else, anything at all, would have pushed him into darkness. But her quiet, velvet voice worked like a balm, and his fury retreated like the ebb of a violent wave.

"I did turn the horses, Morvan."

"You almost died."

"As did you."

"That is different."

"Not to me. I love you, and I see no difference."

It was the first time she had said it. The last of the anger soaked away into the sands of his soul.

She still sat on the bed. The sensual light of hearth and candles played off her hair and flickered over the pale skin of her leg, visible where the robe had parted. The wave of fury had gone, but the tide of his blood still flowed high and other waves replaced it, just as violent, just as driven by the emotions of battle. And with them came images of her, erotic visions remembered and fantasized, and a hunger that he knew could be just as cold as the anger had been.

He had more experience at controlling this madness. He knew how to deal with it. "We will talk tomorrow," he said, opening the door.

"Please do not go."

His arm stopped, the door partly open. He glanced to where she had risen to her feet. The robe, loosely tied, threatened to fall open. He remembered the first time he had seen her in it, tall and brave, sword in hand, wild and free. Magnificent.

"It is best if I do, Anna."

She walked over to him. The vision of her legs kicking through the slit of her robe entranced him. Breathtaking. He should leave now.

She stopped an arm's span away and looked into his eyes. What he saw in her face was unmistakable. He held on to his sanity with effort. She placed a hand on his chest. "I want you to stay. Do not turn from me because of this."

He took her hand and kissed it. Even this small touch of her devastated him. "I don't leave because I'm angry with you, but because I am not fit for your company tonight. I am in no mood for courtly seductions."

She considered what he said.

"Neither am I. Stay."

His resolve began to crumble. But he had been very careful with her in their brief marriage and she was, in the end, still very ignorant.

"Nay. It is different after battle. I am different." He released her hand. "I will go."

She strode to the fire, angry and hurt. He was sorry for that, but he would take care of it later.

"Fine. Leave me to pace the floor like a good wife."

"Anna—"

"On second thought, send me a man. One of the grooms. Or maybe Sir Walter."

Her words cut like a hot knife into his head.

So. No longer ignorant and oblivious.

He moved in a dark, unseeing, furious blur, and found himself beside her, his left hand twisted in her hair and his right holding her face in a tight grip.

"Do not *ever* taunt me thus."

She met his eyes with her level, bold gaze. If he was hurting her she did not show it. "What would you have me do then, Morvan? Ride a horse? I too have been in a battle."

He studied her face in amazement. Aye, she felt what he felt. He could smell it on her. Could smell the remains of the exaltation and glory that only came when you defied violent death. Could smell the forbidden fear that surfaced when the danger ended. Mixed with them, covering them all, was the other scent that spoke of her hunger to feel alive. Her need intoxicated him, and he felt his control washing away.

"You do not know what you are talking about."

"I hope that I'm talking about a few hours." She laughed a little. "Whatever that means."

Her humor and love threw an unaccustomed light onto his dark passions. He suddenly knew that he would not leave. He did not have to. This was Anna, and it would be different with her.

He thrust his hand between her thighs and felt the wetness already there. She rose against him with a groan and her small teeth sank into his neck. The thundering desire claimed him with an immediate need. He began lowering them both to the fur rug, pulling off her robe as they went, turning her body.

"You must stop me when you want." It was a warning he had always given those nameless women after battles and tournaments and fights. But this was Anna, he dimly reminded himself through the engulfing fire. He himself would know when she was done.

"You did not seem surprised by that," he said.

She lay facing the hearth, his body still molded and joined behind her as it had been when they fell following his release.

Nay, not surprised. She had known what he was going to do even as he pulled her to the rug in their ferocious need. No preliminaries and no need for them, and she found her own release for the first time as his hard thrusts had salved this deep restlessness that she felt.

She glanced back at him. He was still dressed. No time for that either. "I am not completely ignorant, Morvan."

He stroked her arm. "Still, some women do not like it. They feel too used."

"Do not worry so much about me. I never feel used by you."

His arms circled her, and he buried his face in her hair and neck. She felt him swelling, and an exciting expectation thrilled through her.

"Again, then." He reached down and raised her knee to her chest. "After we will call for a bath and wash the battle off of us."

It was very late when they called for the bath. After the last bucket of hot water had been poured, Morvan pushed back the bed curtains behind which she hid and carried her over to the tub. He washed her himself with caressing hands that both soothed and excited. He slowly lathered her with sensuous caresses, his hands smoothing over her again and again, circling deliciously around her breasts and down her thighs. She knelt while he rinsed her, and his tongue whisked at the rivulets of water streaming down her body. By the time he lifted her from the tub and began drying her, her whole body was trembling again as if she had not had him in weeks.

He kissed her as he wiped the water away, and his sparkling eyes followed the progress of his hands as his mouth pressed and bit at her flesh. Her body was crying for him before he finished, and then she did for him as he had done for her, washing and drying him, floating the whole time in a tingling stupor of anticipation. When she went to her knees to wipe the water from his legs, her kisses found all of him. His hand touched her head and held her there, and he exhaled a response of ragged breath. It was the first time in all of their lovemaking that he had ever made a sound.

He lifted her up into his arms and carried her to the bed. She wanted him desperately, painfully, and as he laid her down she tried to pull him to her, but he restrained her with an arm over her stomach and kissed down her length. He pushed her legs apart and then, first with his hand and then with his mouth, caressed and probed, sending arching white lights of excitement through her.

Her release came violently. It crashed through her, almost tearing her apart. He held her hips firmly and kept his mouth to her, extending the incredible pleasure into a series of higher peaks.

He moved up, bringing her legs with him. Lifting them over his shoulders, he rose on extended arms and entered her with hard thrusts, slowly at first and then more fiercely, until finally his strength threatened to move her whole body before him. She closed her eyes to savor the power, and her own passion rose again to meet his and tense toward that deeper, different release that she had learned about this night.

In her delirium, her body thrashed out of control. She grasped at him frantically, screaming into the timeless, airless oblivion where he had taken her. If not for the tremendous force of his body claiming her, she would have lost awareness of reality completely.

They made love all night. Over and over, during fierce hours of long joinings and brief separations, they both buried the emotions born in the battle. She never stopped him, no matter what he did. There was no real submission in her obedience, only new pleasures and satisfactions that soothed primitive parts of her soul.

Finally, as the first light of dawn replaced that of the guttering candles, they lay side by side, bodies entwined.

"Do you sleep?" she whispered.

"If you will finally permit it."

"Oh."

He laughed and shook his head. "Hell, woman, you are insatiable. I recall Ascanio once telling me that you would match me in this as all else. Prophetic, although this isn't quite what he had in mind."

"Go to sleep. Dawn breaks. I could go ride a horse now."

He laughed again, and pulled her up and held her shoulders above him. Her breasts grazed his chest, tantalizing her. "Seduce me," he said. "I can probably show some patience now. And then you can ride me instead of a horse."

CHAPTER 23

ANNA SAT ON A STOOL BY the solar hearth, smoothing Morvan's favorite red pourpoint over her lap. While their night of passion had subdued their battle, she had hardly given up the struggle. Eventually some form of compromise would be his only choice.

She held up the pourpoint and eyed it critically. He had worn this the day that he sealed their bargain at David's house. The color brought attention to his eyes, and he looked magnificent in it. She remembered the effect well, and the disadvantage his appearance had put her in that morning. Aye, this garment had a lot to answer for.

Morvan looked up from the table, where he was working with a quill. "What are you doing?"

"Woman's work." She flattened the sleeve on her lap

and tilted her head back to imagine what she would do to it. "Gold, don't you think?"

"Gold?"

"Thread. Very visible and rich. Good contrast."

"I have always liked it as it is."

"Your garments are much too plain for a lord. What will people think if I let you go about thus? Gold it will be."

"I find that I prefer plain garments. I was impressed by David's. The total lack of adornment is very appealing and distinctive."

"David is a merchant."

"Still, I would keep a few items thus. Like that pourpoint."

"Are you implying that you do not want me to care for your things? That you do not trust my womanly skills?"

He laughed. "I am saying that I would prefer that you didn't ruin my favorite garments, Anna. Have a little mercy."

He came over and lifted her up, drawing her to his chair and settling her on his lap. He never seemed to notice that she was really too big to sit like that. "How did you manage to become the worst needlewoman in Brittany?"

"I avoided it whenever possible. One just sits for hours counting threads, plying a needle. It was enough to drive me mad. So I made it a point to never do it well. Even at the abbey they soon found other work for me."

"What kind of work?"

"Not ladies' work, I'm afraid. I tended the garden. I helped in the infirmary. Sometimes I even scrubbed floors."

"You fought off brigands."

The mood suddenly changed. The air in the room seemed to thin.

"That too, once."

His smile was gone and a thoughtful expression had taken its place. A strange stillness came from him.

"You were happy there."

"Contented."

"You are not contented now."

An odd feeling stirred in her. Almost a foreboding. His sudden seriousness unsettled her.

"Nor could I be there anymore," she said.

His gaze fell to her arm, where his fingers were gently stroking her. He studied the patterns that he made on her sleeve.

"Do you know that you have never asked me for anything? One time you asked for advice about Gurwant. Other than that, nothing. For as long as we have known each other."

"I asked you to marry me. It is not a small thing."

"The benefit was more mine than yours."

"You argued otherwise very well, as I remember." She laughed, hoping to lighten the mood.

"I told you once that men are weak, and most generous, when most pleased. Yet after we make love you ask for nothing."

"Is that what you expect? Is it common for wives to do this? Lie with their husbands, and then ask for things? Besides, what would I ask of you? Jewels? A new gown?"

"After I have been with you, you could ask for anything. Everything."

She suspected she knew what he was offering, what he was telling her. It frightened her, and she kept silent, hoping to end this conversation.

It was not to be.

"When I was with Baldwin, I visited your property at Rennes," he said. "The castellan is a good man. With some more men-at-arms, it would be well protected, and Baldwin is not that far away. I would come if ever you needed me."

"Are you saying that you want to send me away?"

"I am saying that I would let you leave. I never thought that I would, but I cannot see us like this forever. I do not like the anger, Anna, or your unhappiness. At Rennes you could live the life that you had here. I would ask that you not endanger yourself, but if you did at least I would not see it."

She looked away, stunned. He had been waiting for her to ask for this. He had already known his answer. But why bring it up now? Had their talk of Saint Meen opened a door that he felt compelled to walk through? Or had he tired of her already?

"And if I do not ask for this?"

"Then I would have you be my wife in all ways. No more bargain. No more games."

She had been negotiating for a compromise. Instead, he was now giving her an ultimatum. He was actually doing it. He was asking her to choose between him and herself.

She sensed the emotions in him and knew that he fully expected her to take this gift. Everything, all that she had demanded when they first spoke of marriage, waited a few words away. She pictured herself at Rennes, managing the property, riding as she wished, using her judgment and even her weapons. Independent. Free. Separate.

She wondered if he expected her to make a decision right now. She dreaded that he might force her to.

There came a scratch on the door. Josce stuck his head in. "A messenger has come from Sir Haarold."

"It is very late. He must have ridden all day," Morvan said. "Bring him here."

Anna slipped off her perch and returned to her stool.

"Does Sir Haarold have trouble?" Morvan asked when the man arrived. Anna knew that he worried about Gurwant's family still, even though they had agreed to the ransom.

"Nay, my lord. But we received your warning about the thieves, and I was sent to tell you that we have caught one."

"You are sure?"

"Aye. Found him with three of the horses. One was a palfrey. Sir Haarold recognized the saddle as the workmanship done here. And he recognized the man as once being in your service. It be a young guard named Louis."

"Does he know of the others?"

"He says only that the others are still nearby and that he will tell all he knows, but to Lady Anna and no one else. Sir Haarold wants to know if the lady will come, or if he should just hang the boy."

"Go and find some food. I will decide by morning."

When he had left, Morvan gazed thoughtfully at the fire. "It appears that you were wrong about him, Anna."

"So it seems. But I would hear about it from him. And if he can lead you to the others . . . They still know the way to the farm. It will never be safe again while they are at large."

"Only because the boy betrayed your trust in the first place."

"I am aware of that."

"You know that no matter what he says now, he will hang."

She knew that.

"I will go, but you will not," Morvan said. "I will take a

few men with me and borrow Haarold's to search out Louis's friends. When I come back, I will bring Gurwant. It is time to fetch him anyway."

"Louis said he would speak only with me."

"Then he hangs without speaking. You do not go."

He came to her, and lifted her into his arms. "If I do it this way, Gurwant will be here for a week or so before the ransom comes after Easter. Can you bear having him here? If not, say so and I will go back for him later."

It seemed that a lifetime had passed since she had faced that blond giant after the battle. She realized that she no longer feared him. The reason stood in front of her, his fingers resting gently on her cheek.

"Bring him. But I will not be in the yard to greet you when you return. I told him that we would not meet again."

He drew her back to the chair. She let him hold her, but she did not think about poor Louis, or even Gurwant. She calculated how long she had before she had to make a choice.

Morvan left the next day, accompanied by Haarold's messenger and four other men. It wasn't clear how long he would be gone. Even if Louis did not lead him to the other thieves, he intended to find them. Under any circumstance, however, he told Anna to expect him by the beginning of Holy Week.

His offer weighed heavily on her mind as the days stretched on without him. She tried to imagine her life both ways, looking for some reaction inside her heart that would tell her what she really wanted. Sometimes she hated him for forcing such a choice on her. She had never asked him to decide between her and anything.

Her little games of rebellion lost their appeal, and she spent one afternoon putting the looms and stools in the weaving room back where they belonged. The cooks had never obeyed her, so she had nothing to rearrange there. She decided that her rooftop garden would stay, however. She had grown fond of the idea.

By the Friday before Palm Sunday she knew what her decision would be. The choice carried some sadness, for she knew well what she saved for herself, and what she gave up. She felt neither happiness nor triumph in the decision when it came, but she found a contentment in simply having made the choice at last.

On Palm Sunday itself, the Sunday before Easter, she was disappointed that Morvan had not returned. She paced the time away, waiting for him, anticipating him. Even the thought that Gurwant would come with him could not impinge on her building expectation. She wanted very badly to make love with him one last time before she told him her decision and things changed forever.

When Tuesday passed and he had not come home, worry replaced anticipation. By the afternoon of Maundy Thursday, she knew that something had gone very wrong.

Morvan stood and stretched and turned his face to the dim light seeping through the high small window. He ran his hand over his beard, and was grateful that his senses had long ago dulled to the fetid smells that filled this damp chamber.

Ten days. The bastard had kept him here ten days now. But it was Maundy Thursday, and Anna would finally know there was trouble. He prayed that she would not come herself to discover what had happened. Gurwant counted on her doing so. Morvan counted on her being too smart to walk into the trap.

He himself had not been that smart, but then he had never anticipated Haarold's betrayal. Only when he rode into this castle's yard had he known that something was amiss. He had been greeted with the honor befitting an overlord, but there had been too many men in the bailey and they had been too carefully positioned. He had drawn his sword instinctively, without thinking of the costs. When it was over, and they dragged him into the keep's hall, two of his men lay dead.

The sight in the hall had explained everything. There at the high table, taking their evening meal, sat Haarold and Gervaise and young Paul. With them, in the honored position beside Haarold, lounged the cold-eyed man who was supposed to be a prisoner in close confinement here.

"Where is your wife, Englishman?" Gurwant asked. "She surprises me. I was sure that she would come to speak with her young guard to find out what had happened." He tapped the table thoughtfully. "Perhaps she follows you, as she did with the horses. Aye, I know that she was there. She does not accept the will of a man forced on her by a foreign king, does she? She is Breton, and does not accept an English lord."

"She does not follow," Morvan said. He turned his gaze to Haarold. "You break oaths of fealty easily, Haarold. I did not expect it of the man who was the right arm of Roald de Leon."

Haarold's frown deepened. "Roald would never have accepted you, and I do not. Nor does she."

"You know that is not true, that Anna de Leon would have no man against her will. What has this man promised you to make such dishonor worthwhile? Has he said that he will give her to your son when I am gone? That your bloodline will become the new lords?"

"It is a match that Roald would have approved."

"You are a fool. Look at him. Do you really think that he goes through all of this trouble to put your son in the lord's chair?"

He turned to Gurwant. "Do what you will, Gurwant, but you have lost. Your family will not lend you an army to besiege La Roche de Roald. Your attempts to enforce a spurious betrothal were one thing. This is another."

"If she comes to me, I will not have to lay any sieges. If you are dead, we are back where we were."

Surprise flashed on Haarold's face as the old vassal realized that Gurwant had been lying to him. But there would be no help from him now, Morvan knew, even with him knowing he had been duped.

"She will not come."

"You are so sure, Englishman?"

"I am sure."

He wasn't the least bit sure, of course. It would be just like Anna to borrow some knight's tunic, sling on her bow, and come searching for him. She would never suspect her father's trusted vassal of betrayal, and might well ride into that bailey with a handful of men, just as he himself had done.

The light through the small window grew stronger, and the other bodies in the chamber became visible. His two men huddled in their sleep along one wall. Morvan turned his attention to the last figure, lying on a pallet under the window.

He and his two men had been brought here after his meeting with Gurwant and Haarold. It was a rude cellar dungeon, the kind that men could die in.

They had found young Louis already in the cellar. He had been beaten badly, and fever from his wounds racked his body. Examining him, Morvan had seen the twisted, misshapen right hand. Louis had been tortured, and every finger broken.

Requests for Lady Gervaise to aid the boy finally bore results. Three days later she had slipped in, carrying salves and potions. From her fear and quick work, Morvan guessed that neither her husband nor Gurwant knew that she had come.

She did not stay long, but Morvan learned from her how Gurwant had ingratiated himself. He had impressed Haarold by speaking often of the need for Breton independence. When the message came announcing Anna's marriage, Haarold had been furious, and Gurwant had played on it. By the time Haarold left for the wedding, an alliance had been formed.

Louis stirred, and Morvan brought him some water and helped him up, propping his shoulders against the wall. The youth appeared alert and finally able to talk.

"I am sorry, my lord. It is my fault that you are here. Finally, the pain was too much."

"No man withstands these things long. How did you get here?"

"Three of them were waiting when I came through the trees to the path. They had been waiting for days, I think, for someone to come back alone from the farm. They'd been looking for the route for some time, and not succeeded. So they took me."

Morvan thought of the extra tracks he had seen the day he went for Anna. "Who were they?"

"Haarold's men. New men he has recruited these last months. They brought me here, and it was clear that Haarold had thrown in with Gurwant. They wanted me to tell them how to get to the farm. I think that they sought to steal the horses, and then take you when you came searching for them."

Morvan looked down at Louis's crippled hand. The youth grimaced. "Aye, it was that what did it. The beating I could take. After a while you don't hardly feel it anymore, and I figured I'd die and that would be that. Then Gurwant found a new pain, didn't he? Still, I kept worrying about the lady. I knew that she went there still, and might be there when they came. But in the end I told them."

Morvan touched his shoulder. "When this is over, you will always have a place with us."

Louis glanced at his hand. "I won't be much use, my lord."

"There is always a use for a loyal man."

Morvan slowly paced the small confines of the cell. By tonight she would know for sure. He closed his eyes and tried to find some connection with her, but she was too far away. Still, he focused his thoughts on her and willed with all of his soul that she not come.

For Gurwant was right. If he had her, and Morvan was dead, they would be back where they had started.

On the day of the Resurrection, guards came and bound his hands with rope. They slipped a noose around his neck and led him out into the light.

No gallows waited. Instead they took him into the keep. Servants were preparing the hall for the Easter feast, and he was brought through the large room to a door at one end. The lord's solar flanked the hall, as it had at La Roche de Roald before the upper level was built.

Inside the solar, Haarold and Gurwant sat waiting for him. Standing near the window was a blond-haired man with dark eyes, wearing priest's vestments.

"He would not speak until he saw that you were alive," Haarold said.

Ascanio looked him over. He reached under his robe and withdrew a dagger. Glaring a challenge at Gurwant, he walked over and cut the rope. Morvan slid off the bindings, then went to stand beside Haarold. He wanted his face to be visible to his friend during the parlay.

"You find being a priest convenient when it suits you, Sir Ascanio," Gurwant said.

"I am always a priest, especially on this holiest of days. Perhaps you wish to confess?"

Gurwant laughed at that. "You are alone. What kind of woman refuses to come to a wounded husband when he sends for her?"

"An intelligent woman who knows he would never ask her to come here. She saw the truth of it at once. She knew the message did not come from him."

Gurwant smiled ruefully. "I underestimated her."

"Men often do."

Gurwant gestured to Morvan. "So. Now you see that the English thief still lives."

"Sir Morvan is many things, but no thief."

"He stole what is mine. This would have been easier if she had come with you, but she only delays things. I have terms for you to bring to Anna."

"The only terms that she will hear are those that secure his release."

"He dies. I will hang him for the thief that he is."

"Then this castle becomes your tomb. And yours too, Haarold. Even now she gathers an army."

Despite his perpetual frown, Haarold's face could be

very expressive. Impatience flashed. "Tell him the terms, Gurwant. Enough of these games."

Gurwant glanced over as if Haarold were a boring adult taking away a child's fun. He looked at Morvan with a thin smile. "You think that she is yours? We will see. Just what will she give to save you?"

Morvan didn't acknowledge the question. He kept his gaze on Ascanio, and hoped that his friend read the commands that he silently communicated.

"Tell her that she can save her husband in exchange for the treasure of La Roche de Roald."

Ascanio didn't flinch. "Is that all? It will be brought."

"That is not all. She is to bring it herself. She is to come to me. With no guard." He paused thoughtfully. "Naked."

Haarold, and only Haarold, reacted. "Good God, man. Enough."

"Fine, my friend. I will respect your counsel. She is to come wearing only her shift." He turned to Morvan. "If you use her army against me after you are released, I will kill her."

"Why not ask for the child while you are at it, Gurwant," Morvan snarled sarcastically.

"Why not, indeed. Aye, she is to bring the serf girl with her."

Ascanio's shock at the goad faded quickly. He glanced his comprehension to Morvan. She might well have come herself, but she would never give up the child.

Gurwant extended his legs, a man content with himself. "Six days hence. If she has not come, I will hang him."

"She will not enter this castle while he is held. If she exchanges herself for him, it must be outside the walls."

"We will do it on the plain in front of this castle."

"Beyond the range of the bowmen on the battlements. If she does this for him, she will not risk treachery."

"Six days hence. At daybreak. If I see an army, or any knights, if she brings ought but servants with her, he is dead."

Ascanio nodded. "Six days then." He gestured to Morvan. "I would see that he is cleaned up. Anna is fascinated by his beauty, and if she sees him like this, there is no telling what she will do."

"She will come then?" Haarold asked anxiously.

Ascanio shrugged. "Who knows? She never wanted to marry, and was content without him. Even now she has retaken the place that she gave up to him. But he has bound her to him with pleasure, and she may be besotted enough to do this for him. Then again, she may decide to let him die and then enjoy herself avenging him. For your sake, Haarold, you had best pray that she is indeed a saint."

CHAPTER 24

ANNA LISTENED TO Ascanio's report. Josce, Catherine, Carlos, and the knights were with her. A shudder of relief had passed through the castle when Ascanio returned and announced that Morvan still lived, but as he listed the details of Gurwant's demands a dark sobriety returned.

Anna had no trouble visualizing his meeting with Gurwant and Haarold, and could see her husband standing silently through it all, aloof to the negotiations over his life.

Through the solar windows came the sounds that signaled the arrival of Fouke and his retinue. She expected Baldwin and Gaultier by the morning. The English garrison had already sent twenty longbowmen from Brest, and she had met with the town elders and demanded that they commit their guard as well.

Yesterday she had ridden to the nearest villages, asking their aid. Faced once more with the threat of Gurwant, the farmers had decided the English lord was not so bad. They would come, to help their saint defeat the devil.

"It is his will that you do not meet with Gurwant, or try to exchange yourself for him," Ascanio concluded. It was the third time in his story that he had inserted that.

"You mentioned nothing of speaking with him privately."

"He said nothing, but he made his will known."

Aye, he could do that, she knew. But she didn't have to agree that it had been made clear. Not that she would have obeyed a direct command anyway.

"Will Gurwant accept an individual challenge? Will he meet me one-on-one?" Sir Walter asked.

She shook her head. "This is no longer about this castle and this estate, Sir Walter. It is about revenge."

"And jealousy," Ascanio added.

She would have found that suggestion preposterous not so long ago. Now she accepted the observation without comment. Ascanio's assessment, however, meant that Gurwant wanted Morvan dead for more reasons than to reopen his claim to her and the estate. That only made the situation more precarious.

"Remind me how the land lies there, Ascanio," she said.

"The castle is on a hill overlooking a plain. To the west, about a quarter of a mile away, there are more hills. No doubt they will have someone on them watching, so we can forget about hiding the army behind them."

"What if we take the watchmen?"

"If our army comes over the hills, there will still be time to kill Morvan before we reach him."

"But Gurwant will be there, you think? With Morvan?"

"I doubt that he will be able to resist."

"We can lay siege for months, Anna," Josce said. "We can starve them out. Gurwant and Haarold are dead men."

"If we do it that way, so is Morvan."

Ascanio looked into her eyes. "He is anyway, Anna. You are not to go."

She rested back in her chair. The muscles in her arms ached, for she had spent many hours the last days practicing with the bow at the farm. Shadow was in heat, and so she had yesterday used the lead stallion as her mount, training him to her commands as she imagined her bolts coursing into Gurwant's black heart.

Since that bleak Maundy Thursday she had retaken command of the castle. No one, not even the new knights, had questioned the sense of it. It had suddenly been like before, but with two differences. For one thing, now she understood the complex reactions that men had to her, and knew the power that it gave her. The other difference had been that she no longer wanted this authority, at least not under these circumstances. A part of her, a big part, wished that one of the vassals or knights would show the strength that Morvan had always shown and step forward to at least share the burden.

"There will be no long siege," she said. "I will not hold this army there all summer, and I will not have Gervaise and the other innocents in that castle suffer. We will attack when Gurwant is on the field waiting for me."

She spoke with more determination than she felt. Surely there must be an alternative to letting Morvan die. "Leave me now. I need some time alone. Tell Fouke that I will see him shortly."

Ascanio held back as the others left. "If you do it this way, Anna, you must not lead them."

She glared up at him.

"He would not want you to see his death. And he could get no satisfaction from this retribution if he knew that you rode into danger."

Tears blurred her vision. Silent tears, that she held in only with fierce determination. Weak tears that no one but Ascanio would ever see.

"I would speak with him one more time," she whispered.

"He already knows all that you would say."

"He does not. I want to see him again."

"Not like this. Give him that."

Helplessness and anguish ripped through her. She gritted her teeth and pounded her fists on her knees. "I want to kill Gurwant."

His hand gripped her shoulder. "Morvan wants him dead too. But for your sake, and not by your hand."

Ascanio stood by her until her breathing calmed and the tears stopped. "Go now, dear friend," she said. "I have much to think over still."

Leaving the solar, she went down to her chamber, where she so often had found the solitude and strength that she now desperately needed. Lying down on their bed, she tried to ignore the space beside her where Morvan should have been. Yet something of his presence still lingered there, and she turned her body toward it.

A drowsy peace claimed her and her dulled thoughts wandered, aimlessly and scattered, over Gurwant's demands. The treasure of La Roche de Roald. There was no such thing. She had searched the entire castle for it on the small chance that it actually existed. Two days ago, torch in hand and rope in tow, she had gone down to the foundation vaults and passages and opened every door of every chamber just to make sure it was not all legend. She had found only rotting pallets, rats, and rusting armor.

Herself in a shift. He wanted her humbled and conquered before the world. She would do it, except that she was sure Morvan would die in front of her eyes as soon as Gurwant had her. The man had no honor, and neither he nor Haarold could risk releasing Morvan alive.

The child. The worst part, really. Without that, she might take her chances. On her own, she would go to Gurwant, and try to kill him before he could execute Morvan. But the child . . .

The terms and their images floated through her mind again and again. And then they began playing out like a pageant, combining in new ways, the shapes of the pieces transformed to fit with the others in new, unexpected ways. She began directing these thoughts, considering their possibilities.

She went out on the gallery and looked to the sea. She went through it once again. Maybe, just maybe . . . It was a huge gamble, especially for Marguerite. Still, if the child played a role in this revenge on Gurwant, might it not give her back something of what he had taken from her?

It could work. And if it didn't . . . well, they could all die together.

Gurwant had a knack for the dramatic gesture. An elaborate scaffold had been constructed on a high dais out in the middle of the plain. It was oriented so that the condemned could face the western hills and watch for the woman who would rescue them.

Morvan climbed the stairs and Gurwant fitted the noose around his neck. He expected and wanted no rescue, and even if it came, he knew he'd receive no quarter from this man. They had to kill him now.

He glanced over to where Louis and his two men stood beside him. He doubted that Haarold had approved of that. Gurwant had probably included them because one hanged man made a poor display and four looked impressive.

Gurwant checked the rope tying Morvan's hands behind his back, and then went to do the same on Louis.

"This is between you and me, Gurwant. There is no need for the others," Morvan said.

"This one gave me too much trouble."

"Nonsense. Torturing him gave you great pleasure. You should release him for that reason alone."

Gurwant's cold eyes shifted to him. "I think that I will let you live for a while after she comes. I will let you watch me take her before I kill you."

"She will not come. There is no treasure to bring. She will not let you have the child."

"If she wants to save you she will find a treasure. She will weigh the girl against you and give her up."

"She knows that you have no honor and will kill me anyway."

"She is Breton, and that is something you do not understand. She will come—if not to save you, then to kill me." He walked down the steps and took a position in front of the dais to wait.

Morvan glanced down at the gaping hole cut in the floorboards in front of him. Not a deep drop. No quick snap of the neck. Under the circumstances, the bath and shave that they had given him last night seemed very pointless. Perhaps Gurwant had decided that if he died looking like a common criminal the drama would lose some of its effect.

He let his mind wander to Anna. The regrets that he had about her had been laid to rest last night. Today the thought of her only brought him tremendous peace, and gratitude that between his last deathwatch and this he had been granted something that gave life and even death some meaning.

He had already decided that he would fill his mind with her at the end.

"My lord."

He turned to Louis. The youth looked straight ahead to the western horizon. Dawn's mist still shrouded the far plain and hills, but Morvan's eyes found what Louis had seen.

His breath caught. *Nay.* If he thought that his voice would carry that far, he would have hurled the command at them.

Cresting the hill, lumbering into view, came a large wagon pulled by two horses. He cursed inwardly as it rolled slowly down the slope.

Below him Gurwant snapped alert, and the twenty men with him deployed themselves in front of the dais.

The wagon moved into clearer view. Carlos held the reins. Beside him, swaddled in a long cloak, sat Marguerite.

Morvan couldn't believe that he was seeing this. He had been sure that she would never give up the girl—and it had been his own doing that Gurwant had even asked for her. The child's terror would follow him to the grave now.

Carlos drove the wagon right up to the dais, forcing Gurwant's men to move away, and stopped it alongside.

Morvan looked down into the wagon. Piled inside was the movable wealth of La Roche de Roald. Every item of any value, from the silver dinner plates to the tapestries that hung in the solar, had been thrown in. Atop this mound sat an open chest full of gold and silver coins, many more coins than the estate reserve.

Carlos glanced down behind his seat in a meaningful way. Morvan let his own gaze follow. Under the tapestry, its edge barely visible beneath the clutter, lay a shield. He also saw the very tip of a sword's hilt.

Damn it, what was she up to? Twenty men guarded this dais. Even if he could get the weapon . . . But maybe Anna just wanted to give him the right to die fighting. It would be like her.

Gurwant walked over to the wagon and surveyed its contents. "The treasure of La Roche de Roald," he said.

"Part of it. The rest arrives soon," Carlos said.

"She is coming then?"

"Aye. She is coming." His tone suggested that Carlos thought Anna had made a bad choice. Morvan agreed. His head and heart almost burst from the turmoil in them. The relief that he would see her one more time fought with fear for her.

Marguerite descended from the wagon, holding her cloak tightly around her. Gurwant looked down at her. She did not even acknowledge his presence, but kept her gaze fixed on Morvan. Gurwant touched the girl's head. Morvan's stomach turned.

"I am not yours until the exchange is made," Marguerite said stiffly. "I will wait with my lord." She marched over to the steps, straight-backed and proud. She bore such dignity in her manner that no one thought to stop her. She came up and stood between Morvan and Louis.

Everyone waited, milling around expectantly, the men eyeing the coins pouring out of the chest. Then the air on the plain changed and a soundless noise poured toward them from the west. Morvan knew what was happening, and Gurwant and the other battle-experienced men recognized it as well. This was the way a field felt when the enemy charged but had not yet become visible.

But the western hills did not fill with soldiers and knights. Instead, snaking over the crest came a long line of horses tethered together, herded by six grooms.

The real treasure of La Roche de Roald. Their value would easily surpass the coin in the chest.

The front of the long file drew near, and the lead groom jumped down from his mount. The other horses were not drawn up, but kept strung out. The grooms dropped to their feet and untethered them, holding them in groups by their reins. She had sent only the stallions.

The horses in one of the distant groups moved a bit. From his raised position Morvan saw the faintest glint of steel on the groom's saddle under a leather flap. His glance quickly shot around the rest of the herd. Except for the lead man, these were not grooms at all, but five of his own knights and soldiers. They stayed out of view, blocked by the horses, slouching to look servile, but he picked out Walter and several of the other recent additions to his retinue.

"My lord, look you to my cloak," Marguerite whispered. She lifted one edge of her cloak to reveal a dagger hung around her waist. "When she comes."

"It is too risky for you, child."

"When she comes, no one will be watching us."

Perhaps she was right. Indeed, no one watched them now. Certainly not Gurwant, whose gaze examined the western horizon, searching for the woman he both hated and wanted.

Suddenly, on the most distant hill to the north, two

men appeared. One was Ascanio. They dismounted, as if to announce that they would come no farther. Their presence created a new air of anticipation. Gurwant paced forward, away from the dais to the fore of his men.

And then, out of the thinning mist that surrounded the southern hill, a white horse began to emerge. It stopped for a moment, and the early morning sun picked up the gold of long blond curls blowing in the breeze.

The white stallion walked forward into view. The woman riding it became visible. A breathless hush fell over the assembled soldiers. Morvan's own breathing almost stopped too.

She looked like a gold and white goddess riding out of the mists of time. She sat on the stallion as straight-backed, dignified, and authoritative as ever. Her strength and nobility covered her like an invisible cloak, but in truth she wore little else. A golden band encircled her head, and a thin short shift, cinched at her waist with a golden cord, clung to her breasts and rode high on her thighs. The strap of her quiver crossed over her chest, outlining her body. Her loose hair was not yet long enough to cover those breasts and arms and spreading hips. Naked thighs and legs dangled down either side of the horse.

Morvan had seen her completely unclothed many times, but even he was stunned by this confident, erotic image. This was not the same girl whom he had first kissed. This was an Anna fully aware of her desirability and willing to use its power. She frankly challenged every man to dare to want her and try for her.

As she came closer the grooms turned to face the dais so as not to look at her. The stallions at the back of the herd began showing restless agitation.

Her slow progress provided the distraction that they needed. Morvan was jolted out of his reverie by the cuts of Marguerite's blade on the ropes that bound his hands. From his right, he heard Louis mutter, "Holy Jesus."

Morvan gestured for Marguerite to cut the other men's ropes. "I think that the men loyal to me are supposed to look away, Louis." He reached up and slipped the noose off his neck.

"You wouldn't deny a condemned man a view of paradise, would you, my lord?" Louis asked sheepishly before he became aware of Marguerite's dagger behind him.

The agitation of the stallions grew, spreading like a ripple in a lake. The horses around the dais became affected.

Suddenly, the white stallion broke into a gallop. Anna charged at the stallions and then pivoted away, arching around to the left and heading directly at Gurwant. The stallions of La Roche de Roald followed her, and a herd of horses began stampeding toward the dais.

Walter and the others held on to their mounts and rose to their saddles. Swords appeared from under flaps, and the knights allowed their horses to follow the others. Confusion broke out as the enemy tried to retain their panicking steeds. Gurwant turned, cold eyes hard with anger, and began pushing his way to the dais. And still Anna rode toward them, a bow in her hands now.

Morvan jumped into the wagon. Gurwant ran toward him, battle-ax raised.

An arrow thudded into the ground in front of his feet. Gurwant halted and turned in fury. Anna galloped past, turning in her saddle with another arrow aimed at her adversary's head. Morvan grabbed the sword and shield and held it aloft. She nodded and urged her horse onward, the trailing herd blocking Gurwant's movements more surely than the arrow had.

Carlos had freed the wagon's horses. "The other one is for you," he shouted as he swung up on one.

"Get the child out," Morvan yelled, but already Marguerite was jumping into Carlos's arms.

"Louis, take the other horse. I will be better on foot," Morvan commanded. He stood on the wagon, protecting Louis's retreat, and his other two men jumped to the ground and ran to the field north of the melee. Anna waited there, arrow ready, to cover the group scurrying to safety.

The herd of horses caught the scent of their leader. They flowed toward him, taking some of the horses belonging to Haarold's men with them. From his perch on the wagon, Morvan could see the northern plain clearly. Anna raised her bow in salute, then turned her horse and headed toward Ascanio.

Swords began to meet each other with ferocity. Walter and the other four were seriously outnumbered, but they were playing for time rather than fighting for their lives. There was an army nearby.

Morvan knew that he should wait for it too. But Gurwant had found his horse and mounted and was coming toward him, battle-ax gripped in an outstretched arm. Jumping down from the wagon, Morvan faced the bulk of the destrier.

The ax fell with a terrific force on Morvan's upraised shield, the impact bringing him to his knees beside the horse. He rolled toward the animal's rump, away from Gurwant's next blow. While his adversary strained to turn the animal, Morvan struck at thick legs with his sword. The huge weight of the destrier sagged to the ground.

Cursing, Gurwant disentangled himself from the saddle and rose. He faced Morvan over the length of the fallen horse.

Shouts went up and men began streaming away from the dais. Morvan did not take his eyes off Gurwant to look behind him, but he knew what he would see. The army had arrived.

Morvan stepped away from the horse, and Gurwant did likewise. They faced each other in the open space in front of the scaffold. An eerie silence fell upon the plain, and Morvan glanced to the western hills. Strung out along its crest stood Anna's army, and at one end Anna herself, her body cloaked now, beside Ascanio and the stranger.

Walter and the others circled around behind Gurwant. Morvan gestured for them to stay back.

Gurwant glanced toward Anna and grinned. "She is one hell of a woman, isn't she?"

"Aye, she is that," Morvan said.

"Brittany will ever regret that she didn't marry me and bear my sons."

"Brittany does not need such as you."

Gurwant made a taunting gesture with his ax. "Will you kill *all* the men who looked at her?"

"Only the one who brought it on her."

"Perhaps not, Englishman. Your wife is not here to save you this time."

"Hope that I don't fail, Gurwant. If I do she will claim you for herself. Future generations will know you as the only Beaumanoir killed by a woman in battle." He gestured for Walter. "Help him remove his armor."

"You are not so sure of your skill then?" Gurwant taunted.

"I am sure. I just don't want to waste all morning killing you."

A horse approached while Walter helped Gurwant remove the plate. A man Morvan had never seen stopped his horse between them.

Gurwant glanced up. "Greetings, cousin."

The stranger looked over the small assembly, pausing a moment to take Morvan's measure. "I am Robert de Beaumanoir. This is my kinsman."

"You brought the ransom, then. You will not leave empty-handed. He is yours, after we are done here. You can bring his body home," Morvan said.

Robert smirked sourly. "You are fortunate, Gurwant, that Sir Morvan fights you with honor. If this man hanged you on the gallows that you prepared for him, I would be hard pressed to object."

Gurwant shrugged. "It was a good plan. Who expected a woman and a girl to thwart it?"

"Anyone who learned, as I have, what the woman and girl held against you." He looked down at his kinsman. "Die well, cousin."

"I don't plan to die."

Robert glanced at Walter and the other mounted men, and then at the waiting army. "The how and when may not yet be written, but it is safe to say that you die this day." He stepped his horse back.

Morvan faced the western horizon, and fixed his gaze on Anna. He sent his heart and soul out to her and let himself bask in the warmth of their living bond. After a moment, she raised her arm, turned her horse, and disappeared down the back of the hill.

He turned around and faced Gurwant.

CHAPTER 25

ANNA SAT AT A TABLE in the hall watching the closed solar door. By the time she arrived in the castle, Morvan and the vassals had already sequestered themselves inside that chamber with Haarold and Paul. She knew what was happening, just as she knew how it would end.

She glanced down at her blue gown. Underneath she still wore the scandalous costume that had been part of her plan. She wondered what Morvan would say to her about that particular detail of his rescue. Actually, she wondered what he would say about all of it.

He was alive and Gurwant was dead and nothing else should really matter, she told herself. Eventually, however, he would begin assessing the risks and realize that she had taken tremendous chances. After the initial exhilaration of not dying wore off, how would he react?

She was not surprised that he had not come for her immediately after dealing with Gurwant. She knew that his mind had been filled with what was occurring in the solar right now. An unpleasant judgment awaited him there, and she couldn't blame him for wanting to be done with it before any celebration or reunion took place.

The mood in the crowded hall was very sober and the noise at a minimum. Everyone within the walls, victors and vanquished alike, waited in morbid fascination for the news that they all expected. Haarold had broken the most sacred oath a knight could give, the only one that most men really honored. In the world in which they lived, there was only one punishment to be expected, and the continued order of their world depended on its being meted out. The rule was very simple. If a man violated his fealty to his lord by bearing arms against him, he died.

The door opened and Paul came out. Anna caught a glimpse of Morvan sitting in a chair, looking stern and resolute, before the door closed. Paul walked to a chamber off the long wall of the hall and entered it.

A woman's wail pierced the quiet. The chamber door flew open and Gervaise rushed out, pushing aside her son's restraining arms, fighting to be released from his hold. She broke free and ran to the solar. Anna jumped up to try and catch her, but Gervaise plunged in, leaving Paul and Anna grabbing at air from the threshold.

Gervaise ran to Morvan and threw herself on the floor, grabbing his legs and whispering entreaties. Anna could not hear what he said in return as he bent over her. Finally Haarold lifted her up and brought her over to the door. He kissed her gently, and handed her into Anna's arms.

The door closed again, but it would not be long now.

Gervaise insisted on sitting in the hall where she could see her husband emerge. She grabbed Anna's hands in her own, twisting them all together on her lap. "He has disseized the estate," she whispered hoarsely. "We have been here almost as long as your family has held La Roche de Roald."

It was the least that they should have expected. A traitorous vassal does not keep his lands.

"Your son will not be harmed, though," Anna tried to console her. It had been the offer to spare the son that had gotten Haarold to surrender.

"He must leave by nightfall. Your husband said he could take only his weapons, armor, and horse."

Anna thought that was generous. It left Paul ready to take service at least, and not impoverished. Still, for Gervaise's sake, she would find a way to slip Paul a few coins.

"They are going to execute him. A sword to the neck. He doesn't even get to meet someone in combat and die honorably."

Anna didn't know what to say. Gervaise gripped her hands harder. "Morvan would listen to you," she pleaded. "Haarold was seduced by Gurwant into this. As soon as they took Morvan he began regretting it, but he said that it was too late. Please, Anna. He was your father's friend, and loyal for years. He came to you when you called in November."

Anna pulled the weeping woman into her arms.

Her heart went out to Gervaise, but also to Morvan. She could feel his mood. No matter what the justice of it, he had no stomach for this, and a cold-blooded execution of a vassal was one lordly duty he would have preferred to avoid.

Perhaps if he had been lord for a number of years he

could show mercy, but his authority was still not secure. What message would it send to Baldwin and Gaultier if he let Haarold live?

The solar door opened and the four vassals emerged. Gervaise walked over to her husband. He drew her aside and spoke quietly to her. It occurred to Anna that this man had probably not shown so much gentleness to his wife in the last twenty years combined.

He pulled away and glanced at Anna meaningfully, silently requesting her help in keeping Gervaise away from the bailey. Then, with clenched-teeth resolve, he joined the other vassals and left the hall.

Anna looked into the solar. Morvan stood there, his back to her. A bandage bound one upper arm.

She had played their reunion out many times in her mind. Her imagination had usually filled it with joy, but sometimes with anger. Never had she expected it to occur in this shadow.

She had only to leave and take refuge in one of the chambers and her happiest fantasies might unfold later this day.

She went over to Gervaise and spoke quietly. Gervaise retreated to her chamber.

Anna walked into the solar and closed the door behind her. Gliding up to Morvan, she placed a hand on his back. He turned, startled out of his thoughts, and a smile wiped away the frown that had creased his brow. He pulled her into an embrace.

"I am sorry that I did not come to you right away," he said, burying his face in her hair.

"I understand why." His hold created a timeless spell. She gave herself over to his assault on her senses, letting his presence fill voids in her soul and renew memories too quickly half forgotten.

He touched all that was alive in her. She did not want even a just death intruding on this bliss.

"You don't have to do this," she said softly, sorry to break the mood.

"Nay, but it was decided that even with my wound my sword arm is the strongest. No one wants him to suffer."

"That isn't what I mean. It doesn't have to happen at all. I know that his crime is great, but a lord can be magnanimous if he chooses, can't he?"

"Is that why you came here? To ask for his life?"

"He was one of my father's closest friends, Morvan. And a loyal vassal for many years."

"But not loyal to me, Anna."

She didn't know what to say to that. Haarold had handed Morvan over to be killed. It was too much to expect mercy.

He took her face in his hands and stroked her cheeks with his thumbs. "If it had just been me, it would be one thing. But he was ready to give you to that madman."

"Did none of the others speak for him?"

"Nay. Not even Fouke. Not even his son Paul. You are the only one to have done so except his wife."

She knew she should hate Haarold for the role he had played in Gurwant's scheme. Morvan might be dead if her plan hadn't worked, and Haarold would be responsible. But her plan had worked, and Morvan was alive, and the man she really held responsible had already been killed. She wanted Morvan to stay in her arms, and not walk away now to wield his sword again today.

"You said that I never asked you for anything. Well, I am asking you for this."

His eyes flashed with annoyance. "Do not do this, Anna."

"I am doing it."

He shook his head in disbelief. "The one time that you want something from me, and it is the life of the man who would have destroyed us?"

She held on to him tightly and forced his gaze to meet hers. "I do not ask for myself, or for Gervaise, and especially not for Haarold. Someday the child that I carry will hear of this day. I want him to be told of his father's generosity and not of his wrath."

He went utterly still. She watched her words sink in. His dark eyes brightened and a slow smile formed. Briefly, for no longer than a blink, another expression and realization flashed, but the pleasure won out for now.

"You are sure?"

"I consulted Catherine and Ruth. I am as sure as a woman can be."

He caressed her cheek. "You did not want this."

"You said that your ancestor hailed from Brittany. Surely at least one drop of his blood still flows in you. I will have my Breton heir, Morvan."

He gave her a sweet, grateful kiss. She reveled in the comfort of his warmth.

He smiled. "I suppose that it would be churlish for a man to be ungenerous on the day that he got such news."

"I suppose so."

They walked into the hall arm in arm. With each step Morvan's elation grew. By the time they reached the bailey stairs he was grinning and holding her so close that he was practically carrying her under his arm.

At the bottom of the steps he gave her an encompassing embrace and a deep long kiss, and afterwards let his gaze and hand drift curiously to her belly. "There is no sign yet," she whispered, aware of the eyes watching them.

In the middle of the bailey the four vassals waited in

morbid silence. Ascanio had joined them, and Fouke held a heavy two-handed sword. Every face wore the hard lines of control and duty.

Anna and Morvan walked over laughing. Everyone exchanged appalled looks. Haarold's face held an expression that said he found it in very bad taste for Morvan to interrupt an execution in order to fondle and kiss his wife. That it was Haarold's own execution that had been delayed didn't seem to matter.

Fouke began to unsheathe the judgmental sword. Morvan held up a hand and shook his head.

"My wife has just given me good news. For nothing less would I pardon you, Haarold, but to honor Anna and the child that she carries I will do so. You must leave at once, though."

A tremor of relief passed over the bailey. Fouke slapped a hand down on his old friend's shoulder.

Morvan looked past the group to the far end of the yard. "It would seem that a squire is bringing your mount already, Haarold."

Haarold and the others pivoted to watch the slow approach of two horses. On one sat a skinny youth in a baggy cotte and high boots, a broad-brimmed hat almost obscuring his face.

"What the hell . . . See here, woman," Haarold sputtered.

"Don't 'see here' to me, husband," Gervaise snapped, handing him the reins as she looked down from beneath her hat.

"Go and dress decently at once. I'll not be seen riding over the country with you like that."

"And I'll not ride saints know how long and how far in clumsy skirts. This is very practical. It is even safer for a woman. Lady Anna says so."

Haarold glanced furiously at Anna.

"You want to say something, Haarold?" Morvan asked. "Perhaps you want to announce that you would rather die than be seen with a woman in man's garments? The sword awaits. We can still accommodate you." He turned to Gervaise. "My lady, if you prefer you can stay with us. We will see that you get to your kinsmen."

"Nay, my lord, I will go with the old goat. I wouldn't know what to do without that scowling face frowning at me all day."

The other vassals gave up all pretense of not enjoying themselves at Haarold's expense. They teased him as he cursed and mounted the horse. Gervaise reached down and grasped Anna's hand before falling in beside her husband. Low bickering could be heard until they passed below the portcullis.

Morvan turned to the circle of men in front of him. "Is there anything else that requires my attention right now? Nay? Good."

Anna gave a startled shriek as Morvan abruptly scooped her up in his arms and turned to the keep. Then he kissed her, and she barely heard the hoots and whistles that followed them through the hall to the solar.

"You risked too much."

His voice caught her in the middle of a sensual stretch. They had made love fiercely, savagely, and then slowly, gratefully. The chamber was still drenched with their poignant emotion, and with their profound awareness that they had almost lost each other.

His quiet statement startled her. She froze. She had hoped that he wouldn't think about that for a day or so.

"Any number of things could have gone wrong," he added.

"But they didn't. It worked." She had decided that her success would be her best defense.

"Gurwant might have stopped the wagon away from the dais."

"I assumed that he would want you to see it."

"He might not have let Marguerite stand beside me."

"He needed her out of the way, not underfoot."

"The horses might not have followed your stallion."

"They did before."

"Gurwant might have just killed you when he saw you. One arrow from a longbow would have done it."

"That would have been too simple. He enjoyed humiliating people too much for that." She stroked her fingers through his hair. "Aye. I risked much. It was not without danger. But it worked, Morvan. And I would do it again."

He rose up on his arm. His gaze drifted along her body, and his hand touched her belly.

Now they were down to it.

"You endangered more than yourself. You should have stayed at La Roche de Roald." His voice sounded more thoughtful than angry.

"And let you die? Then what? I raise this child alone? Or perhaps your King sends me another husband?"

"If your plan had not succeeded, and Gurwant had killed me and taken you, he would have claimed that the child was his."

"I left a document, witnessed by Ruth and Catherine and the town priest. I left a sworn statement that I carried your child."

"Did anyone else know? Ascanio?"

"None other, especially not Ascanio or Carlos. They

would never have let me come if they did. They are both getting as protective as you."

He pulled her to him, embracing the length of her, his rough hand caressing from her shoulders to her knees. Her kiss met his greedily. Still, it seemed that this conversation had not really been completed.

"So how angry are you, Morvan? Are you going to forever blame me for putting your unborn child in danger?"

"Considering that I am alive and not dead, it would be ungrateful of me to blame you for anything. I find no anger in me. There aren't many men whose wives would risk so much for them." He was quiet and thoughtful, his fingers stroking absently along her back. "The child changes things, though. I cannot let you leave now."

"I never asked to leave. You are the one who found living together too hard."

He turned her on her back and rose up over her. "That is not true. I wanted you to find contentment."

"You wanted to throw out our bargain. You gave me a choice, Morvan, and the choice was to change or to leave. Well, I can't leave now, so the choice is gone. But I can't change either, nor do I want to. You knew what you got in me, and I gave you fair warning on this."

His eyes sparkled in amusement as he listened to her little speech. She couldn't imagine what he found so humorous about being told that she planned to make his life miserable for the next forty years.

"And if not for the child, Anna, what would you have done?" he asked softly.

She looked into those bright eyes that could mesmerize her still. "What would you have had me do, Morvan?"

He lifted her hand and kissed each finger and then the palm. "I have been in love with you since that first night." He said it simply, as if he had done so many times before. He did not speak of mere desire, or the love of friendship. She wondered if her surprise showed, and if he could tell that her breath had caught.

"It is a rare love that we have, Anna, and not given to many, I think. Certainly never to me before. I would have let you go, but it would have broken my heart. I would have had you stay."

She pulled him down, holding him tightly and kissing him desperately.

"And I could never have left."

CHAPTER 26

ANNA WALKED ALONG the battlements bordering the field, relishing the warm sun and cool morning breeze. It promised to be a glorious day, and she decided to enjoy a long ride later. She would have to take an escort. Nothing had changed there, even with Gurwant gone and the estate peaceful.

It could have been worse. During the weeks since Morvan's rescue she had been holding her breath, waiting for more protective measures because of the unborn child. She had expected him to refuse to let her ride at all now. But whatever Morvan's inclinations, he had let things remain much as before.

She made her way along the wall walk to where she could survey the end of the field. Within days of their return men had begun raising a high fence down there, enclosing the northern third of the yard. When she had asked Morvan why, he had said that he was building a breeding corral for Shadow and Devil.

But this fence was too high for such a purpose, and the space it enclosed too large. The mystery fascinated her, and she had come each day to watch the men cut the trees in the forest and hew them to shape, then haul them in and set them in the ground.

It was finished now. She decided she would go and see if anything had been put inside.

Morvan entered the bailey just as she reached the stairs. She ran down to him.

"I wish that you would stop wearing that brown pourpoint," she said, tugging at the garment in exasperation. She had tried once more to embroider it, with painstaking care this time, but it still looked horrible.

"I find that I favor it. It is comfortable in the warmer weather."

"Then at least allow one of the women to redo the stitches."

"It suits me as it is."

He draped his arm around her and they strolled toward the sea. He sat on a large rock, and pulled her onto his lap. He still never noticed that she was too big for that.

"The first day that you came, I watched you sitting on this very rock," she said. "I remember it well. There had just been a glorious sunset, astonishing in its beauty. Watching it had been like seeing a glimpse of heaven, and I felt as though I had melted into the sea and sky itself."

A serious, speculative expression passed on his face, as if he found her story fascinating. "I remember that sunset, like everything else about that day."

"While it passed I gazed down and here you were, completely unaware of me."

"Not so unaware. I had always thought our love was born of my deathwatch, but I realize now that my full awareness of you began on this rock, in the glory of that sunset. I sensed you in it, as I always sensed you afterwards."

She remembered the profound empathy she had experienced while she watched him on this rock. Perhaps he was right. She had never been completely separate from him after that.

"Then I am thankful that I stepped out on the gallery that evening," she said.

He kissed her sweetly. "As am I. It opened my heart to learning that paradise can be found in love."

They held each other in a mood as intimate as she had ever known, both looking out to the vast sea and sky. She noticed that Morvan gazed in the direction of England, as he often did when they stood together on the gallery. Their delicious unity led her to broach a worry that had formed in her heart. "Do you intend to try for Harclow this summer?"

"Nay. It will take a few years to prepare for that. We will let the world right itself first, and make this estate strong again before we turn to Harclow."

"We? You speak as though we are together in this."

"We are together in everything now. I find that I do not mind the delay, but welcome it. I want to see my son through his first years. When I leave, I want to know that another succeeds me."

"It may not be a son, Morvan."

"God help that Scottish laird then. If he is wise, he will surrender at once to avoid the chance that your daughter may one day carry my standard."

Despite his jest, they were speaking obliquely of realities that might come. "I also welcome the delay. I would not interfere with your destiny, but I want to live awhile in our love before you embark on that dangerous quest."

"That sounds very womanish, Anna."

"Aye, doesn't it. Perhaps it is the child making me feel thus. Or love."

He caressed her face and turned her gaze to his. "Harbor no fears for me. We will live in our love a long while, until we are old. I am as sure of it as I am that the sun will sink into the sea again tonight. I was not led to this rocky cliff to only know a brief love."

She believed him. The worry disappeared, consumed by the certainty in his fiery eyes.

She gestured to the new fence. "Now that it is finished, are you going to tell me what it is?"

"I already told you. When we breed the two of them I will want Devil here in case I need him."

"It is much too elaborate for that. A simple post and rail would suffice."

"I thought that would be too public for the virginal Shadow. I assumed that she was modest like her mistress." He set her on her feet. "Let us see if it meets with your approval."

The enclosure was larger than it looked from the battlements. There was nothing to see inside, except an old chest in one corner.

"Actually, I thought that you could plant a garden here," Morvan said. "A rose garden."

"I already have a rose garden, but, aye, some fruit trees and bushes. Flowers in the summer—"

"I was jesting. It is not for a garden, love."

"Then what?"

"I have been talking with Carlos. I have asked him to become steward for all the farms. He will have less time for the horses. I thought you might help with them."

She was speechless with surprise.

"Don't you want to do it?" he asked.

"Of course I do."

"The rotation of the guards will change so that each morning a relief guard rides out and each afternoon the one that he replaces comes back. When you need to go to the horse farm, you can ride with them." He gestured around the enclosure. "When the child is born you may not be able to go so often. Horses can be brought here for you to train."

She assessed the space. For close work it would be big enough. The high walls would keep the horses from getting distracted by the bailey activities.

"Aren't you afraid that I will fall off a stallion and harm myself or the child?"

"A woman who can lead an army has the sense not to risk her neck or her unborn child. I think that you will know when to stop in the months ahead, and that you won't take any chances with dangerous games."

"I won't stand on a horse's back, if that is what you mean."

"That is what I mean."

He walked to the chest, threw it open, and called her over. There were some sacks inside, and on top of them a brown tunic. He lifted the garment and handed it to her. "Put it on, Anna. Catherine sewed it for you."

She stared in confusion. He reached down and pulled a sword from one of the sacks. "This was a gift to me from David. Now it is my gift to you. It is lighter weight than most. You should be able to handle it with one arm and learn to depend on your shield more." He slid a new shield from the other sack and propped both weapons against the chest.

"You can practice with the bow at the farm," he said.

"But you may use the sword only here and only with me. I want your promise on that. It is intended only for exercise, and for your pleasure. No matter how skilled you get, you will never be strong enough to face a trained man and you must avoid doing so whenever possible."

The implications astonished her. "You will teach me?"

"Aye."

"Sooner or later I will get hurt, you know."

"With my skill it will be much later, and I will be careful."

"Not too careful, I hope. I'll never learn anything then."

He laughed. "Are you going to change, or should we go back to the keep?"

She began stripping off her gown. She glanced over her shoulder.

"It is too high," he reassured her. "None can see. Ascanio helped me check the sight lines while the first wall went up."

So Ascanio had been consulted too, as well as Catherine and Carlos. Everyone who mattered most to her had helped Morvan plan this surprise.

She stepped out of the gown and tossed it aside. Her shift followed. Naked except for her gartered hose and shoes, she reached for the tunic, but paused.

"Looking for this?" Morvan pulled a long silk scarf from the front of his pourpoint. He helped her bind it around her breasts. "But I get to take it off," he added quietly.

She thrust her arms into the brown tunic. It was short-sleeved and came to her knees, but it had been made to fit her.

Morvan was enjoying her surprise and pleasure. She

skipped over and embraced him. "Why are you doing this?"

He wrapped his hand in her curls. "I had much time to think while in Haarold's cell, my love. All of this seems very unimportant now. Twice you have snatched me from the jaws of death, and both times you then gave me a magnificent gift. First it was yourself, and now it is this child. These are simple things in comparison."

"They aren't simple to me, Morvan. I don't think that I've ever loved you more than right now."

"Nor I you. But it would be a sad thing if my love kept you from being the woman I fell in love with. In truth, I have always thought the sight of you in a tunic and carrying a weapon exciting. That was the image I held in my heart the night I waited for Gurwant to kill me." He gestured to the sword. "Let us start. God willing, you will never need weapons for other than sport, but in the hell that is the world today, one never knows. If my protection should ever fail, I would have you and the child be no man's victims."

"If we work at this seriously, it will be much like being in battle. It will leave me very restless, I expect."

The lights that entered his dark eyes made her heart skip. "I am counting on it."

She picked up the sword and shield. They felt good and natural in her hands.

Exulting in her strength and love, she faced him.

ABOUT THE AUTHOR

MADELINE HUNTER is a nationally bestselling author of historical romances who lives in Pennsylvania with her husband and two sons. In a parallel existence to the one she enjoys as a novelist, she has a Ph.D. in art history and teaches at an East Coast university. Readers can contact her through her web site, www.MadelineHunter.com, where they can also learn more about the characters and historical backgrounds found in her stories.